RED SKY HILL

A JAKE CASHEN NOVEL

DECLAN JAMES

Red Sky Hill

A Detective Jake Cashen Novel

By
Declan James

ONE

Pain is a song most cannot play. Most cannot hear. But make no mistake, there is a melody to it. A harmony. There is beauty of form. Each person is different. Like each instrument. No two notes sound exactly the same, if you know how to listen.

Tonight, it began when the killer stepped into the room. Slow. Quiet. Taking care not to let his victim know he was there. The element of surprise. Because fear is a type of pain. The power in bringing it formed the very first notes. The very first movement.

He stood there, watching. Waiting. His victim sat at his desk, typing up invoices in front of a large computer monitor.

His victim was happy here. At peace. He'd worked hard for the things he had. Or so he told himself. The expanse of acreage at the foot of Southern Ohio's Red Sky Hill. His hobby farm with horse stables and the chicken coop. The garden his wife liked to putter in. The very barn he worked in. He'd spent six figures converting it into a state-of-the-art home office. A man cave. A warehouse for all of his extravagances. The vintage cars. From here, he could look out the window at the rolling hills, surveying his kingdom. Satisfied. Smug.

The killer took another step. He waited. He wanted to. The longer he stayed undetected, the closer he got to his victim. It felt good. To be in control.

The phone beside his victim's computer rang. The killer froze. He took a step back, but stayed directly behind him.

He answered, his tone one of annoyance.

"Hey, Gemma. It's not a good time. No. No. You don't need to bother Rachel."

Silence. His victim grew agitated, shaking his head.

"Yeah. I'm just finishing up a few things in the office. I'll leave the keys in the lockbox when I go. Just make sure you don't let anybody touch anything back here. I know what I have. I don't want to see so much as a fingerprint on my Mustang. And you tell them if they're really interested, they better be ready to write an offer."

The killer took one step back. He slipped his 40 millimeter Glock out of its holster and aimed it at the back of the man's head.

"Yeah. Talk to you tomorrow morning. Call me as soon as the showings are over. Sure. I expect multiple bids as well. I'm counting on it. I expect you to deliver on your promises."

He hung up the phone. He pounded something on his keyboard then shut his computer down. The killer waited. He took a step forward, then pressed the barrel of the gun to his victim's head.

He would wait. A moment. He would savor the fear in his eyes as he let him turn and realize who would end him tonight.

Only it wouldn't be quick. It couldn't be.

The killer's blood heated. His whole body began to tingle with the promise of the kill. No. Not the kill.

The coming pain. The music.

Craig Albright put his hands up and tried to rise up out of the chair.

"I don't know what they told you," he said. "Let's just calm down, okay?"

"The house," Albright said, his voice cracking. "There are cameras all over the property." The killer knew it was a lie. Albright thought he was safe out here in his fortress.

The killer reached into his back pocket with his free hand and pulled out the first zip tie.

"Tie your right wrist to the arm of the chair," the killer whispered. He pulled the hammer back, letting Craig Albright fear that distinctive sound.

He wouldn't shoot him. That wasn't the plan.

"All right. All right." He was too compliant. Almost calm. Almost like he had expected things to get to this point sooner or later.

Albright took the zip tie and secured his own wrist to the arm of his chair. It took him two tries.

The killer stepped back. He delivered the first blow. A quick, clean snap across Craig's temple with the pistol. He knew exactly how hard to hit. Not enough to knock him out. Just enough to make him see stars, stupefy him so the killer could secure his other wrist and his ankles to the chair without him putting up a fight. As Craig's head lolled forward, the killer rolled the chair into the corner.

Now his work could truly begin.

He holstered the gun. It wasn't his weapon of choice for what had to be done. He slid his backpack off his shoulder. Took out his hammer. His blow torch. The drill.

His instruments of pain.

The killer took a deep breath. Slowed his own pulse. He would not break a sweat. He would not let his heart rate go above seventy beats per minute.

He checked his watch. It was seven p.m. exactly. He could take all night if he wished. But he would finish in exactly two hours.

When Craig came to the first time, he screamed, eyes widening with fear. The time after that, he cried. Then, as the killer applied the torch, Craig Albright merely moaned.

"Why? Why? Why!" Craig whispered. He said a lot of things. The killer paid no attention. It only took the first burn to turn him. He sang out the combination to the safe in the corner. He told him where he would find the other thing he sought hidden behind the paneling in the corner of the barn. He made promises that were long past time to keep.

He thought it would save him. He thought it would end things. Begged for it.

The first hammer blow cured him of that hope.

God. It felt good. The power. The rhythm. Each bone that broke. The tiny ones sometimes hurt the worst. Each drop of blood that fell. Even that felt like art.

He bore up better than the killer would have given him credit for. He went numb. Hung his head low. His right eye had swollen shut. The left eye stayed wide and clear. The killer thought about ways to blind him.

But that was not the plan.

"Please," Albright said as the second hour drew to a close. He'd given so much of himself. His blood. His tears. His agony.

Now there was just one last thing.

As the killer approached, Albright tried to lift his head. Tried to meet his eyes. The good one anyway.

"Please," he said again. The killer put his weapons down. His instruments. He pulled the final one out of his pocket and arced it in the air, letting the blade gleam under the ceiling lights.

Albright had moved through his fear. The killer had wrung it out of him. Or so Albright would tell himself. But as the killer held the blade to Albright's neck, Albright tried one last thing.

"You have no idea what you've done," he whispered, crying. "It'll be the last thing you do. They'll come for you. You think I don't have a plan? They'll take everything you love."

It shouldn't have mattered. They were just words. For the first time since the killer had walked in, his anger rose. He punched Craig Albright as hard as he could, bruising his cheek with the ring he wore under his gloved hand, tearing the latex.

"Shhh," the killer said. "You've done well. You've done enough. The rest is up to me."

And so it was. He slashed Craig Albright's neck in a single, clean cut, opening the vital arteries, so the last of Craig Albright's blood became the final refrain.

Because that was always the plan.

TWO

T he quickest way to spread gossip within the walls of the Worthington County Sheriff's Department was to tell someone else to keep a secret. Though Detective Jake Cashen didn't know what it was, he could see it on the faces of everyone he passed as he walked down to his office. There were whispers. Fake smiles. Conversations that stopped mid-sentence the moment he came into view.

Jake just kept on walking. He didn't have time for bullshit today. For the last week, he was the only detective Worthington County had working. Gary Majewski, who normally handled property crimes, had taken three weeks' worth of vacation to go meet his first grandchild in Fort Worth. Ed Zender, Jake's partner, had been in and out of the office on medical leave for the last six months. When he was here on the top of his game, Ed tended to leave the real detective work to Jake anyway. Jake himself hadn't taken a single vacation day since he joined the department nearly two years ago on the back of his stint with the FBI. But that was a story for another day. Today, Jake had forty-three unanswered urgent emails and a full voicemail box. They would have to wait until tomorrow. He was already into his second hour of unapproved overtime.

"Jake," Darcy the dispatcher called out as he made his way down the hall. Quite a few of his messages were from her.

"I'm ten minutes from clocking out, Darcy. It's been a long day."

"Jake!"

He froze. Darcy stepped out and stood between him and the door to his office.

"It can't wait until tomorrow?" he asked.

She had her hands crossed in front of her. She gave him her best schoolmarm expression. "Trust me. I like to avoid dealing with you after a long day too. It's the sheriff. She wants to see you in her office before you go."

"What'd I do now?"

"Beats me. But she's practically wearing a hole in her carpet storming around in there. We need you to talk to her."

"We? Who's we?"

"We're worried. She snapped at Moira down at the commissioner's office. She practically bulldozed over the new civilian clerk trainees. Actually made one of them cry."

"Landry?" Jake said.

"Yeah. That's what I'm saying. It's not like her. Go talk to her."

"Why me?"

"Because you're her favorite," Darcy said, batting her eyes at him.

Jake grumbled. "Nice try. Y'all are just a bunch of cowards."

"Come on," Darcy said. She took Jake by the arm and turned him away from the door. "If you're nice to me, I'll bring you pastries tomorrow morning."

"Well, now I know hell's about to freeze over."

"I'll even get them from Papa's Diner. Tessa's baklava?"

"And coffee. The biggest to-go cup she's got," Jake said.

Darcy kept pushing him toward the stairwell. "Fine," she said. "But then you come to me first when you're done with the sheriff. Let me know what she said."

"So I'm a spy now."

"Don't be so dramatic."

"Two pieces of baklava," Jake muttered. "Big ones."

By the time he got to Landry's office, her door was closed. He could see her through the frosted window glass, pacing, just like Darcy said.

Steeling himself for whatever had Meg Landry angry enough to scare off the civilian clerks, Jake raised his fist to knock on her door. Landry swung it open just before he made contact with it.

He'd never seen Meg Landry like this. Her face was flushed, lips pursed into a tight line. Behind her, papers were scattered over the floor as if she'd swept them off her desk in a rage. Maybe she had.

"Jake," she said. "Get in here."

Jake looked behind him. Darcy and a couple of the other clerks darted out of view behind doors, desks, and down the hallway.

Jake straightened his tie and went into the lion's den.

"Uh. How's your day?" he asked, not bothering to hide the sarcasm in his tone.

Landry turned on her heel and charged over to her desk. She picked up a tablet and thrust it at Jake, practically slicing it through his chest. He caught the thing and looked at the screen.

"Sit down," she said.

"Okay." Jake took a seat at one of the chairs opposite Landry's desk. He had to side-step scattered paperwork.

"It's hitting the internet in about an hour," she said. "A friend of mine at the *Daily Beacon* ... some friend ... gave me an advance copy hoping I'd be willing to comment."

Jake scanned the article she'd pulled up on the tablet. The headline read, "Is Blackhand Hills's Top Cop in Over Her Head?"

Before Jake could get very far, Landry pulled the tablet out of his grasp and started reading from it.

"Meg Landry was never supposed to be a permanent replacement for beloved Sheriff Greg O'Neal. Sources close to her say not even she wanted the job. Now, it appears the citizens of Worthington County may have to pay the price. In the two years since the interim sheriff ..."

"Interim?" Jake interjected. "You're not interim ..."

"In the two years since the interim sheriff clipped on her badge," Landry continued over Jake's comment.

"Well, more pinned than clipped," Jake said.

"Crime in the county has only risen. Call response times have tripled. And there is a growing dissatisfaction among the rank and file. The whispers through the halls of the public safety building echo with a common theme. Meg Landry may be in over her head."

She tossed the tablet onto an empty chair.

"It's a hit piece," she said. "A three-part exposé that's rolling out this week."

"Landry ... since when have you operated based solely on public opinion? And that's not even public opinion. That's one reporter. And it's not like the *Beacon* has ever been pro law enforcement."

"Jake, they're talking to people inside the department. The sources quoted have pulled details from private conversations I've only had behind these four walls. Internal statistics. Things that were never meant for public dissemination."

She sat down hard in her desk chair.

"They're blaming me for everything that's wrong with the county. Manpower issues. Slow response times."

"Which are a direct result of county and state budget cuts and attrition outpacing new recruits. That's a nationwide problem. Not something you caused."

"The *Beacon* is gearing up to endorse whoever decides to run against me when I'm up for re-election next year. This is just them laying the groundwork."

"Looks like it."

"It's veiled misogyny. Phrases like *in over her head*. There's a passage where they call into question whether I have the right emotional temperament, for God's sake."

"And I've known you to have a thicker skin than this, Landry. It'll blow over. You knew you were probably gonna have a fight on your hands next term."

"Jake, if the command and deputy's unions don't back me, I'll be out of a job and you'll be looking for a new boss."

"Maybe so. But that's not a problem you can solve today. Also, this sounds like one or two idiots bending some reporter's ear. That bit about the rank and file? It's crap. It's not reality. It sure as hell isn't what I hear."

"Thanks," she said. "But you're probably biased. Everyone thinks you're my favorite."

Jake laughed, recalling Darcy's earlier comment.

"Thanks for letting me vent. I was gonna call you in here earlier, but not about this, if you can believe that. This little turd salad just sort of dropped in my lap. There's something else I wanted to talk to you about actually."

"What's up?"

"Ed Zender," she said. "I had a long talk with him last night. It's supposed to be hush-hush, but ..."

"So that's why I was getting all those looks all day," Jake muttered. "What's Zender done now?"

"He put in his paperwork. He's planning on retiring at the end of the year."

The news hit Jake like a thunderbolt. Zender had been threatening to retire for two years now and probably should have at least five years ago. But nobody thought he'd ever go through with it.

"I know his timing couldn't be worse," she said. "We're short-staffed enough as it is."

Jake didn't want to say it, but even on a good day, Zender wasn't much help to him. Jake had been carrying Zender's load for months.

"I have an idea who I'd like to bring up to replace him but I wanted you to hear it from me. It impacts you more than anyone else."

"Who's your pick?" Jake asked, bracing himself for the answer.

"Mary Rathburn."

Jake took a beat.

"What do you think?"

"I think that's gonna ruffle more feathers than you probably want to right now. Gary Majewski has hinted for years he'd like to move over into crimes against persons. I've heard from Broadmoor and Corbin too. They've got more seniority. But ... if you're asking for my pure opinion."

"I am."

"I think you couldn't have made a better choice than Rathburn. She's solid. I've worked with her a few times. She's smart. Tough. Ambitious."

"You can work with her?"

"Absolutely. To be honest, if you'd asked me for my pick at the outset, she would have been on my short list."

"Good. Your support is going to matter."

"Yeah. You get you're gonna catch heat for it though, right?"

"I do. Mary's young. She's female. This place is still very much a good ole boys' club. I know she's not the safest choice."

"But she's the right one."

"It could get ugly," Landry said. "I could get some pushback. Mary could get some pushback. Are you up for that?"

"I'll have your back," Jake said. "More importantly, I'll have Rathburn's. When are you going to tell her?"

Landry's office door opened. Deputy Mary Rathburn came in.

"Pretty much now," Landry said.

"Hey, Jake," Rathburn said. By the confused expression on her face, Jake guessed she had no idea why she'd been called up.

Jake's cell phone buzzed. The caller ID told him it was his sister, Gemma. Jake clicked the volume off and slipped his phone back in his pocket.

"Thanks for coming up, Mary," Landry said. "Have a seat."

Rathburn came into the room and made her way to the empty chair beside Jake.

His phone buzzed again but Jake didn't pull it out. At the same time, there was a knock on Landry's office door.

"Sheriff?" Darcy called out. "I'm sorry to bother you but I need Jake. It's urgent. And you should hear it too."

Jake and Landry exchanged a look. Mary Rathburn rose from her seat. Darcy opened the door. Worry lines creased her face. She held a small note in her hand.

"What's going on?" Jake asked.

"We got a 9-1-1 call," she said. "Out at the Albright farm at the base of Red Sky Hill. Jake, your sister's out there showing the house."

Jake got to his feet.

"She's okay," Darcy said. "It's not that. It's ... well ... she found a body. It sounds pretty bad. There was a lot of blood and ..."

"I'm on my way," Jake said.

"Mary," Landry said. "You might as well go with him. Trial by fire and all."

"What?" Rathburn asked.

"Come on," Jake said. "I'll drive. I'll explain on the way."

THREE

Deputy Chris Denning's cruiser blocked Jake's entrance to the driveway at the bottom of the hill. A good sign.

Jake and Rathburn got out of Jake's vehicle. Denning met them halfway.

"Nobody's been in or out, Detective," Denning said. "I made sure. Deputy Snow and I were first on scene. He's still up there at the barn. He's got your sister and the couple she was showing the house to. They're all pretty shook up."

"What'd you see when you got here?" Jake asked.

Denning's color was off. The man looked gray. He cleared his throat. "I've ... I've never seen anything like that, Detective. I hope to God I never do again. There was a lot of blood. The victim's got kind of a man cave, home office in part of the barn. That's where Gemma said she found him. He's tied to his desk chair, covered in blood. As soon as I saw that, me and Snow backed right out and got Gemma and her clients out of there. Made sure there's nobody else in the house. Gemma said they'd just come from there. The barn was the last place she was showing. Anyway, I taped off the barn and we've been waiting for you."

"Good man," Jake said. "Stay right where you are, okay? You log anyone coming in or out. And nobody has permission to come in or out unless you hear directly from me. I'll get you some help down here as soon as I can. You okay, Denning?"

Denning's throat was dry. It took him two tries to get his words out. "Yeah. I'm okay."

Rathburn reached out and put a hand on Denning's shoulder. "It's bad, Mary," Jake heard him whisper to her.

"You ready?" Jake said to Rathburn.

"Sure thing, Detective."

"Stop with this Detective crap," Jake said. "I'm just Jake."

Jake and Mary went up the rest of the driveway on foot. The woods were thick on either side of it. Jake kept his head on a swivel, looking for anything out of the ordinary. Footprints. Broken branches. Anything.

"Do you know the family?" Jake asked Mary.

"My dad knew Craig Albright's old man. But he's been gone for at least twenty years. I can't say I really know ... um ... knew Craig."

"Me either," Jake said. He was twitchy. As they approached the main house, Red Sky Hill loomed ahead of them, stretching across the horizon, its peak forming the highest point in Worthington County. Beyond that were cavernous valleys and smaller hills that held some of the oldest secrets and legends of the region.

The old red barn behind the main house had been built at least a hundred and fifty years ago. The Albrights restored it to its former glory though the land itself hadn't been properly farmed in decades.

Gemma's For Sale sign hung in the front yard, his sister's smiling face flapping in the breeze as he and Deputy Rathburn approached.

He found Deputy Snow just where Deputy Denning said he'd be. He had his cruiser angled so no one could get to the barn doors without passing by him. Gemma herself sat on the back porch, consoling a young couple sitting on a long porch swing. The woman was sobbing into the man's shoulder. Gemma saw Jake and rose. He gave her a wave and gestured to her that he'd be over in a minute. She nodded and turned her attention back to the couple on the swing.

"Don't let her or anyone else come back here," Jake said to Snow. He and Rathburn approached the open barn door. There were lights on inside. Snow came up behind him.

"Albright's home office is walled off to the back left," Snow said. "That's where you'll find him. The lights were on when we rolled up. We didn't touch anything, Detective. I made sure."

"That's good, Deputy," Jake said. He'd get with Gemma soon to find out who else she brought through here in the last few days.

Rathburn handed him a pair of gloves and booties, then put on her own pair as Jake did the same.

It was a barn in name only. Over four thousand square feet, the place hadn't seen a stall or a hay bale in years. Now, Craig Albright kept a collection of classic cars in the front section. Jake spotted a red Mustang and shined a light inside.

Further in, Albright had installed a fully stocked bar with a live edge bar top and seating for a dozen. He had a pool table and pinball machines against the wall. Jake walked around the bar and opened the door to the bathroom. A sink. A single shower stall and a urinal. Jake couldn't smell anything but pine cleaner until he shut the door and walked toward the back of the structure.

Another section had been walled off for Craig's home office. Mary got to the door first.

"That smell," Mary said. She put the back of her hand to her nose. Jake noticed it, too. Metallic. Sour. It was blood. A lot of it.

As Jake came to her, he spotted a giant gun safe against the west wall. It stood wide open. Jake looked inside. He saw stacks of papers, bonds, handguns, and two AR-15 rifles untouched.

"That's a lot of firepower," Mary said.

Jake shone his Maglite inside but nothing looked disturbed. Then, he turned and followed Mary to the small home office laid out in the back of the barn. He found Craig Albright's desk and the strongest scent of blood.

For a moment, he could almost see through Gemma's eyes. She might have thought Craig Albright was simply sitting in his chair waiting for her. But his head slumped forward at an odd angle. Dark blood soaked through his shirt, making it impossible to tell what color it had originally been. It dripped down the side of the chair, forming a large puddle at Albright's feet.

"That's gotta be just about his entire blood volume," Mary said.

It was gruesome enough. But the gaping wound in Albright's neck wasn't the worst of it. Not by a mile. Craig Albright no longer had fingers. They were flattened, smashed, and both palms looked cored out.

"What did that?" Rathburn asked.

"I'm guessing a drill," Jake said.

"His feet," Rathburn said. "Oh God. Do you smell that?"

Jake did. Burned flesh. Albright wasn't wearing any shoes. His toes were blackened.

"One by one," Jake whispered. Rathburn stepped away.

"Who would do this?" she said.

Jake shined his Maglite along the walls. They were made of reclaimed barn wood. Gorgeous, really. Only now, a section had been ripped out in the corner. Mary saw it at the same time Jake did. She moved in.

"It looks hollow back there," she said. "Like someone ripped something out of the wall."

"What else do you see?" he asked her. Rathburn stepped away from the hole in the wall. She clipped her light to her belt and surveyed the scene.

"He has so much stuff here. The computer. The guns. The cars. We don't know what was in that wall, but they didn't take anything. And to do that to him."

"It took time," Jake said.

"Do you think he was alive for all of that?"

"We'll know soon enough. We need BCI out here. The Medical Examiner. I need to talk to my sister. Can you talk to that couple? It's unlikely they know anything if she was just showing them the house, but I need you to take their statement."

"Of course," Rathburn said. She held her hand to her nose again.

"You gonna be okay?"

"Yeah. Just give me a minute. This is just ..."

Jake pulled out his cell and made a call to Darcy. As soon as she responded, he said, "Darcy, this is a homicide. We need BCI out. Also, call the M.E. and get him out here. Tell him we're all gonna be in for a long night."

"Copy that, Jake," she said.

"Come on," Jake said to Mary. "I don't want to take another step through here. Let Agent Ramirez and the crime scene lab do their thing. There's plenty of work to go around."

Jake led Mary out of the barn and back up to the house. Deputy Snow was waiting for them. "They're from Ann Arbor," he said, pointing to the couple with Gemma. "Names are Karl and Daphne Birdwell. They just came down for the day for a showing."

"I'll take it from here," Rathburn said. She walked up to the Birdwells and pulled them aside. Gemma stepped off the porch and came to Jake. He put a hand on her back and led her away where they could talk in private.

"Tell me what happened," he said.

"I don't know," she started. "I just ... we had a showing scheduled at five thirty. The Birdwells came down from Ann Arbor. The listing just went live at four. They wanted to be the first ones in. The husband was practically ready to write me an offer over the phone."

"Gemma."

She nodded a little too fast. "Right. Sorry. I called Mr. Albright. Craig. I called him last night. Right after dinner."

She pulled out her phone and unlocked the screen. "Six fifty-five. I called him at six fifty-five. I confirmed the showings for this evening. Wanted to make sure he'd be out of the house. He said he would be. It was brief. Not even thirty seconds, I don't think."

"What time did you get here?"

"Um ... five o'clock. I did a quick walk-through up at the main house. Just to make sure the stagers did a good job."

"When did they come through?"

"Two days ago. Nobody was supposed to be here, Jake. The Albrights haven't been living in the house. Anyway, the Birdwells were right on time. We went through the house. Maybe twenty minutes. They weren't lingering. The husband wanted to see the barn. That's the draw. With that man cave. Anyway, we walked back and just found him there. Like that. Mrs. Birdwell passed out, Jake."

"Did you touch anything?"

"No! God, no. They were behind me. I shoved them back out as fast as I could. As soon as we got the wife back on her feet."

"Good. That's good, Gemma. What about Albright? What's his story?"

She shrugged. "I mean ... he runs that electrical contracting company. All-Brite. You know it."

"I've heard of it."

"This place has been in his family for like fifty years. He inherited it from his father. Donnie Albright. Tragedy that one. My God, Jake. He died on this farm, too. Some kind of accident with the tractor or something."

"Gemma, focus. What about Craig?"

"Oh. Right. I don't know a lot, Jake. He was selling the place because he wanted to move down to Florida. They've got a daughter in college somewhere. I may have a note back at the office. But Rachel, Craig's wife. I used to do her hair, gosh, like twenty years ago. She liked me. That's how I got the listing."

"Do you have her number?"

Gemma shook her head. "Just Craig's. He was very insistent that I only deal with him. I saw Rachel like three weeks ago when we first signed the paperwork. But she's been down in Florida scouting out wherever they're moving to. Destin, I think."

"Can you find her number? I need to locate her. I need to talk to her."

"I'll try. I just had an email for her for when I sent documents back and forth for signatures."

"All right. Just try and get me whatever you have. What else do you know about Craig? How did he seem when you talked to him last night?"

"Fine. He's never been very friendly. All business when we talked, which is fine with me. It bothered me that he wouldn't let me talk to Rachel. Seemed kind of misogynistic but she was okay with it too. He said she just didn't want to be bothered with anything to do with selling the house. He made comments about how she doesn't have a head for business, that sort of thing. But I never got a sense that anything was wrong. It was all pretty normal. They were easy to deal with. Cooperative. He was motivated to sell the house and excited about the showings I had lined up. Oh God. The showings. Jake, I have to make some calls. I've got two more scheduled to start in ..."

Gemma looked at her phone again. "Like twenty minutes!"

"Make the calls," he said. "Cancel everything. Gemma, who's got a key to this place other than you?"

"No one. Well, there's a lockbox at the main house. I have the combination and it's in the MLS listing. So anyone with access to that listing, other realtors."

"You're sure nobody else has shown the house?"

"They weren't supposed to. The listing just went live this afternoon. Plus, it's mine. Nobody is supposed to go in or out without me knowing."

"Supposed to. But that doesn't mean they couldn't. Do you know if he's got security cameras installed?"

"No cameras," she said. "I asked him about that. He was really proud of this property, Jake. Said nobody can get in or out without him knowing the way it's situated."

"Can you make sure no other realtors accessed that lockbox, Gemma? I need to know everyone who's been in or out of here in the last couple of days."

"Nobody, Jake. Just me. And the stagers. I can give you their card. I used a new firm."

She pulled a business card out of her purse and handed it to him.

"Thanks. When did you put the lockbox up?"

"Two days ago. The stagers came in that day. But Jake, I was here with them. Did I do something wrong? Do you think whoever did that got in here using my code?"

She was starting to hyperventilate.

"Relax," he said. "You didn't do anything wrong. I'm just trying to look at every possibility. Anything you can remember will be helpful. Are you okay?"

Her lip quivered, but Gemma straightened her back. "I'm okay."

"Good. You did good, Gemma."

"What if I'd gotten here too early?" she whispered.

"You didn't."

He went to his sister. They didn't hug often. Or rather, he didn't. But today, Gemma folded herself against him. It was brief. She squeezed him back and pulled away.

"It's okay," he said. "Just head home. I'm going to have more questions for you, but not right now."

"No," she said. "It's not okay. Jake. He's out there, isn't he? Whoever did this?"

Jake looked back at the barn.

"It's cursed now," she whispered. "Maybe it already was."

Jake didn't believe in curses. But that evening, a mist rose around the peak of Red Sky Hill and clung to it. Ominous. Sinister. Some might have called it a sign.

If you believed in that sort of thing.

Four

"I've got everyone staying after school," Landry said as she met Jake and Mary back at the station. "Darcy cleared out the conference room next to your office for your war room."

"I appreciate it," Jake said. He followed her into the room. Sergeant Jeff Hammer and Lieutenant Beverly from day shift were already there. Two other deputies from field ops sat at the table. They were good picks. Matt Corbin and Tom Stuckey. Deputies Snow and Denning were charged with securing the Albright's property until Mark Ramirez and his team from the Bureau of Criminal Investigations made their way up from Richmond. They should be there within the hour.

"Thanks for staying over," Jake said to the group. "What's happened at the Albright farm is as bad as the rumors you're gonna hear. Worse. I'll know a lot more once Ramirez's team does their thing, but this is about as brutal a killing as I've ever seen."

Jake ran through what he and Rathburn found and the condition of Albright's body. Landry never sat. She stood against the wall beside a blank whiteboard. Soon, Jake would have the thing covered with a timeline and suspects.

"It's looking like my sister Gemma might have been one of the last people to talk to Craig Albright," Jake said. "I'm trying to find his wife and daughter. They were in the process of moving down to Florida. I don't know the Albrights well myself. What about the rest of you?"

Stuckey raised his hand. In his mid-thirties, like Jake, Stuckey was young, but seasoned. He'd make a good command officer when he was ready.

"My old man knows Craig pretty well. They play ... um ... played in a golf league together. I know they work plenty of jobs together, too."

Jake remembered Stuckey's father owned a heating and cooling business.

"You know if they've worked on anything together recently?" Jake asked.

"I can find out. I know they got some of the contracts for Arch Hill Estates. That's been my dad and brother's main work this year. Craig doesn't go out to the sites much himself anymore I don't think. Let me make a call."

Stuckey pulled out his cell phone and stepped out of the room.

"Have you talked to Andrew?" Sergeant Hammer said. "Andrew Harter's Craig's brother-in-law. Craig brought him into the business after he married Rachel."

"How well do you know him?" Jake asked. "My immediate concern is finding her. Gemma couldn't say for sure whether Rachel was at the house yesterday. She thinks she might be in Florida. Though whoever did this left a lot of valuables in the main house and that barn, there's a hole kicked out and a hollow space behind it. My gut is telling me somebody was looking for something."

"You think they tortured Craig Albright to find it?" Landry asked.

"I think anything's possible right now. I need to make sure Rachel Albright's safe, number one. But somebody's gotta tell her her husband's dead before this hits the internet. And that's another thing. I want to keep this locked down as tight as we can. No leaks. I'm not worried about Gemma saying anything. But that house being for sale was news around here because of its list price. People are going to start talking. Mary, what's your read on the Birdwells, the couple who came down to look at the place?"

"They don't know anything, Jake," she said. "And they're completely traumatized. They had no connection to the house other than seeing Gemma's Zillow listing. They came down from Ann Arbor and were ready to make an offer on it. I mean ... not anymore. But they didn't see anything other than what we did. I'd say your sister did a really good job getting them out of that barn quickly."

"She's good in a crisis," Jake agreed. "What else do we know about this family? Other than seeing that All-Brite Electrical van around town, I'm in the dark. I don't remember any Albrights from high school."

"You wouldn't," Lieutenant Beverly said. "The old man, Craig's dad Donnie. He had Craig working on the farm as a kid. He was home-schooled. Good family."

"How big a family?" Jake asked.

"Just Craig. He had a brother but he died young. Leukemia or something. Craig was supposed to take over the farm, but never had an interest in it once he grew up. Went to trade school instead to be an electrician, then started that business."

"Gemma said he inherited the place from his old man," Jake said. "That he died in some kind of accident."

"Yeah," Beverly said. "Grisly. Somehow got part of his overalls caught in his tractor's PTO revolution. Got wound up into the machinery like a meat grinder. I was in field ops at the time. I've seen the photos. Frank Borowski's the one who cleared it as an accident."

Jake bristled. He had a long history with Detective Frank Borowski. One that had recently ended in a way that still haunted him.

"What about the immediate family?" Jake said. "How well does anyone know Rachel and Craig as a couple? What can you tell me?"

Stuckey came back into the room. Jake repeated his question.

"Just talked to my dad," Stuckey said. "I didn't tell him why I was asking. Don't worry. He knows how to keep his mouth shut anyway. He said he hasn't seen Craig or Rachel in a couple of weeks. But Drew Harter's been doing most of the day-to-day stuff for All-Brite. He actually had a conversation with him out at one of the job sites in Arch Hill earlier in the week. Nothing out of the ordinary. Drew said Craig's been working on closing up shop. Turning the business over to Drew. He was still planning on being a silent partner, but Drew was gonna eventually buy him out. Your sister's intel is right. Albrights were getting ready to retire to Florida."

"Do we know if there's been any talk of them having trouble?" Jake asked. "Rachel and Craig?"

The men around the room murmured, but no consensus emerged until Beverly spoke up. "There's nothing, Jake. Nothing I've heard. Craig's never been the most social guy. He's pleasant enough, but I don't know. I think maybe it's to do with the way he was raised. Something about that hill."

"Come on," Jake said. "Don't tell me you're one of these people who believes in curses."

"It's Red Sky Hill," Beverly said. "Not cursed. It's haunted, Jake. People who go up that hill tend not to come back down. And Donnie Albright saw fit to live in that house and work that farm. Rumor was Donnie was related to hill people a couple of generations back. There were some who didn't like that Donnie and his family farmed the land. That they came down from the hill and went into town in the first place. Then you add to that the way Donnie died. People say he was tempting fate."

Jake couldn't entirely tell whether John Beverly was kidding or not.

"How much interaction did the Albrights have with anyone who lives in those hills?" Landry asked. "Does anyone know?"

"Craig's dad, Donnie, was always an outsider," Beverly said. "His family up the hill didn't want him. The people in town thought he was odd. Donnie used to go around town telling ghost stories but nobody really took him seriously. As far as he was concerned, his cousins up the hill were all a bunch of inbred weirdos. There's a report somewhere. Maybe twenty-five years ago. Donnie had a run-in with one of the Knox boys. I don't remember the details. Some kind of boundary dispute that came to violence. As far as I know, that's the last time anyone from the hill had anything to do with the Albrights. Or anyone from town, for that matter."

Jake had heard the stories his whole life. A group of families still lived in the hills and kept to themselves more or less off the grid. A generation or two back, they were related to Rex Bardo, kingpin of the region's organized crime family. It's how his crew got its name, the Hilltop Boys. Though as far as Jake knew, none of them actually lived in the hills anymore. The name just stuck.

"Maybe somebody up that hill wasn't too keen on the idea that Craig was going to sell that land to outsiders," Mary said. "Maybe they thought he should give it back to his cousins on the hill."

"It's a good theory anyway," Jake said. "But in the meantime, I'm more interested in what was going on in that house. I don't have a cell phone on Rachel Albright. Gemma had no firm idea where in Florida they were thinking of moving to."

Stuckey raised his hand. "I know Drew Harter well enough. We're not friends, but let me get him for you."

"Do it," Jake said. "Sounds like he's someone I need to talk to sooner rather than later. And hopefully he has a way of getting a hold of his sister."

Stuckey left the room again. "Tell us what you need, Jake," Sergeant Hammer said.

"I need to know who Albright was talking to besides my sister over the last twenty-four hours. A lot of that will come from BCI's report on his cell and computer. I need to know who had access to that house. Gemma's got a lockbox out there. She gave me the name of the firm who staged it for her. They're local." He pulled out the business card Gemma gave him and handed it to Mary Rathburn.

"I'll track them down now," she said.

"Work a timeline. Gemma talked to Craig Albright at six fifty-five last evening. Agent Ramirez should be able to give me an approximate time of death but we know it was in the last twenty-four hours. I need to know if either anyone from that firm was in the house prior to Gemma's showing or who else had access to that lockbox code."

"On it," Mary said, ready to excuse herself. She looked at Lieutenant Beverly. He in turn looked at Meg Landry.

"Consider all overtime approved," she said to Beverly. "Whatever you need, Jake. I hope to God this was just some isolated incident. A personal beef. But by morning, I'm going to have to start fielding a lot of questions. We can all agree to lock this down but you know how things work around here. The details of what happened at the base of that hill are going to get out. People are going to want assurances that they're safe in their homes, Jake."

"And I'll do my best to give it to them."

"It's not just that," Beverly said. "I'm telling you. This is going to stir up a lot of ancient history about those hills."

"It just better not come from us," Jake said. "I don't believe in ghosts, John. Or curses. I don't want bigoted people thinking they need to take the law into their own hands with this and charge up that hill with pitchforks and AR-15s."

"God," Landry said. She finally sat down. "I hadn't even thought of that. No. We cannot have that, Jake."

"It doesn't do any good to think too far ahead on this," he said. "Priority one is getting Rachel Albright secured."

"Do you think she's in danger?" Deputy Corbin asked.

"I think at this stage of this, we can't make any assumptions," Jake answered. His head was starting to pound. There would need to be a press conference. Soon. Jake hated the things. But he knew Landry would rely on him to help her project calm. The citizens of Worthington County would need to know they were safe. At the moment, that was something he couldn't guarantee. Whatever else was going on, Craig Albright's death was enough to scare anyone.

Deputy Stuckey came back into the room. "I've got him, Detective. Deputy Paulson was on patrol a couple of blocks from Drew Harter's house. He said the Harters just came home a few minutes ago. He pulled Drew aside and let him know we needed to talk to him. He can have him here in five minutes."

"Good," Jake said. "Tell Paulson to bring him in to interview one. I'll meet him down there."

"Rathburn, you should listen in," Landry said. Jake nodded. He grabbed his suit jacket off the chair and headed downstairs.

FIVE

Andrew Harter waited in the only chair against the wall in the hallway outside interview room one. He wasn't alone. Beside him, an older man stood, bent-backed, leaning on a cane.

"Mr. Harter?" Jake asked. Both men looked up.

"I'm Mick," the older man said. He held out a blue-veined, gnarled hand. "This is my son, Andrew. Is he in trouble?"

"Uh ... no," Jake said. "Your son. So you're Rachel Albright's father as well? I don't want to assume ..."

"That's right," the elder Mr. Harter answered. "Is she here? Is there something wrong?"

"Mr. Harter." Mary stepped forward. "Why don't I set you up somewhere more comfortable? Detective Cashen will explain everything."

Mary swooped in and put a hand on Mick Harter's sleeve. He eyed her, but slowly went along with her as she led him to the break room at the end of the hall. Jake mouthed a thank you to her.

"Andrew?" Jake said. The younger Harter hadn't so much as rose from the chair.

"Drew," he said. "He's the only one who calls me Andrew. Are you going to tell me what this is all about?"

"I am," Jake said. "Follow me."

Drew Harter heaved himself out of the chair and followed Jake into the interview room. He was tall. Fit. Light-brown hair combed straight back. He took a seat at the table and swept his arms across the top, folding his hands.

"Drew," Jake said. "I'm Jake."

"Fine."

Jake tucked back his tie and took a seat opposite Drew Harter. He set his phone face down on the table between them.

"I understand you work with your brother-in-law, Craig Albright."

"Yeah. We run the business together."

"Drew. I need to ask you. When was the last time you saw Craig?"

Drew raised a brow. "Yesterday."

"What time?"

"When we quit work for the day. Four. Maybe five?"

"Where is work?"

"Craig's office. At his house off of Lassiter Road. We work out of the barn."

"Can you be more specific about the time? It's important. You said four or five. Which was it?"

"Why are you asking me this?"

"Drew, please. Let's get through this."

"Right before five. That's as close a time as I can give you. We own the business. I don't punch a clock. But it was Craig's last day. He's stepping back from the business. We had a beer together and then I left."

"Where was Craig when you left?"

"It's his house. He was gonna head up to the kitchen and make himself dinner."

"So he was still in the office ... still in the barn when you left?"

"Yeah."

"Was Craig alone?"

"Yes," Drew said, his tone sharp. "What the hell is all this about?"

Jake picked up his phone. "Drew. Something's happened. I'm very sorry to be the one to tell you this, but your brother-in-law was found dead this evening out on his property."

Drew Harter's face stayed blank. Jake pulled up a picture on his phone. "This might be rough. I don't really have a way to soften the blow. But I need to show you a photograph. It's graphic. If you need to take a minute."

"Let me see it," Drew said. He reached across the table and snatched Jake's phone right out of his hand.

"Drew ..."

Drew Harter turned the phone over and stared at the photograph. He blinked once. Twice.

"Jesus!" Drew said. He dropped the phone as if it were on fire. "Jesus! What the hell is that?"

"Drew. I'm sorry. But I need you to confirm for me. Do you recognize the man in that photo?"

"That's sick. Jesus. Yes. That's Craig. What the fuck, man. How can you just shove that in my face like that?"

"I'm sorry. I know. We're still trying to figure out what happened."

"Somebody sliced him open. That's what happened."

Drew Harter vaulted out of his seat. He started pacing, clawing at his shirt. "Oh man. Oh man."

"Drew, I need you to think. Is there anyone you know who would want to hurt your brother-in-law?"

"What?"

"Did he have any enemies? Anyone who would have wanted to do something like that to him."

"What am I supposed to do? He's dead? He's dead?"

"Yes," Jake said. He sat back while Drew Harter continued to spin out. Drew smacked his palm against the wall.

"I can't be here. I gotta get out of here. I can't breathe."

"Drew, please, take a seat. I know this is rough. But I need some information."

"What am I supposed to do?" he asked.

"Sitting here and helping me figure a few things out is what you need to be doing."

"Craig can't be dead. We work together. He was leaving the business to me. How am I supposed to ..."

"Drew!" Jake said. "Take a seat. Now."

He did. Drew tore his fingers through his hair and leaned forward on his elbows. The whole table shook as he tapped his heel against the floor.

"Where'd you go after you left work yesterday, Drew?"

"Out of town," he said. "I've got a girl in West Virginia. We met up. Christ. I need to make some calls. We've got contracts. People Craig was supposed to lock down before he left for Florida. If he's not here to help with the transition ... they might leave."

"Drew, look at me. Your sister, Rachel. When was the last time you spoke to her?"

Drew Harter looked at Jake, but through him. The man was clearly more concerned with whatever business dealings might be jeopardized by Craig Albright's passing.

"What?"

"Rachel. Your sister. Craig's wife. Where is she?"

"You don't know?"

"No. Do you have a number for her?"

"What?"

"A number. For Rachel. Craig's wife."

Finally, Drew took his phone out of his pocket. "Yeah." He opened his contacts. Scrolling through, he turned the phone toward Jake. Rachel Albright was listed merely as "Sis" in her brother's phone.

"I need you to call her for me right now," Jake said.

Drew pressed the call button. The phone rang four times, then went to Rachel's voicemail. "Tell her to call you."

"Rach ... it's Drew. Either pick up or give me a call. It's important." Drew clicked off. Jake wrote down the number on Rachel's phone.

"Where is she, Drew? Where's Rachel?"

"I don't know. She was headed down to Destin. She and Craig are ... uh ... were moving there. That's the whole thing. Craig was turning the business over to me. It was all set up. He was going to make sure all our biggest clients understood. So it would go smooth, you know? Now ..."

"I understand. That's tough. But right now, don't you think there are more important things to deal with? He's dead, Drew. Your sister doesn't know her husband is dead. I need to find her. Do you get that?"

"Yeah. God. Sorry. Yeah."

"You have a niece? I understand Craig and Rachel have a daughter?"

"Lex. Yeah. Alexis. Uh. She's not here. She goes to school. A senior, I think. University of Colorado. She's in Boulder."

"Do you have a number for her?"

Drew shook his head furiously. "No. No. My dad does though. They text. Shit. My dad."

"My colleague, Deputy Rathburn, is with him."

"This is gonna kill him. You gotta find Rachel."

"We're working on that. This helps. Do you know where in Destin she was staying? A hotel?"

"No, man. No." Drew Harter started to cry. "I can't be here. I can't breathe."

There was a pitcher of water and paper cups at the end of the table. Jake poured some for Drew and slid it to him. With shaking hands, he took a drink.

"Thanks."

"I know this is rough for you. Shocking. But we need to figure out who did this. And we need to make sure Rachel and Alexis are safe, okay?"

"Yeah. Yeah."

"So, think. Do you have any idea who might have wanted to hurt your brother-in-law?"

"Did they take anything?" Drew asked.

Jake flipped to a different photograph on his phone and showed it to Drew. "Do you recognize that?"

Jake had snapped a quick picture of the hole ripped out of the wall near the body.

Drew covered his mouth with his hand. "I don't know. I don't know."

"Do you know what was behind that panel in the wall?"

Drew kept shaking his head. "No. Nothing."

"All right. What about Rachel? Is there anyone else she might be in communication with? Did she go down to Florida alone? Did she take a friend? Was she talking to a realtor?"

"I don't know. We can ask my dad. They're close. Maybe he's talked to her. I'm sorry, man. I just can't be here right now. This is too much. Too heavy. I need a cigarette. I need air."

Jake stiffened. Drew Harter seemed very good at articulating everything *he* needed.

"Drew. Listen to me. From how things are shaping up, I think there's a pretty good chance you're one of the last people to have seen your brother-in-law alive. So I need your help. I need you to clear your head. If that means you need to take a smoke break, fine. I don't care if you light up in here. But we should talk to your father now, okay? You think you can help me out with that? He doesn't look well."

"God."

Jake rose. "Come with me, then you can have your smoke." Drew got up and followed Jake out into the hall. He led him down to the break room. Mary had Mick Harter seated at the table. His color had gone ashen. Mary leaned over and patted him on the back.

"We'll do this together," Jake said.

"He's on pills," Drew said. "His heart."

"Mr. Harter?" Jake said.

"Is he in trouble?" Mick Harter said, looking at his son. "This lady won't tell me anything."

"It's Craig," Drew blurted. "He's dead, Pops. Somebody cut his throat open."

Jake winced. Drew delivered the news with the grace of a sledgehammer.

"Where's Rachel?" Mick Harter asked, sensibly. "Andrew, where's your sister?"

"Mr. Harter." Jake stepped forward. "That's what we're trying to figure out. She wasn't at the house. I have no reason to think anything bad has happened to her. But we need to get a hold of her. She isn't answering her phone. Do you know where she was staying?"

Mick Harter erupted into a deep, hacking cough.

"Jesus," Drew said. "Pops, you can't do this. Not now."

Mary held a glass of water out for Mick Harter. He batted it away.

"Mr. Harter," she said. "Jake, I don't like his color." She reached out and tried to loosen his collar.

Harter shoved her away and tried to get to his feet. He took two staggering steps forward then keeled sideways. Jake rushed forward, catching the older man before he hit the floor.

"Mary, call for an ambulance."

"Rachel," Mick croaked. "Where's my baby girl?"

"We'll find her," Jake assured him. "I need you to try to breathe for me, okay?"

Jake helped Mick back into a chair. He was sweating. Jake checked to make sure the old man's lips weren't turning blue. He checked his pulse. It was racing. Drew Harter backed himself out into the hallway.

The fire department was housed directly next door to the sheriff's. Within a minute, two EMTs came charging in. Jake moved away as they assessed Mick Harter.

Jake and Mary gave them room. Slowly, Mick Harter's color improved. They'd had him hooked up to oxygen.

"Your blood pressure went through the roof, Mr. Harter," one of the EMTs said. The other looked back at Jake and gave him a quick thumbs-up.

Beside him, Mary whispered in Jake's ear. "Jake. Drew Harter's gone."

In all the commotion, Jake almost forgot about him. But as he turned and looked down the hall, he saw Mary was right.

"That shit," he murmured. "He just left his old man here?"

"I'll bring him back," Mary said.

"I want someone following him," Jake said.

"You think he had something to do with this?"

"I don't know. But the guy was a lot more concerned about himself than anyone else. I want to pin down his alibi. He just said something about a booty call with some woman in West Virginia. We need to find Rachel Harter and her daughter. Can you get a hold of the campus police at the University of Colorado in Boulder? Alexis Albright is a student there."

"On it," Mary said.

Mick Harter was better. Thank God. He took off his own oxygen mask and locked eyes with Jake.

"You feeling okay, Mr. Harter?" Jake asked.

"He took off, didn't he?" Mick asked. "My son." He bit down on the last word.

"It appears so."

"Find my little girl," he whispered. "Please."

"I will," Jake promised, praying Rachel Harter, wherever she was, hadn't suffered a similar fate as her husband.

Six

J ake managed a quick four hours of sleep then hit Saturday morning running. Agent Ramirez and the medical examiner finished their preliminary reports at the same time. Jake asked Ramirez to meet him at Dr. Stone's office so he could hear what they had to say together. Plus, he figured it wouldn't hurt for the two of them to be on the same page if anything new came up.

Jake pulled into Stone's office parking lot at the same time Mark Ramirez did. Ramirez looked like he'd gotten even less sleep than Jake. On a hunch, Jake had stopped and grabbed four coffees on his way in. Though he could have probably used all four, he handed one to a very grateful Ramirez.

"It'll probably do me more immediate good if you just threw the damn thing in my face," Mark said.

"You look like you slept in your suit," Jake said as Jake used his security badge to key them into Stone's building.

"You're half right," Mark said. "I'm rolling on thirty-six hours with no sleep."

Ramirez lifted one side of his jacket and smelled his own armpit. He wrinkled his nose. Jake laughed and cut him a wide berth.

Dr. Ethan Stone's office was at the end of a long hallway, two doors down from his lab. Jake knew Craig Albright, or what was left of him, was still in a cooler drawer behind one of the other doors.

Stone opened his door just before Jake was about to knock. Stone had a day's worth of white stubble sprouting along his jaw. He looked even worse than Ramirez did. Jake pulled another cup of coffee out of the cardboard drink carrier and handed it to him.

"Good man," Stone said.

"Ethan," Jake said. "You've met Agent Ramirez?"

"Of course," Dr. Stone said. The two men shook hands anyway and Stone ushered them into his office. Jake was glad of it. He was hoping not to spend any more time in a room with Craig Albright's corpse. He'd seen enough of the live show and pictures were bad enough.

"Who wants to go first?" Jake said as the three men settled. Stone took a seat behind his desk. He had his Army medals in a display case on the credenza behind him. The man had served two tours in Vietnam at an Army hospital and reached the rank of captain. Nearing eighty, the powers that be had been on him to retire. But Jake knew the only way Ethan Stone would leave his lab was on a slab right beside the cases he worked on. They didn't make them like Stone anymore. For this case, Jake knew what an asset that was.

"Let me give you the highlights of what I found out at the scene," Ramirez said. "My full report will be on your desk by Monday morning."

Ramirez came prepared with handouts. He gave a copy to Dr. Stone and the other to Jake. Jake quickly flipped through the stapled pages. Ramirez had flagged certain photographs from the crime scene. The wall next to Albright's desk. The floor under his chair. His tool bench on the far wall. Then there were the grisly images of the body itself. Close-ups of the black zip ties around Albright's wrists and ankles, securing him to the chair. His hands, little more than mottled, purple lumps of flesh. Jake wouldn't have recognized them as hands if he hadn't seen them himself.

"Somebody really did a number on that poor fellow," Dr. Stone said.

"We found blood spatter against the wall behind him," Ramirez said, pointing to that photograph. "From the angle, most of that was probably from when they drilled into his hands."

Jake winced and put that photograph face down.

"Our rapid DNA came back indicating it's only Albright's blood. Whoever did this, did it clean. Probably wore gloves and maybe a hazmat-type suit. We didn't find any foreign blood or hair samples. No fingerprints other than Albright's and one other."

Ramirez pointed to another photograph. There were two glasses on the counter to the left of Albright's desk. One was empty, the other was half filled with gold liquid.

"Beer," Jake said. "Harter said he and Albright had a beer at the end of the workday Thursday night."

"Well, it tracks with what we found. One of the glasses had Albright's prints on it. I need prints for Harter, but I'll go out on a limb and say the other set belongs to him."

"What about the house?" Jake asked.

Ramirez let out a defeated sigh. "Jake, it was pristine for the most part. The bigger problem is the furniture. You said your sister says the Albrights moved most of their stuff to storage a few weeks ago?"

"Yeah. Ahead of putting their house on the market."

"Right. So what's in there now is everything the house stagers brought in. I talked to the woman who runs that company. Kathy Byers. She said they staged the house with items from their collection. The couches. Kitchen table. Bedroom sets. It's all stuff that's been used multiple times in other houses. It's garbage in terms of having any evidentiary value."

"I assumed as much," Jake said. "Plus the odds are the killer or killers never went inside the house."

"Well, you'll never be able to prove whether they did," Ramirez said.

"What else you got?" Jake asked.

"Well, the problem is what we don't got."

"What do you mean?"

"The tools of the trade on this were missing. Albright had a workbench in the corner. Basic stuff. Hammers, screwdrivers. A few power tools. But none of them were used on him. His hands were drilled. His feet burned. Doc can speak more to what caused those injuries, but whatever it was, the killer took them with him. Or more likely ... brought his own kit and took it with him. Or her."

"A professional," Jake said.

"This man was tortured, Jake," Dr. Stone said. "Over a prolonged amount of time. His fingers were smashed one by one. Probably with a hammer. His nail beds were pulverized. The killer used a three-eighths-inch drill bit through the tops of each of Albright's hands. The scorch patterns on his toes. It was most likely a blowtorch, something with a steady flow of flame. And again. One by one. He cooked 'em like sausages."

"Jesus," Jake muttered.

"This took a while," Dr. Stone said. "And this poor son of a gun was alive during it. I can't tell you if he was conscious but I'm guessing he was. At least for part of it."

Dr. Stone picked a tablet up off his desk. He swiped the screen and turned it, showing Jake and Ramirez various photographs from the autopsy. He settled on one, showing the zip ties cutting into Craig Albright's wrists.

"These lacerations above and below the ties," Dr. Stone said. "Craig Albright was fighting against his bindings. Struggling. And the lividity patterns. The man was sitting upright in that chair for a prolonged period of time. My best guess, your killer wanted him awake and alert for a lot of what happened to him. Now your cause of death is pretty obvious."

Stone scrolled forward, stopping on a picture of the gaping wound to Craig Albright's neck.

"This man's throat was slit with one clean cut from a very sharp blade. I'd say some type of fillet knife. The cuts were precise, slicing through both major arteries in the neck. And it wasn't a slashing gesture."

"What do you mean?" Jake asked.

"I mean it was a deliberate cut, ear to ear. The depth of the wound is almost uniform from one end to the other. Albright would have died pretty quick after that. Total exsanguination. He lost his entire blood volume down the front of his shirt and pooled on that barn floor, Jake."

"His face," Jake said. "That bruising to his cheek. Do you think that would have been enough of a blow to render him unconscious?"

"I didn't find significant swelling in the brain. No sign of a concussion. I think that blow would have been hard enough to ring his bell, to put it unscientifically, but not enough to knock him out. See that scraping? My guess, the killer might have been wearing a ring."

Jake and Ramirez looked closer. It was hard to make out with all the discoloration to Albright's skin but Jake could barely make out tiny red lines along the man's cheek and temple.

"Can I get copies of all of these?" Ramirez asked. "I can have my techs take a look and see if they can come up with a theory as to what made those marks."

"I'll have my full report to you Monday morning as well," Dr. Stone promised.

"Somebody wanted information from him," Jake said. "I'm betting it had to do with whatever was behind that wall paneling." Jake had Ramirez's photo of the hollowed-out space in the wall behind Craig's desk.

"We couldn't find anything useful there either," Ramirez said. "If it was a crowbar, we don't know. I have no evidence for you of what was used to rip off that portion of the wall."

"What about the digital forensics?" Jake asked. "His phone. His computer."

"His laptop was powered on. Our guy at the lab will do a full forensic report for you. Our initial eyeballing didn't pull up anything unusual. Albright was running his business software on it. He had tabs opened for his work email, his invoices, his accounts receivable. Doesn't look like the guy was even playing

Tetris or anything during work hours. As far as his phone, our digital guys did a basic quick forensics report on it. Last call was from your sister, just like you said. It only lasted forty-five seconds. There are some pretty benign texts between Albright and his wife, but even those stopped Wednesday morning. Some calls to and from Drew Harter. One from his daughter on Tuesday afternoon. But nothing alarming in the days leading up to his murder. I'll know more in a few days. And we're looking into the landline he had hooked up on the desk. The number goes to All-Brite Electrical and it doesn't look like they had a personal landline to the house. Just the business."

"Thanks," Jake said.

"It's not much," Ramirez said. "Only ..."

"Only what?" Jake said.

"Jake ... I don't know who wanted to kill Craig Albright. But the way he was killed. I've seen it before. The drill holes. The burning to the feet."

Dr. Stone met Ramirez's gaze. "I've seen it before too," Stone said.

Jake knew what they were thinking. He'd been thinking it too, but hadn't wanted to give voice to it. He still didn't. Not here. Not in Worthington County.

"This is the kind of thing you see from some of the cartels, Jake," Ramirez said.

Jake squeezed his eyes shut and let out a breath. There it was. He didn't want to believe it, but the truth was, he had seen this kind of thing before himself when he worked for the Bureau.

"Yeah."

"You need to find out whether Craig Albright was mixed up in something like that."

"Yeah."

Jake's phone rang. His caller ID read Deputy Rathburn.

"Yeah," Jake said. He put her on speaker.

"Detective," she started.

"Mary," he said. "If we're gonna work this case together, I told you to start calling me Jake."

"Jake," she said. "Okay. Well. I just got off the phone with a deputy down in Okaloosa County, Florida. Destin. They've found Rachel Albright. She's been staying at their new house but there's no landline hooked up. Apparently, she lost her phone two days ago and that's why she hasn't been responding. But she's okay. She's safe."

Jake let out a breath he hadn't realized he'd been holding.

"They're putting her on a plane. She'll be back in Stanley by this afternoon."

"Good. That's good news, Mary."

"I have more," she said. "The daughter, Alexis. Campus police at the University of Colorado got to her as well. They've informed her what's going on. She's on a different inbound flight and should get here this evening."

"Thanks, Mary. Can you make sure we've got a presence at the airport when both of those planes land? I don't want either of those women headed to the Albright house. I want them brought straight to the station."

"Already on it," Mary said. "I'll bring them right to you."

"Good work, Mary," Jake said, then clicked off.

"God, Jake," Dr. Stone said. "I know Rachel Albright. We used to go to the same church. Little Lex? She was a soloist in the children's choir. Sweet kid. Pretty. Really smart. Do you think they could be in danger too? Is it safe for them to come back here?"

"They could still be in danger," Jake said. "If that's what this is."

He could only pray that it wasn't. Or Blackhand Hills was about to be turned on its ear.

SEVEN

At ten a.m. the next morning, Rachel Albright walked into the sheriff's department, clinging to Deputy Erica "Birdie" Wayne. Birdie had been there, waiting at the airport. Rachel had latched onto her and had yet to let go.

"Mom?"

At the other end of the hall, Alexis Albright raced toward her mother. Even then, Rachel wouldn't let go of Birdie. Jake walked in as Rachel threw her free arm around her daughter and sobbed.

"It's going to be okay, Mrs. Albright," Birdie said. She locked eyes with Jake and mouthed, "She's a mess."

"You're okay?" Rachel said. "Lexie, you're okay?"

"I'm okay," the younger Albright woman assured her mother. "But Daddy. Mama ... they said ..."

"Mrs. Albright," Jake said. "I'm Detective Cashen. I'm very sorry for your loss. I appreciate you coming down here. We can ..."

"Who did this?" Rachel cried. "Who did this? They won't let me see Craig. They won't let me go home."

"Mom, they can't," Alexis said. "They don't know who did this."

Despite her concern for her mother, Alexis had been remarkably composed since arriving at the police station. It was Alexis who comforted Rachel, translating whatever Jake or Birdie had said to her. It was an interesting role reversal, Jake thought. Alexis acted more like a parent than Rachel did.

"Mrs. Albright," Jake said. "I know this is difficult. I'm sure you have a lot running through your head. But I need you to sit down with me. There are some things I need to ask you."

"I can't," she said. "I can't be here. I can't. I want to see Craig."

"Mom, it's all right," Alexis said. "The detective needs your help. For Dad. Okay?"

Alexis turned to Jake. "Can I come with her? Would that help?"

"For now, I need to talk to your mother alone. Deputy Rathburn needs to ask you some questions as well."

"I'll come with you, Mrs. Albright," Birdie said, looking at Jake. He nodded. If Birdie could provide a calming presence to the woman, he was all for it.

Alexis gave her mother another hug, then went with Mary to another interview room. With her hand still fastened to Birdie's, Rachel followed Jake into interview room one.

"Can I get you anything?" Jake asked. "A glass of water? A soft drink? Something to eat?"

"No. No. I don't want anything. I'll throw up. I just want ... I don't even know what I want."

She took a seat at the table. Finally, she let go of Birdie but gravitated to her as Birdie sat beside her.

"You've been so nice to me," Rachel said to Birdie. "The police officer in Destin, too. I couldn't think. I couldn't even remember where I kept my driver's license. They wouldn't have let me board the plane."

"Mrs. Albright," Jake said. "I know this is very tough. But it's my job to try to piece together who might have done this to your husband. So the first thing I need to ask you is, can you think of anyone who might have wanted to hurt Craig?"

Rachel wiped her tears away. "He ran an electrical contracting business. Everyone likes Craig. Most of our business comes from word of mouth. He's reliable. He does good work."

"Did he owe anyone any money that you know of?"

"No ... if anything, people owed him money. Collections were never his strong suit."

"Were you involved in the business end much?"

"No," she said. Rachel leaned back and placed a flat hand over her stomach. For a moment, it looked like she was about to be sick. Birdie reacted. She poured Rachel a glass of water and handed it to her. Rachel's hand trembled so badly, drops of it spilled on the table before she could get it down.

"No," she finally said. "I didn't have anything to do with the business. I had no interest in it. I kept the house. The farm. Craig likes ... liked the look of the place. But he hated dealing with the yard. The chickens. The gardens. He would have let everything grow over if it weren't for me. That's ... how we do things. Craig runs the business. I handle the homestead. But it was all just getting to be too much. I'm fifty-two. Craig just turned sixty. I'd been on him for a few years. The winters here are just so darn cold.

He promised me when I turned fifty, we could move to Florida for good."

"That's why you were down there?"

"Yes. We bought a house in Destin a few months ago but it needs major renovations. I've been going back and forth dealing with the designers and the contractors."

"When was the last time you spoke to Craig?"

Rachel Albright put a hand to her cheek. "Wednesday morning. I lost my phone. Wednesday night. I've been staying at the house. Making sure the workers know what they're supposed to be doing. Picking out paint colors. But I went out for a walk along the beach to watch the sunset. I took some pictures, but I must have dropped my phone somewhere along the way. I didn't realize I didn't have it until the next morning. Craig is always yelling at me about that. He can't figure out why I don't have the thing glued to my hand like most women."

"We were worried when we couldn't locate you," Jake said.

"I know. I talked to my dad. I'm so sorry. So so sorry."

"Is he doing all right? Your dad? We were worried about him too."

"This is killing him, too. His heart's not in the best shape. He had a heart attack three years ago that almost took him from us. That's one of the renovations the house needs. They're converting one section of the house into a suite for my dad. He won't commit yet, but once it's done, we're going to talk him into coming to live with us. Florida would be good for him, too."

"Mrs. Albright ..."

"Please, call me Rachel."

"Rachel. Can you tell me where you were Thursday evening?"

"My interior designer and I were picking out countertops for the kitchen and mudroom. Then she took me out to dinner."

"Can you write her name down?" Jake slid a pad of paper across the table to Rachel. She opened her purse and took out a business card.

"Cindy Shore. Isn't that funny? Her name's Shore and she specializes in redecorating beachfront property. You can have this."

Jake took the card from her.

"Thank you. So you said you spoke to Craig on Wednesday morning and you lost your phone Wednesday evening?"

"It was Wednesday at around ten, I think. I called him while he was in the office."

"How did he seem?"

"He seemed like Craig. He was busy. In a rush. He was supposed to fly out this morning. So we could finalize some of the design plans. He was trying to finish up work. They were going to start showings at the house here. He was annoyed. You know. Distracted. Just trying to get everything done."

"Sure. How was the business doing? If you know."

"Fine. Craig was busy. Always busy. But if you're asking me about numbers, I don't know. Craig handled all the books. All our finances. He told me what I could spend on certain things."

"As part of my investigation, I'm going to need to take a hard look at Craig's business dealings ..."

"Anything," she said. "Whatever you need. If you need me to sign authorizations ... I don't care. You have to find out who did this to us."

"I appreciate that. What about a family feud? I've heard rumors that maybe Craig didn't get along very well with his side of the family. I've heard something about an argument or dispute with his father's family?"

"The hill people?" Rachel said. "Sorry. I shouldn't call them that. Craig used to get angry with me. Like I was calling him a redneck or a hillbilly. I wasn't. I swear. Only those people on the other side of that hill are odd. Everyone knows that. Craig was always kind of ashamed of that side of the family."

"Have you ever met them?"

"No. I barely knew his father. They were estranged by the time Craig and I started dating. We didn't spend a lot of time with him. He didn't even come to our wedding. But despite all of that, Craig inherited the farm from his dad. Donnie. He didn't really want anything to do with it. He hated it there. God. I should have listened to him. I'm the one who talked him into moving to his family's farm and making it what *we* wanted it to be. Converting the old barn to his office space. Starting a hobby farm. That was for me. He did it for me. He said that place was cursed."

"Because of how his father died?"

"Just ... he didn't have anything to do with his family after his dad died ... or before for that matter. He said when he was a kid, his father had some bad blood with *his* father's people. I never even met them. I don't think any of them are still alive."

"I'm hearing there was a boundary dispute on the farm," Jake said.

"You're talking fifty years ago, maybe longer," she said. "I'm sorry. I can't tell you what you want to know. I don't know what the details were. I just know my father-in-law was disowned by his family a long time before I met him. And they're all dead now. Even my father-in-law. He was killed in a tractor accident out in the field. Craig was the one who found him. It was terrible. He'd been out there for days. Some animals got to him. Craig said he never wanted to live like that. His dad was mean. He pushed everyone away. But even with all of that, Craig was a good son. He checked on Donnie. Tried to look out for him. If he hadn't ... God knows how long Donnie would have lain out there rotting in that field. Craig was going to sell the farm but I talked him out of it. We *did* make it into something wonderful. We raised our daughter there. And now? God. I don't think I ever want to step foot on that land again. Only now, how are we supposed to sell it? Who would buy it after all this?"

"So as far as you know, none of the Albrights were in contact with Craig recently?"

"There aren't any Albrights left. Craig didn't have any living siblings. His mom died before I met him. There might have been an uncle or two but they're long gone as far as I know. I don't think Craig could have even named any cousins if they existed. Craig was it. That's one of the reasons he and his dad had a falling out. Because Craig wanted to go his own way. He went the trade school route instead of taking over the farm. And he married me. A city girl. Isn't that funny? Like I'm from Manhattan or something. I'm from Stanley. Literally ten miles away from the farm where Craig grew up."

"Families can be complicated," Jake agreed. "But the barn. Obviously, it was renovated. But it's the original one from when Craig's family farmed it proper?"

"Yes."

"Rachel, there was one thing out at the crime ... out at the barn that I'm trying to puzzle out. There was a large section of the wall paneling removed. A hollowed-out space behind it. Do you have any idea what might have been stored there?"

Jake showed Rachel a single photo of the hollowed-out wall space. She shook her head.

"No. No idea. Do you think they stole something?"

"Maybe. Robbery can always be a motive."

"We had a safe out there. That's where Craig kept any valuables he had there. I don't know what this is."

"Did you spend much time out in that barn?"

"Not really. It was Craig's space. He didn't like me out there, honestly. But you should talk to Drew, my brother. He was going to take over the business. The day to day. Craig was going to keep a hand in and mentor Drew. But he was finally willing to step back and give Drew his time to shine. It's been such a relief. I wish we'd have done this ten years ago."

Her voice caught and Rachel Albright began to sob again. Birdie reached over and put a hand on her arm.

"If he'd listened to me. If he'd retired ten years ago, we'd be gone. This wouldn't have happened, would it?"

"You can't wrap yourself up with too many what-ifs, Rachel," Birdie said. "When my brother was killed, I asked myself that a thousand times. If I'd come to visit him more. If I'd answered him the last time he called me. It'll swallow you up if you let it."

Rachel nodded. "Thank you. You're right. I know. You're right. But what am I going to do now? Lex. She and her dad weren't in the best place. It's hard raising teenage girls. She was just starting to come back to us. Craig and Lex were just starting to find common ground with each other again. She should have come home. She was supposed to visit this summer but she couldn't get off work. She's got an apartment in Boulder now. A job. He was so proud of her. She seems so strong. So calm. But this is going to hit her later.

Hard. She's going to start blaming herself for all the arguments she and her dad had. It was just typical stuff. Their politics. Lex's lifestyle."

"Her lifestyle?" Jake asked.

"Lex is, um ... fluid. I think that's the term. She has a boyfriend now, but the last one was a girlfriend."

"Ah," Jake said.

"He wasn't a bigot. Oh God. I don't want you to think that. It's just ... you worry about your kids. You want them to take the easiest path and people can be so cruel. Even now. It's better now. But you just worry."

"Of course," Jake said.

"I need to see him. Will you let me see him?"

"Rachel, whoever killed Craig ... his injuries are very severe. I honestly think it would be better if you remembered him the way he was. In my experience, that will be better for you in the long run."

"Rachel, don't," Birdie said. "As I've told you, my brother was the victim of a violent homicide. I understand your instincts, but it really is going to be easier for you if you don't see Craig right now. Not like this."

"Okay. Okay." Rachel sniffled. Jake handed her a fresh tissue. "Thank you. Thank you both. Oh gosh. I've been so wrapped up in my own thing. Detective ... um ... Jake. I know you're Gemma's brother. This whole time I haven't asked you how she's doing. She found my Craig. She saw him ... how he was. Is she okay?"

"Thanks for asking," Jake said. "Gemma's pretty tough. But yes. It was rough for her."

"Will you tell her ... God. I don't even know what to tell her. I'm sorry. Tell her I'm sorry she had to go through that. Tell her thank you. I'll try to call her in a few days, maybe. I just need some time to think."

"Of course," Jake said. The difference between Rachel's reaction compared to that of her brother couldn't have been wider. Rachel's concern for others seemed genuine. Drew had only been concerned for himself.

"Are we done here? Do you still need me? I've got to go be with my dad. He needs to see Lex. It'll do him good. It'll do us all good."

"Is that where you'll be staying?" Jake asked. "With your father?"

"Yes. Gosh. Yes. I guess so. I hadn't even thought of it. I can't go back to the house now, can I?"

"No. Not yet. Maybe not for a while."

Rachel gathered her purse and held it to her chest.

"Right. Of course not. I don't know if I can ever go back there. Yes. Anyway, yes. I'll be staying at my dad's place until ... I don't ... I don't even know what to do."

"Take care of your family," Jake said. "That's what you can do. I'll be in touch. And here's my card. Please don't hesitate to reach out to me if you have any questions. Or if you think of anything that might be helpful. And I do mean anything. Even if it seems insignificant."

"Right." Rachel rose. She reached out and hugged Birdie. "Thank you. I'm so sorry I kind of adopted you this last hour."

"It's okay. I truly don't mind."

Deputy Rathburn poked her head into the room. "If you're finishing up, your daughter's waiting outside for you. She'll drive you over to your father's house."

"Thank you," Rachel Albright said. She blew her nose and joined Alexis Albright out in the hall. Mary stepped into the interview room and shut the door.

"Did the daughter have anything useful to say?" Jake asked.

"Not really," Mary said. "She hasn't been living with her parents for over a year. She got an apartment and took a job in Boulder near the university this past summer. She hasn't been home to visit since last spring."

"That's what the mother said. Birdie, how was she on the way over?"

"A complete wreck. I honestly worried she wasn't going to pull it together enough to have a coherent discussion with you."

"Well, that's in part thanks to you. You were great with her. Thank you."

Jake was worried about her. When he asked her to meet Rachel Albright at the airport, he hadn't even thought it might dredge up painful memories for her about Ben Wayne's murder. He could kick himself for that.

"I'm glad to help," Birdie said. "Let me know if you need me for anything else on this one."

Birdie said goodbye to Mary and excused herself.

"Did Rachel have any theory as to who might have killed her husband?" Mary asked.

"Not so far. I want to look hard at their financials. Specifically their credit card habits. You can tell a lot about a marriage from how they spend their money. But as of now, I'm not getting a bad vibe from her. Except for one thing. She said Craig didn't like her coming out to the barn. It makes me think he was hiding something out there."

"Or maybe there was something going on he didn't want her to overhear or walk in on."

"Maybe," Jake said, letting his voice trail off. His wheels were turning. Hard. Mary had hit on it. What was Craig Albright hiding out in that barn? Jake's instincts told him finding it would be the key to solving this case.

EIGHT

By Tuesday, everyone in Worthington County seemed to have a theory as to what happened to Craig Albright. Rumors flew and most of them led nowhere good. Jake stayed away from the media and let Landry field any and all questions about the investigation. So far, the new prosecutor, Corey Ansel, had stayed out of Jake's way. That was one small blessing that came from the turmoil of Jake's last murder investigation. Former prosecutor Tim Brouchard had been forced to resign in the wake of a scandal. If Brouchard were still at the helm in the building next door, he would have made Jake's life a living hell.

Now, at six o'clock on Tuesday evening, Jake turned down the private drive at the bottom of his grandfather's wooded oasis. Two hundred rolling acres nestled at the foot of Blackhand Hills. Grandpa Max had turned the small, two-bedroom cabin over to Jake upon his return a year and a half ago. In exchange, Jake took care of the property and Grandpa, to the extent the older man would let him.

He was late. Jake had dinner with Grandpa two nights a week. Though Max was completely blind in one eye and nearly so in the other, he still knew his way around his own kitchen. The doctor said the practice was good for him. Tonight, he was making venison chili, one of Jake's favorites.

As he drove up the hill to the big house, Jake saw Gemma's car in Grandpa's driveway too. He hadn't had a chance to talk to her since Friday evening out at the Albright crime scene. They'd exchanged a few quick texts. Just enough for Jake to know she was all right.

"There's too much cayenne," Grandpa Max shouted as Jake wiped his shoes off on the mat in the foyer. "I told you not to touch anything, woman. I've got things under control."

"It's perfect," Gemma shot back. "You're getting old. Everything you eat is bland."

Gemma's two boys sat in the front room with their faces in their phones. The older boy, Ryan, looked up and nodded his chin at his Uncle Jake.

"How long have they been at it?" Jake asked.

"An hour!" Aiden, the younger boy, said. He was turning eight later this fall. Ryan would soon turn eighteen. That was hard for Jake to believe. He had started his senior year in high school a few weeks ago. Sometimes Jake felt like his own was just a day ago. And sometimes, a hundred years.

"Do I need riot gear, or is it safe to head in there?"

"Proceed with caution," Aiden answered.

"She's just goading him," Ryan said.

"How's she been?" Jake asked Ryan, lowering his voice. He was sure Gemma told her oldest son about what happened last Friday. She would have likely kept it from Aiden though.

Ryan shrugged. "She's keeping busy. Won't sit still. You know how she gets."

"I do," Jake said. He tousled Aiden's hair and headed into the kitchen battlefield.

"It's fine!" Gramps said. "Here. You. Taste this."

Grandpa Max had heard Jake come in. He held out a spoonful of chili. Jake stepped forward and tasted it.

"Seems pretty good to me," Jake said, though he'd damn near burned his taste buds off. He took a seat at the kitchen table and watched his sister and grandfather do their dance. Every time Gemma tried to get a spice from the drawer, Grandpa would try to smack her with a towel. She would neatly dodge him, then shove her way past him. To anyone else, this would seem hostile. It was. But cooking and bitching was Max Cashen's love language. Inserting herself in everyone else's business was Gemma's.

Finally satisfied that Grandpa had indeed added enough pepper to the sauce, Gemma left him to mind the pot and took a seat opposite Jake. He reached over and took his sister's hand.

"How are you doing? I'm sorry I've been off the board for Ryan this week." Though wrestling season wouldn't start in earnest for two months, Coach Purcell had started conditioning a week ago. With the Albright murder on his plate, Jake hadn't had time to pop in.

"He's doing fine," Gemma said, then lowered her voice. "He knows everything, didn't you know?"

She deflected. Jake squeezed her hand. "How are *you* doing?"

She slipped her hand out of his. "I'm doing fine. I'm just ... everyone in town knows I'm the one who found that body. My showings are starting to dry up. I don't know what's wrong with people. As if it was my fault what happened."

"Screw 'em," Grandpa said. He put the lid back on his chili pot and took a seat at the table beside Gemma.

"Is it ready?" Aiden poked his head around the corner.

"A half an hour," Grandpa said. "I told ya I'd call you when it was time to stuff your face."

"But I'm hungry now! Can I just make some nuggets or something? Or get some chips?"

"I don't care what you shovel into your face at home, but when you're at Grandpa Max's, you'll eat properly, and you'll eat what's put on the table."

Aiden grumbled, then sulked his way back to the front room.

"You got a real mess on your hands with this one, don't ya?" Grandpa said. He had a way of doing that. Starting conversations in the middle of them. As if he were too old to be bothered with preambles and expected you to just keep up. Jake was familiar with and could translate his grandfather's shorthand. People in town often thought he was losing his marbles with his riddle-speak.

"It was a rough crime scene," Jake said, meeting Gemma's eyes. He hated that she'd had to see it.

"I don't mean that," Grandpa said. "I mean with the idiot rumor spreaders."

"I was going to ask you both about that," Jake said. "I've been in the office with this one so far. What are you hearing around town?"

"People are saying a demon came down from the hill and ripped poor Craig Albright to pieces. Gutted him."

Gemma winced. She reached across the table and grabbed the pitcher of lemonade Grandpa had sitting there.

"A demon, huh?" Jake said.

"Not a real demon. But there are plenty of bigots in this town. They're thinking Albright's shirttail relations came down and finally taught him a lesson about what happens when you betray your family."

"Betray?" Gemma said. "How did Craig Albright betray them?"

"By not taking over the family farm when his daddy asked him to," Jake said. "By his granddaddy coming down the hill and going civilized in the first place."

"That's ridiculous," she said.

"You hearing any buzz that anybody's planning to head up the hill to see for themselves?" Jake asked.

Gemma poured their grandfather a lemonade and stuck it in front of him.

"There's been some talk," Max said.

"From whom?"

"Just ... old farts sticking their noses in places they don't belong. Craig made a lot of the old-timers mad when he set off and tried to make a life for himself."

"He didn't exactly set off," Gemma said. "He never left the county, Gramps. He just became an electrician instead of a farmer."

"I didn't say I agree with the argument. I'm just saying that's why his old man tried to disown him. When Donnie died, nobody was more shocked than Craig that he left the farm to him. I think Donnie's brothers figured it would revert back to them."

"You ever met Donnie Albright's brothers? Craig's uncles? Or cousins? Because I haven't."

"They don't come down from the hill. Far as I know, they're dead. If Donnie were alive, he'd be a good ten years older than me. So I don't think there's any credence to the rumors that those boys came down from the hill to do Craig harm. Still ..."

"Still what?"

"We live in dangerous times is all I'm saying. People don't just disagree with each other anymore. Everybody digs their heels in. People get tribal. So who knows? This might be just the excuse a few of the zealots around here use to go marching up that hill with pitchforks and torches."

It's what Jake feared, too.

"Nobody's ever going to want to buy that house," Gemma said. "Jake, that's the warning I got from some of the other real estate agents around town. I didn't pay it any mind. But it was one thing for Craig and Rachel to run that electrician's business out of that barn. Craig was at least distant kin to the people living on the other side of Red Sky Hill. What if someone killed Craig like that to send a message? Make it so nobody would ever want to buy that property."

It was a good theory. Only so far, Jake didn't have a shred of proof.

"That just seems pretty extreme," Jake said. "We're a death penalty state. How crazy would you have to be to torture and murder someone like that over a real estate transaction?" Though Jake wouldn't say it, that theory also didn't explain the hole cut out of Craig Albright's barn wall or what was behind it.

"Well, maybe extreme. But effective," Gemma said. "That property will never sell now. Not for a long time anyway. I feel terrible for Rachel. On top of all the rest of it, she's probably going to have to move back here. I don't see how she'll be able to afford to keep her place in Florida."

Jake had no good answers for her. Grandpa excused himself from the table and went back to stir his chili pot. He proclaimed in a booming voice for the benefit of the ears in the other room, "Chili's on! Wash your filthy mitts and get on in here!"

Ryan and Aiden came running. Jake's own stomach rumbled.

"That goes for you too," Grandpa said, pointing his ladle at Jake. Jake took his turn at the sink and washed his hands.

"Enough talk about Red Sky Hill," Grandpa said as everyone served themselves a bowl of chili. "It's not suitable for dinner conversation."

Jake couldn't argue. He sank his teeth into the warm, homemade bread Gemma had bought from the European bakery off County Road Fourteen. It melted in his mouth. He could have eaten just that and been stuffed in five minutes.

"You'll get no argument from me," Gemma said. "Besides, there's another matter I've been meaning to talk to you about, Jake."

"Oh boy," he said, recognizing the tone in his sister's voice. She was winding up for a good and proper nag.

"What'd Uncle Jake do now?" Ryan asked through a mouthful of bread.

"It's what he hasn't done," she said. "And what I'm going to help him do."

Jake paused mid-spoonful. He already didn't like where she was going.

"What are your plans for next weekend?" she asked.

"Gemma, I can barely think past tonight. I'm in the middle of a major ..." He stopped himself as Grandpa glared at him. He was about to violate his "no murder talk at the table" edict of five minutes ago.

"Things are busy at work," Jake said. "I'll probably be working overtime and weekends for a while until things are resolved."

"I heard they cut off Craig Albright's head," Aiden said. "Is that true?"

"Hush!" Gemma shouted. "No. That's not true. And you better not repeat that nasty talk, Aiden."

"Well, people at school are asking. I'm kind of famous because you saw it."

"That's ghoulish," Gemma said. "You just tell anyone who asks to mind their own business."

"I like being popular," he said.

"Not like that, you don't," Gemma said. Her son didn't seem to take the point, but he at least knew better than to argue with her.

"You, baby brother," she said. "This is exactly why you need to do what I say for your own good. You're taking Saturday night off next weekend if I have to come down there and drag you away from the sheriff's department. If I have to enlist Meg Landry herself."

"For what?"

Gemma put her spoon down in exasperation. "You know for what. Geez, Jake. Dominique Gill."

"What?"

"Dominique Gill. My friend. The one who's perfect for you."

Jake did a double take. He vaguely recalled Gemma yammering about some woman she wanted to set Jake up with.

"Gemma, if I find the need to start dating, I'm perfectly capable of arranging my own."

"Really? When's the last time you got … um … went on a proper date?"

Beside her, Ryan tried to hide a giggle behind his hand.

Jake kept his head in his chili and continued eating.

"That's what I thought. You've been living like a monk since you came back home. It's been a year and a half. It's time for you to go out. Live a little. All you do is go to work and come home."

"What's wrong with that?" Jake asked.

"Everything," Gemma said. "Dominique's a sweet girl. She has trouble meeting people because she works so much. You should be able to relate. So you're going to ask her out. I'll give you her number."

"Gemma …"

"Don't Gemma me," she said. Gemma rose and took Jake's plate from him. She walked over to the stove and slapped another ladle of chili in his bowl. She set it down in front of him with a clamor.

"One date," Gemma said. "If you don't like her, and you will … then I won't bug you about it again."

"Yes, she will," Grandpa Max, Ryan, and even Aiden all chimed in together. Undeterred, Gemma sat back down across from her brother. "One date. I'll tell her to expect a call from you. I'll send you her picture and her contact number. She likes Italian food. You can take her to that pizzeria over in Putney if you don't want to run into anyone from the county. Maybe a movie after if it's going well."

"Gemma ..."

His sister gave him her winningest smile. Part of him was glad to see it. Despite her brave face, his sister had been completely traumatized by what she saw in Craig Albright's barn.

Before Jake could mount a proper protest, his phone rang. Grandpa gave him a stern look.

"Sorry, Gramps. I have to take this." His caller ID read Mark Ramirez.

Jake excused himself from the table. "Cashen," he answered.

"Hey, Jake. Sorry to bother you after hours. I thought you should know. We've got the financials back on Craig Albright's business and his personal bank accounts. I can meet you at your office in the morning. There's something in here I think you're going to want to see."

Jake's head immediately started to pound. "Sounds good. I'll be in by eight. And thanks."

The two men said their goodbyes. Gemma was at the sink, starting to clean dishes. His grandfather caught his eye and made a shooing gesture.

"Go," he whispered. "While she's not looking. Now's your chance to make a clean getaway. I'll cover for you."

Smiling, Jake gave his grandfather a salute and ducked out the back door.

NINE

"How's the girl working out?" Ed Zender said. He stood at the entrance to their mutual office. Detective Gary Majewski sat at his desk and looked up after Ed's words.

"The girl?" Jake said. "Maybe we don't call her that."

"Well, she wouldn't be my pick," Zender said. "But I guess I don't get a say in who comes in after me."

"She's solid," Jake said. "I think she's going to make a good detective and I'm glad for the help."

Jake stood at his desk. Since the Albright murder, he'd had to push every other case he had to the back-burner. Ed was in the process of closing out whatever he had left so he could meet his retirement by the end of the calendar year.

"I'm the one who could use some help," Zender said. "If she's planning to step into my shoes, I should be the one training her."

Jake tried to stay stoic. The idea of Zender training anyone horrified him. He'd have to spend the next year trying to break

Mary of Ed's bad habits. On the other hand, she seemed shrewd enough to see through Ed.

"If we get a break in the Albright case, I might be able to peel her off to help you out for a little while. Things are just too fluid right now."

"If you need my ear, I'm available," Ed said.

"Jake?" Mary's voice came from deeper in the hallway. She was right outside the door. Jake wondered how much she'd heard.

Ed jumped. His face hardened as Mary came further into the room. "Detective Zender," she said. "Good to see you."

Ed gave Mary a grunt by way of an answer. It was odd. Ed had his issues, but Jake had never known him to be downright rude.

"Jake," Mary said. "Agent Ramirez is here. I've got him set up in the war room. Are you ready for him?"

Jake grabbed his notepad off his desk. Ed barely got out of his way as he headed for the door. Jake closed it behind him, effectively slamming it in Ed's face.

"Don't pay any attention to him," Jake said. "He's got … senioritis."

He and Mary headed down the hall into the war room. Mark Ramirez sat at the long conference table talking on his cell phone. He held a finger up as Jake entered.

"Got it," Ramirez said to whomever he had on the other end of the phone. "Yeah. That's what I thought. You're sure? Yeah. If you could send me a copy of that deed, I'd appreciate it."

Ramirez clicked off. On the table in front of him, he had three spiral bound reports. He slid two of them to the other end of the table, one for Jake, one for Rathburn. She took a seat and pulled out a pen, ready to take notes.

"What'd you bring me?" Jake asked. He slipped off his suit jacket and hung it over an empty chair. Then he sat opposite Ramirez and opened his copy of the binder.

"Our forensic accountants have finished running their analysis on All-Brite Electrical. And I've got a complete financial analysis on Craig and Rachel Albright."

Jake started flipping through the report. It was thorough. Bank statements, profit-and-loss reports, cash flow analysis.

"There's a lot to dive into," Mark said. "All-Brite's a solid business. It was bringing in a decent profit. It's based on a pretty robust, loyal client list. About half and half commercial and residential. Appendix F has a list of every name on it. You'll find their accounts receivables in there too. And Albright's expense reports."

"Okay," Jake said. "So what's the kicker? You could have emailed all of this to me?"

"The business isn't the interesting part," Ramirez said. "Like I said, it's a solid business. Only ... it's static."

"Meaning?" Jake asked.

"Meaning ... it's afloat due to the loyal customer list. Only, it's not growing. Albright wasn't bringing in much in the way of new clients over the years. It's a pretty flat trajectory."

"It's a pretty small town," Jake said. "If he wasn't expanding much beyond Worthington County, there wouldn't be room for real growth."

"Yeah," Ramirez said. "Only flip to the back half of the report. After the orange tab." Jake and Mary did so at the same time.

"That's a list of Craig Albright's personal assets and how he financed them."

Jake did a quick scan of the list.

"He owned the farm outright. Inherited that from his dad. Fifty grand in a savings account. Ten grand in checking. That's not a huge amount of money in the bank, but it's a nice nest egg. Close to a million if you add in the value of the house."

"He listed only sixty grand as a personal salary. Paying the brother-in-law the same," Ramirez said.

"But the stuff," Jake said as he kept flipping through the report. "He paid cash for the house in Destin?"

"You got it," Ramirez said. "Two million bucks."

"And they're completely renovating it," Mary said. "That's what Rachel Albright was doing down there at the time her husband was killed."

"He's got a new F-150. He paid cash for that, too. Fifty grand," Jake said.

"Jet skis. The vintage cars in the barn. Plus the reno on the barn itself. We compiled the invoices from all the contractors he used. He spent almost a quarter of a million on it five years ago. Plus a bunch of upgrades they did in the house. All cash payments."

"It doesn't track," Jake said.

"That's what I'm saying," Ramirez said. "If you look at the statements from All-Brite's business accounts. They're doing well enough to stay afloat and make payroll. But Albright himself is spending major money on the personal side. Where's it coming from? Because it's not from the business."

Jake ran a hand over his jaw. "This isn't good."

"You know what this looks like as much as I do," Ramirez agreed.

Jake closed his binder. "It looks like Craig Albright's got something going on on the side."

"You mean like ... drugs?" Mary asked.

"Safe bet," Jake answered. He wished he could light the financial reports on fire.

"Between this and the way he was killed ... tortured and killed ... Jake, you know you've got something pretty dark on your hands."

"What the hell were you into, Craig?" Jake muttered. "What the hell did you bring into my backyard?"

"I'm sorry," Ramirez said. "I know this was the last thing you wanted to hear."

"Jake, this is bad," Mary said. "If Craig Albright was running product through here to the point he could afford all this?"

"And you've heard nothing?" Ramirez said. "No rumblings of any type of cartel activity in Blackhand Hills before this?"

"Nothing," Jake said. "Sure, we've got plenty of drugs. We've got the Hilltop Boys and local weed growers. But it's small-time. We're in the middle of nowhere."

"Maybe that's the draw for the cartel," Ramirez said.

Jake wished he could disagree with him. His phone buzzed. He took it out. Gemma sent a text. Jake grumbled and clicked off the screen but not before both Mary and Ramirez saw it.

"She okay?" Mark asked. "Your sister? It was rough her finding the body like she did."

Jake smiled. "Gemma's made of Teflon. This isn't to do with the case. She's been trying to fix me up with some friend of hers. I can't get her off my back."

Ramirez laughed. Mary's cell phone went off. "Sorry," she said. "I should take this. It's one of Albright's subcontractors you wanted me to follow up with. I can try sussing him out on Craig's financials?"

"That's good," Jake said. "Thanks."

Mary picked up her binder and excused herself. Mark Ramirez still had a shit-eating grin on his face after Mary left.

"I think your sister's got a point," he said. "You haven't been seeing anybody since you came back here, have you?"

Jake's phone buzzed again. Gemma was persistent. This time, he flipped his phone over so the screen wouldn't show.

"Not you too," he said.

"Well, if you're in the market," Mark said. "I work with a woman who would be perfect for you. She's one of the accountants who put this analysis together for me. Lydia Penny. I could give you her number."

"No!" Jake said. "Just ... stick to criminal analysis. I've got all the *help* I need."

Mark let out a big, hearty laugh. When he settled, he tapped the binder.

"So, what are you going to do next?"

Jake sighed. "The wife claims she has nothing to do with the business side of things. I get the impression she doesn't ask where the money comes from. Her brother though. Albright was grooming him to take over the business when Craig and Rachel jetted off to Florida to spend their golden years. And he was pretty jumpy about that when he found out Craig was dead. Like he barely showed any concern for Craig and none at all for his sister. He just kept saying stuff like, what am I gonna do now?"

"You think he was in on whatever side hustle Albright had going?"

"Maybe. I think we need to have a deeper conversation. Today."

"Let me know if you'd like me to sit in," Ramirez said. "I've got another case I'm assisting with one county over. I'll be around."

"Thanks," Jake said. He walked Ramirez down the hall. As soon as Ramirez took to the stairwell, Jake dialed Drew Harter's number. It went straight to voicemail.

"Mr. Harter," Jake said. "This is Detective Cashen. If you wouldn't mind, I'd like to ask you a few more questions involving your brother-in-law's case. If you could meet me down at the sheriff's department this afternoon, I'd appreciate it. How about three o'clock?"

He clicked off and went back to the war room. The white board was beginning to fill up. Jake stared at the aerial photo he'd pinned up of Craig Albright's barn.

"Two hundred and fifty grand of reno," Jake whispered. "Where the hell did it come from?"

He hoped the answer wasn't worth killing for.

TEN

"I appreciate you coming back in, Mr. Harter," Jake said. He had Drew Harter set up in interview room one. He'd asked for a cup of coffee. Mary brought it in, then left the room. She would sit in the observation room behind the one-way mirror. It would be good to have a second set of eyes watching Drew Harter's body language.

"No problem," he said. "Whatever you need."

"How's your father doing?"

Drew Harter slouched in his chair. He wore a golf shirt with All-Brite Electrical embroidered on the chest.

"He's okay. It helps that my sister and my niece are here. They're taking care of him."

"That's good. How's your sister holding up?"

Drew shrugged.

"She's a mess. Won't stop crying. She's putting everything on my niece to handle. The funeral arrangements and such. She keeps asking me about what Craig looked like. You know. Those pictures you made me look at."

"She asked me about that too," Jake said. "I'm glad I was able to keep her from going to see him. I don't know that that would have done her any good."

"Sure didn't do me any good," Drew said. "She's always been fragile though. Always had somebody else taking care of her. I gotta be honest. I'm not sure she's gonna get through all of this. She's trying to talk Lex into uprooting her whole life and moving to Florida with her."

"Well, I suppose now's not the time for her to be making big decisions."

"She can't stay here, that's for sure. She can't go back to that house. Christ. That barn. I'm trying to keep the business running from my laptop. I've put off jobs and vendors as much as I can. But pretty soon, I won't be able to. How long are you going to keep that barn tied up? I need to be able to go back in there. I need the files. The computer. This is all falling on me, you know? Craig left a mess behind."

"I'm sure it wasn't his intention," Jake said. "I'm really sorry this has been so hard for you. Rachel's lucky she has you to step into the breach. I'm sure that's what Craig would want."

Drew just shook his head. He was angry. "She has no idea what I do for her."

"It's like that with me and my sister too," Jake lied. "She's raising two boys all by herself. She relies on me a lot."

"Oh, I bet."

"Not a lot of gratitude going around, I can tell you that. Just once a simple thank you would be nice."

"She's a grown woman. She acts like a child. Craig worked his ass off, making sure she had everything she needed."

"I suppose she expects you to do that now. That big house. All those renovations. Craig was shouldering a lot so that your sister could live a comfortable lifestyle. And that house they bought down in Florida. That had to have cost them a pretty penny."

"Rachel's always gotta have the best," he said. Then quickly, "I'm not saying she doesn't deserve it."

"Sure. Sure. Of course not. It's just ... does she really expect you to take care of her like Craig did now?"

"I don't know. I don't know anything. I'm just trying to keep everything going."

"Well, I'll say it again. Thank God Rachel's got you. Even if she doesn't appreciate it. Maybe just give her some time. She's deep in her grief."

"Yeah."

"Would you like more coffee?" Jake asked. Mary had left a carafe at the end of the table. Jake refilled Drew's cup.

"So, the reason I asked you here," Jake said. "I'm trying to get a clearer picture of how Craig's business ran. I figure you'd be the best person to ask, seeing as how he was turning everything over to you."

"We were transitioning, yeah."

"Right. Well, it's just ... our financial analysts have had a look at Craig's books."

"I didn't give them permission to do that."

"No. It was part of a warrant, Drew. Standard procedure in a case like this. And your sister's been very cooperative. She's turned over all the information about her and Craig's personal finances as well. Credit card statements. Bank accounts. You understand it's helpful for me to try to reconstruct what was going on in Craig's life in the last few months."

"Do you have any suspects yet?"

"Not exactly. But a picture is starting to emerge. One that I'm hoping you can help me make sense of."

Jake had a file folder next to him on the table. He pulled out the cash flow report from the most recent quarter for All-Brite Electrical.

"You've seen this before? You're familiar with it?" Jake asked, sliding the document over to Drew. He glanced at it.

"We talked about it, yeah. But Craig's got a bookkeeper. I can't say I was knee-deep in the day-to-day finances."

"Well, this isn't day to day. I had a look at the corporate tax filings as well." Jake pulled out a second stack of documents. He'd tabbed this one and highlighted the figures for last year's profit and loss for the business.

"All-Brite was doing well. Those are some healthy accounts receivable. And Craig wasn't carrying any business debt. Looks like he barely spent any money on marketing."

"We didn't need to. We're a word-of-mouth, solid, local business."

"Sure. Sure. Yeah, that's great. And he kept expenses pretty low. Conservative payroll. I mean, I'm not an accountant. But Craig seems to have left things in a really strong position for you to take over."

"It's not just Craig. We've been running this business together for years. He couldn't have done any of this without me."

"Gotcha. But Drew, here's the thing that's got me stymied. I told you I've had a look at your brother-in-law's personal finances, too. He was paying for a lot of things in cash. The new house in Florida. They closed two months ago. It was over two million bucks and they paid cash. Did you know that?"

Drew Harter didn't answer, but something went through him. His jaw hardened. His eyes narrowed. His face flushed.

"The home office. That barn. He spent over a quarter of a million dollars renovating that. Again, all paid in cash. Improvements to the house too. Cars. Jet skis. These were major purchases being made over the last five to ten years. All cash. It's just ... it doesn't track with the amount of money you were pulling in through All-Brite."

"I don't know anything about that," Drew said through tight lips.

"You don't know anything about how the business is doing?"

No answer.

"Or you didn't know anything about how much money Craig was spending personally? I added it up. In the last eight years, including the purchase of the new house in Florida ... we're talking close to four and a half million dollars. He was only drawing about sixty grand from the business, Drew. Same as you. And he wasn't taking in anything close to that in accounts receivable. I mean, look at it. It's right here."

Drew Harter's whole body started to shake.

"Drew, he's dead. Your brother-in-law was murdered. Tortured and murdered. I believe he was involved in something very bad. I've seen this kind of thing before. I spent over ten years working organized crime cases for the FBI. I know what this looks like. I want to help you. If you know something. Or if you don't.

Whoever did this to Craig, they were looking for something. Information. And this ..."

Jake pulled a photo of the barn wall that had been ripped open. "I think maybe Craig had something stashed in that wall. I think maybe he was tortured until he told someone what and where it was."

"I don't know anything about that!"

"And I'm not sure I believe you. Listen to me, Drew. If Craig was in bed with who I think he was ... these people don't stop. If they think there's more money they're owed, who do you think they're gonna come after next?"

He was sweating. Drew Harter had turned positively gray.

"I can't help you if you don't help me, Drew. What was Craig involved with? What did he drag you into?"

"I can't do this. I can't talk to you, man."

"I'm the only one you *can* talk to. I've got one goal. To find out who did this to your family. And to make sure it stops with Craig. He hung you out, didn't he? Probably told you he had everything under control. Not to worry. He left you alone. With no protection. He got in over his head and now you're all that's left. That means you're in trouble. The kind you can't talk your way out of. The kind you can't run away from. I don't want you to be the next guy who gets his toes burned off one by one. They drilled holes into his hands, Drew."

"No. No. No! This wasn't me. This isn't on me. You tell them."

"Tell who? Drew ... was it the cartel? Was he using the business as a front? With this kind of cash flow, I know Craig was moving serious product. He skimmed too much for himself, didn't he? He never told you. You never got your cut."

"You can't protect me. You have no idea what this is."

"So tell me. Let me help you get clear of it. Let me make sure nobody comes looking for you with zip ties and a blow torch."

"He kept wanting more and more. Taking on more. He said it was never going to touch us. He said we were just providing a meeting place. We weren't involved in anything heavy. We were just a middle man."

"A meeting place. The barn. You were tucked out of the way. Nobody goes up Red Sky Hill. Who was it, Drew? Give me a name."

"I didn't know their names. I never asked. Craig said it was better that I didn't know."

Jake sat back. A meeting place.

"Between the cartel and whom?" Jake asked. "Who was moving product for them?"

"I gotta get out of here," Drew said. "If they find out I'm talking to you."

"Drew, you can't handle this by yourself. Craig thought he could, too. Look what happened to him. So do the right thing now. Who was Craig working for? You said the barn was a meeting place. I know this was the cartel. If you're telling me Craig wasn't the one dealing, who was?"

"He'll kill me. You can't keep me safe. They'll kill me!"

"I can keep you safe," Jake said. "If your information is solid, I can keep you safe. You've got nobody else on your side but me. Do you get that? So tell me. Who was Craig working for?"

Drew's posture changed. He sat straighter in his chair. "I'm done talking to you. You're not here to help me. You're here to find out if I had something to do with killing my brother-in-law. I didn't."

"But you know who did."

"I know my rights. I'm not saying another word unless I've got a lawyer in the room. You hear me?" Drew looked at the one-way mirror. He stood up.

"You hear me?" he shouted. He went up to the mirror and tapped on the glass. "This is me, Andrew Harter. And I am asking for representation. I want my lawyer. I want to make a phone call and call my lawyer right now or I'm leaving."

"No one's stopping you, Drew," Jake said.

Drew turned to him. He pulled his cell phone out of his pocket. With shaking fingers, he punched in a number. Jake pushed his chair back and then made a wide-armed gesture, indicating his openness to Drew's call.

Drew set the cell phone on the table between them, putting it on speaker. The phone was angled so Jake could read the contact name. He took a beat, muttered an expletive under his breath.

The name was Tim Brouchard. "Hello?"

"Tim," Drew said. "This is Drew Harter. I'm at the sheriff's office. I'm in a room with Detective Cashen. He's asking me questions about what happened to my brother-in-law. I told him I wanted a lawyer. You're on speaker."

"Drew," Brouchard said through the phone. "You're not to say another word. Do you hear me, Detective? You're to stop all questioning of my client immediately. You don't even so much as ask him how to spell his name."

"Wouldn't dream of it," Jake said.

"Drew," Brouchard shouted. "I'm on my way."

ELEVEN

Tim Brouchard was a changed man. In the months since his ouster as Worthington County's top prosecutor, he'd grown his hair long enough to wear in a ponytail. He sported a salt-and-pepper goatee. After a thirty-pound weight loss, he rode up to the sheriff's department on a brand-new Harley. Jake waited in the hall as Brouchard stormed down it, his motorcycle boots clomping loudly.

He said nothing to Jake. Barely even looked at him as he strode into interview room one. Just before he slammed the door, he pointed a finger at Jake. "I trust nobody's sitting on the other side of that mirror and there better not be any cameras recording."

Jake stepped back and made a sweeping gesture with his arms. "Have a look."

Brouchard grimaced, then slammed the door.

Birdie rounded the corner. "What was that?" she said.

"The show," Jake answered. "You mind waiting for him to come out? I'll be in Landry's office until he's ready to talk."

"I'll come find you," she said.

Jake thanked her and made his way to Sheriff Landry's office. Deputy Rathburn was already there. At Jake's request, she'd briefed the sheriff on what Drew Harter had to say so far.

Landry sat perched on the edge of her desk. "Do you believe him?" she said. "Do you really think Craig Albright was running drugs through my town for the cartel?"

"Yes," Jake said plainly. "I think it's the only real explanation for his cash flow. And it's not like he just had a heart attack sitting at his desk. Someone wanted to send a message."

Her eyelids fluttered. "Under my nose," she said. "That's gonna be the headline here."

"Probably."

"How's Harter able to afford Tim Brouchard to represent him?" Rathburn said. "Last I heard, he was only taking rich clients."

"Oh, I think Brouchard's been salivating, waiting for a chance to get in my way," Jake said.

"That's what I'm afraid of," Landry said. "Jake ... he's gunning for you. He blames you for his downfall and for the break-up of his marriage."

"Of which I had nothing to do with either."

"Really? Not even Anya?"

"Sheriff, I dated the woman in high school twenty years ago. We're friends. That's it."

"Melissa at the Vedge Wedge says she's probably going to have to close the restaurant down if Anya doesn't come back soon," Mary said. "It's a shame. They have a weirdly amazing vegan taco salad there."

"Have you heard from her?" Landry said. "Anya?"

Jake shook his head. "Not since the day before she left town. She said she was heading to the Outer Banks to stay with friends. I hope she's happy wherever she is."

"Still," Landry said. "Brouchard's going to make this personal if Drew Harter really had something to do with Craig Albright's murder."

"He can try," Jake said. "If this was a cartel hit, he ought to be more worried about his own client's safety."

"You think they'll come after him next?" Mary said. "Don't you think that would be obvious? Albright's murder is big news. It's gotten state-wide press. It's shining a pretty large spotlight on Blackhand Hills."

Jake knew that's what bothered Landry the most. She was right. As bad as what happened was for Craig Albright and his family, it could be catastrophic to her career as well. "I think that all depends on what kind of information Drew Harter has to bargain with. I don't know. My instinct's telling me Albright was the brains of whatever operation they had going. Albright was keeping him at arm's length. I'm going to subpoena Harter's personal financials as well, but the way he reacted when I told him about Craig's expenditures, he was angry. I think good old Craig was holding back on him if Harter was involved, too."

There was a knock on the door. Darcy poked her head in. "Jake, Sheriff? Sorry to bother you. But Corey Ansel just showed up. He said he got a call from Tim Brouchard."

"He what?" Jake and Meg said it together.

"He's trying to end run you," Landry said. "What's Ansel doing following orders from Brouchard?"

Jake brushed past Darcy and headed back down the hall to interview room one. Birdie stood at the door. Corey Ansel came from the other direction. He stopped when he saw Jake.

Ansel had been named the interim prosecutor until a special election could be held to replace Brouchard permanently. Ansel was young. Only five years out of law school. The guy could barely grow a full beard. So far, Jake had found him to be an honest, earnest kid though. If he could survive the sharks, he might make a decent prosecutor long term. If he wanted the job.

"Detective," he said. "If ..."

Jake held up a finger. "Next time you get a call from a defense attorney working on one of my cases, you call me. If Brouchard thinks ..."

The door swung open. Brouchard walked out smirking. "Good. You're all here. Is there somewhere we can talk? Also, my client hasn't had lunch. Do you think you could rustle up a sandwich or something for him, honey?" He stared straight at Birdie. Jake watched a tremor go through her and she clenched her fists.

Jake stepped forward. He opened his mouth to tell Brouchard off but Birdie beat him to it.

"You call me honey again, you're gonna walk out of here wearing your bottom lip as a hat. Now, if you say pretty please, I'll see what I can do to assist your client."

Corey Ansel uncomfortably cleared his throat. Brouchard glared at him.

"My apologies," Brouchard said, though he hadn't dropped his snide tone. "Please."

Birdie patted Tim on the chest with both hands hard enough to push him backwards. "I knew you had it in you."

As she walked past Jake, she shot him a quick wink.

"We can talk in here," Jake said, pointing to the second interview room across the hall. He held the door open as Ansel, Deputy Rathburn, and finally Brouchard walked through.

They all sat around the table. Jake preferred to stand.

"My client had nothing to do with his brother-in-law's murder. Let's get that cleared up straight away. You brought him here under false pretenses, Cashen. So anything he told you prior to my arrival will be inadmissible ..."

"You're talking garbage, Brouchard," Jake said. "Your client came here voluntarily. He was free to leave the entire time. I laid out his brother-in-law's financial situation and your client couldn't figure out how to shut up. The second he asked for a lawyer, he got one."

"Tim," Ansel said. "Enough with the posturing. We know each other. We've worked together. You called me down here so you obviously think Mr. Harter has something valuable to say. Let's get to it."

Jake was impressed. From the get, he'd worried Ansel might feel intimidated by Brouchard's bluster. Like it or not, Brouchard had trained him.

"I want a proffer," Brouchard said. "Full immunity. Drew had nothing to do with any illegal activities Craig Albright was involved with. He only found out about it after the fact. He repeatedly tried to stop Mr. Albright. His concern now is for his own safety. It needs to be made clear publicly that Harter had no hand in any of this."

"Right," Jake said. "The second your client found out Craig was dead, he's been trying to save his own skin. He knew what was going on. He expected a bigger cut of it."

"You have absolutely no proof of that," Brouchard said. "My client is willing to submit to a poly. In fact, I demand it. And it'll be my pick on who administers it. I want Louise Beal. And I want it done within the next twenty-four hours."

Ansel looked up at Jake. Jake spread his hands in a conciliatory gesture. "I've got no problem with that."

"The proffer," Brouchard said. "Full immunity."

"He's said nothing so far," Jake said. "Nothing truly useful anyway. And if he's planning on sticking to the story, he had nothing to do with Albright's illegal activities ..."

"He didn't," Brouchard said. "But that doesn't mean he doesn't know anything. Mr. Harter has information he believes will lead to the identification and arrest of the individual responsible for the tragic murder of his brother-in-law."

"What information?" Jake said.

"Not without a proffer," Brouchard said. He looked directly at Corey Ansel. "I've taken the liberty of drawing up the language myself. Merely as a courtesy, of course. Though I felt it would streamline the process."

Brouchard pulled a folded piece of paper out of his jacket pocket and slid it across the table to Ansel. Jake stepped forward and read it over his shoulder. None of the language surprised him.

"You're basically asking for blanket immunity," Jake said. "If your client had prior knowledge of ..."

Brouchard held up a hand. "Detective, you need my client. You can bluster all you want. But without Drew Harter's testimony, I believe Craig Albright's murder is going to go unsolved. That's not good for you. It's most certainly not good for your boss."

"What's he got, Tim?" Ansel said. "Let's cut to it. What's he offering?"

"Your client admitted to me that he and Albright were facilitating the distribution of illicit drugs into this county on behalf of the cartel and a third party. I want to know who that third party was. I want every name involved. I want dates. Locations. All of it."

"You'll have it," Brouchard said. The door opened and Meg Landry walked in.

"Craig Albright was getting ready to ride off into the sunset," Jake said. "If he was doing business with the people I think he was, you don't get to just retire from that."

"Well, I think we can all agree, he didn't," Brouchard said.

"And these people wouldn't have terminated their relationship with Albright unless they had someone else in place to continue operations. Your client was that someone. Now he's just running scared."

Brouchard locked eyes with Jake. He at least had the decency not to lie again.

"Full immunity," Brouchard said. "In exchange for the name of Craig Albright's killer. That's what we're offering."

"Names. Dates. Locations," Jake said. "Everything he knows about Albright's extracurriculars."

"It ends today," Landry said. "This is bigger than one murder, Tim. This is your town too. I know you don't want this element here, either. So let's stop it. All of us. Today."

"Do we have a deal?" Tim said, looking back at Ansel.

"Yes," Jake said. "If Harter's story checks out. And none of us are leaving this room without the name of Craig Albright's killer. I know he's told you."

Brouchard smirked at Jake. Slowly, he reached into his pocket and pulled out another folded piece of paper. He slid it across the table to Corey Ansel. Jake snatched up the paper before Ansel could reach it.

Landry stepped closer to him so she could read over Jake's shoulder. Keeping his eyes locked with Brouchard, Jake opened the paper and read the name, glancing quickly down. Beside him, Meg Landry let out a hard breath. Then, two words that summed everything up.

"Good Christ!"

TWELVE

"He can't be serious," Meg said. "I refuse to believe he's serious."

The four of them, Jake, Meg, Mary, and Corey Ansel, filed into Meg's office, leaving Brouchard alone with his client. Jake crumpled the piece of paper in his fist.

"Floyd Bardo," Corey said. "As in, the de facto leader of the Hilltop Boys. The biggest organized crime family in the region."

"Floyd's not the leader of anything," Jake muttered. "If anything, he's a figurehead. Eyes and ears to report back to the real boss, his brother Rex."

"King Rex," Mary said. "He's been in federal prison for what ... eight years? How can he still run the show?"

"Trust me," Jake said. "He is."

"This is big," Corey said. The kid was sweating.

Meg walked around her desk and took a seat. "Jake ... this is bad. This might as well be a declaration of war."

"If it's true," he said. "I have my doubts."

"Well, Drew Harter has no reason not to cooperate now. He's got his deal."

"I need to talk to Floyd Bardo. Now. Mary and I will go out to Bardo Excavating and pick him up. He should be out there now."

"You're taking back-up," Landry said. "We cannot afford things to go sideways with this. The Bardos don't exactly have the best relationship with law enforcement."

Landry got up and poked her head out in the hall. "Take Deputies Wayne and Denning with you. They're both down in the bullpen."

Jake nodded. He knew it was the smart thing to do. But part of him wanted to approach Floyd Bardo on his own.

"Nothing crazy," Landry cautioned as Jake made his way past her with Mary in tow.

"Wouldn't dream of it," Jake said.

Fifteen minutes later, Jake pulled into the gravel parking lot of Bardo Excavating at the north end of the county. On instinct, he checked his service weapon. Birdie drove the patrol car with Denning in the passenger seat.

"This is a bad idea," Jake said, looking at the giant Worthington County Sheriff's Department markings on Birdie's vehicle. "I won't be surprised if Floyd's conveniently not available. They saw us coming a half a mile down the road."

Jake got out of the car. Mary followed. With a nonverbal signal from Jake, Birdie and Chris Denning hung back.

Jake walked into the office trailer. A receptionist sat at the only desk. She smiled at Jake.

"I need to talk to Floyd," Jake said. "Is he in there?" Jake pointed to the closed inner door behind her. He read the receptionist's nameplate. Tina.

"Um ... no. Floyd hasn't been in for a couple of days."

Jake paused. "A couple of days? When was the last time you saw him?"

Tina looked behind her at the door. "Um ... not since last Thursday."

Thursday, Jake thought. The day of Craig Albright's murder.

"You mind?" Jake asked. He charged past Tina's desk and pounded on the office door.

"You can't go in there," Tina said. "I told you. Floyd's not here."

Jake opened the door anyway. The inner office was a mess of paperwork. But it was also empty. Jake shut the door.

"He lives next door," Jake said. He jerked his chin toward the window. There was a two-story hundred-year-old farmhouse on the property. As far as Jake knew, it had originally been owned by Rex's great-grandfather, the original Rex. The man who'd first come down from the hill.

"He does," Tina said. "But I'm telling you. He's not there either. He's out of town."

"Where out of town?" Jake asked. He gestured to Mary and walked out of the trailer. Tina trailed behind, wobbling on four-inch-high heels.

"We'll check up at the house," Jake said to Birdie and Chris. The pair of them fell in line behind Jake. There was a small stone path between the parking lot leading to the front lawn of the farmhouse. Jake and Mary went for the front door. Birdie gestured to Chris and had him hang back with her, keeping an eye on the side door.

"Suit yourself!" Tina called out. "I told you, he's not home!" She turned on her heel and went back into the trailer.

Jake pounded on the door. "Bardo? It's Jake Cashen. I just want to talk."

He heard movement inside the house. He tried to peer through the frosted glass window beside the door. A shadow moved. He could barely make out the foyer and the kitchen behind it.

"Bardo!" Jake shouted.

The shadow came closer, stopped, then moved to the back of the house.

"For chrissake," Jake said.

He heard a loud crash.

"Jake," Mary said. He heard a door creak open, then slam shut.

"Jake!" Birdie shouted from the side of the house. "We've got a runner!"

"Dammit," Jake muttered. He stepped off the porch. He got around to the side of the house just in time to see Birdie make a flying tackle, taking down a six-foot man. He landed hard, the wind knocked out of him. Birdie had his arm twisted behind him. She pressed her knee into his back.

"Stop resisting!" she said.

"Kiss my ass!" he yelled at Birdie.

"Lemme guess," Birdie said. "You got a couple of warrants?"

Jake and Mary ran to her. Deputy Denning beat them there.

"All right. All right," the man said, gasping.

Jake knelt down and got in the guy's face. He was young. Probably Floyd's son. He had the Bardo family features. Thick, wavy dark hair, hooded eyelids.

"If she lets you up, you gonna behave?"

"Go to hell," he said. "I know my rights."

"Good. Then I won't have to explain them. I'm looking for your old man. Where's Floyd?"

"Up your ass!"

"Knox!" a woman shouted. Instinctively, Jake's hand went to his gun. She came around the other side of the house, her hands in the air.

"I'm sorry, Detective," she said. "My brother, Knox, seems to have forgotten his manners. Knox, if this nice deputy agrees to take her foot out of your back, you promise to behave yourself?"

She was tall, five eight, five nine. Supermodel good looks. She too had thick black hair but she'd managed to wrangle hers to hang stick-straight down to the middle of her back. She flashed a pair of icy gray Bardo eyes at Jake.

Knox Bardo went completely rigid. Then he exhaled. "Fine," he said.

"He'll behave," the woman said. Woman, yes. But young. Jake thought she couldn't be much more than twenty-five or twenty-six. She extended a hand to Jake's.

"Kyra Bardo," she said. "I'm sorry you've already met my brother, Knox. You'll have to forgive him. He's half feral."

"Half?" Birdie said.

"Let him up," Jake said. "But if you so much as snarl at her, I'll let her at you again."

Birdie pushed herself off Knox Bardo. Feral was a good word for it. The kid vaulted to his feet and took off just like a barn cat let out of a live trap.

"He got any outstanding warrants?" Jake asked. "Denning, go after that knucklehead."

Kyra smiled. "Not that I know of. Maybe a speeding ticket or two. But don't hold our last name against us."

"You're Floyd's daughter?" Jake asked. "You live here?"

"Yes."

"Well, I'm not here for your brother. I'm looking for Floyd. I need to ask him some questions."

Kyra Bardo's smile never faltered. "I'm sorry. He's not here. If you don't believe me, you're welcome to search the house. There's nobody else home but me and Knox. My mother's not in the picture. My other brother, Kyle, is out on a job. It's just me."

Jake hesitated. He wasn't about to step foot in Floyd Bardo's house without a warrant.

"My name's on the deed, Detective," Kyra said as if she could read his mind. "My father put all of our names on it. So you can come inside."

"Where is your father?" Jake asked.

"I wish I knew. He's left a mess for me to clean up. But he does this. Takes off. Usually it's after some woman he met. The last one was a stripper he met in Vegas. Tawny. Tabby. I can't remember. Anyway, I've got her number written down."

"When was the last time you saw your dad?" Jake asked.

Kyra kept that plastic smile in place. "It's been a few days. I'm not sure."

"Can you get a hold of him?" Jake asked.

Kyra took her cell phone out of the back pocket of her jeans. She wore a tight black halter top tied at the waist. She snapped off a large gold hoop earring as she brought her phone up to her ear. Still smiling at Jake, she waited. Then she pulled the phone away from her ear and hit the speaker button so Jake could hear Floyd Bardo's voicemail pick up.

"Hi, Daddy," Kyra said. "Can you give me a call back as soon as you get this? Thanks. Love you."

She ran her finger up the screen then turned it so Jake could read it. "Last time I heard from him," she said. "He sent me a text Friday evening."

Jake read the text. "Knox won't answer his damn phone. Tell him he needs to oversee the Renfield job on Monday."

"That's it," she said, pocketing her phone again. "That's Daddy. He comes and goes as he pleases. He might be back later today. He might not be back for a week. We're used to holding down the fort while he's gone."

"I see that," Jake said. He pulled out his business card. "You tell your old man I need to talk to him. You give him my number."

Kyra reached for the card, her long, red acrylic nails reminding him of claws.

"Is he in trouble, Daddy?" Kyra asked.

"I just need to talk to him. That's all. But you're telling me you haven't seen him since last Thursday?"

"I don't believe I said that at all. I said I haven't seen him for a few days. I don't remember what day specifically. It might have been Thursday. Maybe Friday. But this was the last time I spoke to him. That's what you asked me, Detective."

"Right," Jake said. "I'd like to talk to your brother. You think you can trap him again?"

Kyra turned her head and let out a shout Jake was certain carried to the other end of the property.

"Knox!"

A moment passed, then Knox came strutting around the side of the house with Deputy Denning right behind him, sweating.

"Detective Cashen wants to know if you know where Dad is. When's the last time you saw him?"

"I'll ask the questions," Jake said.

"It's been a few days," Knox said. "He said he was taking a trip to Vegas. I don't remember what day."

"Sure," Kyra said. "Tawny. Tori. What's her name, Knox?"

"Tabby," Knox said.

"There you go."

"A number?" Jake asked.

"Knox, go run into the kitchen and get that piece of paper with Tabby's cell phone number on it, will you? It's clipped to the fridge."

Knox did as he was told. A moment later, he came back out. He handed Jake the paper.

"You need this back?" Jake asked.

"Nope," Kyra said. "I really don't have any reason to talk to her. My father left it there so he'd remember. If he's not sharp enough to put it in his phone, that's not my problem. Between you and me, I wouldn't mind if he lost her number altogether. She's trouble. She's only after my father for his money. Money he doesn't have."

"Well," Jake said. "If you'd let him know I need to speak with him, I'd appreciate it."

"Absolutely," Kyra Bardo said.

Jake gestured to Mary and the others. There was nothing more he would do here without a warrant. As he made his way to his car, Jake had the strongest sense that, just like her Uncle Rex, it was a bad idea to turn his back on Kyra Bardo.

THIRTEEN

"She's meeting you at eight at Wylie's. She's really looking forward to it."

Gemma's text stared back at Jake. He let out a low, rumbling growl.

"Don't be difficult," came Gemma's next text as if she could see and hear him through the screen.

"Not difficult," he texted back. "It's just not a good time right now. I might have to work over."

"You should have thought of that before you agreed to take Dominique out."

"I didn't agree. This was your idea."

Three blinking dots.

"Jake … she's nice. She's cute. She's a nurse. I know there's a thing with nurses and cops. She could be perfect for you. What's the worst that could happen?"

Jake thought of about a million answers to that, but opted not to test them. He finally just settled for a thumbs-up emoji and slipped his phone into his suit jacket.

A blind date. With Dominique the nurse. Jake looked up at the yards of razor wire surrounding the stone prison walls and wondered if the next hour might be the best part of his day.

He climbed out of his car and made the slow walk up to visitor intake. By now, he knew the drill. He flashed his credentials. A loud buzzer went off followed by a metallic clang as the security doors opened and he was let inside.

It was Friday. Four o'clock. Inmate 134391-235 would have just finished his shift in the laundry. A coveted job and one Jake knew he used to get information. Today, with the sun shining and near ninety-degree temps, Jake asked to have his visit outside in the yard.

He seated himself at a picnic table in the farthest corner of the yard. He didn't have to wait long. Not two minutes later, inmate 134391-235 strode out.

At six foot four, Rex towered over most of the other inmates. The few who took visitors at the same time watched Rex as he made his way down the rows until he stood in front of Jake's table.

"You're cutting into my workout time," Rex said.

"Couldn't be helped."

Rex surveyed the yard. Anyone who was still staring quickly looked the other way. Rex took a seat. He leaned casually against one forearm.

"Did you miss me or something?" Rex smiled. "The last time we met like this, I distinctly remember you saying you hoped you wouldn't have to see me for a while."

"I've learned to live with disappointment."

Rex laughed in his deep, rich baritone.

"What do you need this time?" Rex asked.

"It's not what I need. It's what you need. I'm working a murder case. Craig Albright. I think you know him."

Rex arched one dark brow. His niece and nephew really did favor him. Kyra in particular had the same flint-gray eyes.

"Rings a bell."

"Cut the crap, Rex. I know you still get intel on everything that happens on your turf."

"My turf?"

"He was filleted like a fish," Jake said. He reached into his jacket and pulled out the most grisly of the crime scene photos. He laid them out on the table. Rex merely flicked his eyes at the pictures. He didn't touch them.

"I know you know what that is," Jake said.

"Pretend I don't. Did you come here because you think I can somehow help you solve your murder for you?"

"No. I came here because I don't think you know what's about to happen to your family."

Rex's eyes darkened. His whole posture changed, becoming rigid, on guard.

"I've got a credible source telling me some pretty damning things about who did this to Craig and why."

"You gonna tell me or are we gonna keep playing games?"

"My witness fingered your brother, Floyd. Says he's the one who did this to Albright."

Rex didn't flinch. He stared Jake down.

"Floyd," he said. "And you buy that?"

"It wasn't the only thing my informant had to say. I know what's been going on out at the Albright property, Rex."

"I don't know what you're talking about."

"Yeah. You do. Albright was facilitating an exchange of goods, Rex. Dope. Cocaine and pot. And it's been going on for years."

Nothing. No expression on Rex's face.

"Albright wanted out," Jake said. "He had plans to retire to Florida with his wife. My informant says that didn't sit well with Floyd. He was about to kill his golden goose between your family and the cartel. So Floyd made an example out of him. This example."

Jake tapped the photo showing a close-up of Craig Albright's slit throat.

"Your informant is full of shit."

"I don't think he is. He had dates. Times. Names. Enough to expose your family to some pretty hefty federal charges, Rex."

King Rex leaned forward, getting close enough to Jake he could smell what he had for lunch.

"Your informant is a liar."

"Except he's not. And he's willing to testify to what he knows. Your brother Floyd is going to face lethal injection, Rex. And that would be one thing if it were just him. But the feds are going to dig. They're going to want to peel back the lid on your entire family."

"I'm telling you," Rex said through gritted teeth. "Floyd had nothing to do with whatever happened to Craig Albright. We don't kill people. Not like this."

"Then where is he?"

"What?"

"Floyd. I tried to pay him a visit. His employees haven't seen him since the morning of Albright's murder. He took off. Then I went to his house. Your nephew ... Floyd's heir apparent? He tried to run and got into a tussle with one of my deputies. That's not exactly the behavior of someone with nothing to hide."

"Knox is his own man."

Jake stared at Rex. "I never said it was Knox."

"Yeah? Well, Kyle wouldn't have run."

"Is that the plan? You could be in here for another twenty years, Rex. Floyd's made some really dumb decisions that are bad for the family business. Word I'm hearing, he's looking to hand things off to Knox. Only ... from what I've seen, the kid's not cut out for it."

Rex didn't answer. But Jake could tell by the set of his jaw he'd hit on it.

"Kyra," Jake said. "Your niece. You know who she reminded me of?"

Rex sat stone-faced.

"She reminded me of you, Rex. Something tells me she's worth ten of her brothers."

Rex lifted his chin. His steel-eyed gaze didn't falter.

"She's in trouble though," Jake said. "Or she will be."

"She had nothing to do with whatever happened to this idiot," Rex said, stabbing his index finger on the picture in front of him, but not letting his gaze drop.

"The thing is, Rex? I believe you. It just doesn't seem like the Bardo style to torture and kill a man like that. I think your partners tried to send Floyd a message. This is what happens when you try to change the terms of your business arrangement with the cartel."

Rex shoved the photographs back across the table. Two of them slid to the ground. Jake left them there.

"What do you want from me? Why are you telling me all of this?"

"Because, believe it or not, I want to help you. More importantly, I want to make sure Craig Albright's the only casualty of your little business arrangement. I've got the power to make sure the cartel thinks Blackhand Hills is too much trouble for them to stay. But to do that ... I need to talk to Floyd. I need to know what he knows."

"What's that got to do with me? Seems like your beef is with my brother."

"Your brother's gone to ground. But I'm betting you know where to find him. If I pull your call records, I bet I'm going to find out he reached out to you in the last few days."

For the first time since he sat down, King Rex flinched.

"You know where he is. You can get a message to him," Jake said. "Give me access. If Floyd didn't kill Albright, let him prove it to me. Give me the weapon I need to clean up your mess, Rex."

"In exchange for what?"

Jake shook his head. "In exchange for keeping hell from raining down on my town, Rex. I know you care about that as much as I do. If I'm a betting man, I'd say your little brother engaged in some unsanctioned business dealings. Maybe he got in over his head. As powerful as you still are in here, there's a limit to what you can do. So, like it or not, you and I may have to work together to make sure Craig Albright is the last dead soldier in your little war. And if you don't ... you're going to lose everything. If the cartel doesn't come after Floyd and his family, the feds will. And I'll help them."

A tremor went through Rex Bardo. He erupted, slamming a fist down on the table. It drew the attention of the guards in the corner of the yard. Jake put a hand up, gesturing for them to stay back.

"Do you think we're friends, Jake? Do you think it does me any good for people to think that?"

"I don't care what people think. I care about what's happening in my town. I think you do too."

Nothing. No response.

"Did you know?"

No response.

"I think you didn't," Jake said. "I think your little brother is weak. He's play acting at being a leader to your family. But he's not cut out for it. Only you've been in here a long time, Rex. Your brother got restless. Power hungry, maybe. He saw a way to level up. Maybe even get out from under you. Make some real money. Did you warn him? I know enough about how you did business when you were on the outside, Rex. The Hilltop Boys would have never messed with the cartel if you had a say in it. Floyd went against you. Didn't he?"

Rex stared straight at Jake. Only the tiniest twitch at the corner of his mouth betrayed his anger. Jake knew he was right.

"He could have burned the whole house down," Jake said. "Exposed your entire operation, your entire family to something even worse than sitting in federal prison. You don't want a war with the cartel. But you also don't want a war with me. It's coming. If Floyd has handled this as badly as I think he has, he might be next. His kids might be next. Whether you like it or not, I'm your best shot at getting your family clear of this. If Floyd's innocent that is. If he's guilty? Well ... seems to me I can solve another problem for you. It wouldn't be the first time."

"He won't talk to you," Rex said. "Even if I told you where to find him."

"He'll talk to me if you order him to. I'd bet my grandpa's land he came to you scared out of his mind. Begging you to get him out of the mess he's created. If he didn't kill Craig Albright, Floyd knows what happened to him by now. He's in hiding because of it, isn't he? He figures he might be next. So let me prevent that from happening. I'm your way out. I'm Floyd's way out if he didn't kill Albright."

It was there in his eyes. Jake could see it. He was right about Floyd. He'd betrayed his brother.

"You want something from me? You do it my way. You leave those kids out of it."

"Tell me where to find Floyd," Jake said. "Give me that show of faith. I swear to you, I'll do what I can to protect your family."

"A show of faith?" Rex said. "See ... that's what I'm going to need from you, Jake. You want Floyd? You're gonna have to go to him. I know my brother. He ain't coming down from that hill."

Jake went cold. The hill.

"You're saying he's with your relatives on the other side of Red Sky Hill?"

Rex cracked a slow smile.

"You wanna talk to Floyd? Go talk to him. But you and only you. I told you, first you give *me* a little show of faith."

"Tell me where," Jake said. "Tell me when."

Rex folded his hands in front of him, resting them on the table.

"They'll know."

"Who will know?"

"You don't have to worry about finding my people, Jake. They'll find you. When you're ready, you just head up Log Church Pass and don't stop."

"No way. You tell Floyd he better come on down. Unless he wants me to turn over my intel to the feds."

"I don't think you're gonna do that," Rex said. "And if you do, you'll never see Floyd again. You do this how I say, Jake. No other way."

"Time's up, Bardo." One of the guards stepped forward. Rex spread his hands in a gesture of surrender.

"You go alone," he said to Jake. "Or you'll never see or talk to a soul. A man like you is liable to get lost up there."

"Dammit, Rex, I need your word. If I go up there ... you give me your word, Floyd will come out and talk to me."

"He'll talk to you," Rex said. He was still smiling ear to ear as the guards led him away.

FOURTEEN

"I love you. It'll be good for you."

Gemma's text flashed. Jake sat in the parking lot of Wylie's Bar & Grill in the south end of town. It wouldn't have been his first choice for a first date. Too many cops hung out here. He would have preferred to pick a place at least a county over. His instincts told him this was a bad idea anyway. But it made Gemma happy. He wanted her to be happy. His sister had too many things in her life to be sad about lately. And maybe she had a point. Jake couldn't remember the last time he'd done anything social outside of family events.

So, on Friday night at eight o'clock, after spending an afternoon in the federal prison, Jake walked in looking for Gemma's friend, Dominique Gill.

The hostess gave Jake a wide smile. She grabbed a menu and took him by the arm. "Your date's already here," she said. Jake recognized her. Aimee Piehl. She was the older sister of one of the wrestlers Jake coached. She'd been mat side for the last two years.

"Good luck," Aimee whispered as she pointed to a small table in the corner. It was out of the way of the main traffic in the restaurant and around the corner from the bar. There was that, at least. As private as possible.

A woman, Dominique Gill, sat with her back to him. She turned as Jake approached.

She was pretty with thick auburn hair she wore long. Big brown eyes and an upturned mouth. She had a charming dimple in her left cheek.

"Dominique?" he said.

"Yes!"

"Sorry I'm late. Work got a little crazy."

"Can I start you off with something to drink?" Aimee the hostess asked.

Jake looked at the table. Dominique had lemon water.

"You know, I'll just stick with a ginger ale," Jake said.

Aimee smiled and excused herself.

"I figured you'd want to sit with your back against the wall," Dominique gushed. "You know. You being a cop and all."

"Thanks," Jake said. He extended a hand to shake hers. It felt awkward. Jake realized Gemma was right about something. It had been a very long time since he'd done this. He was out of practice.

He took his seat.

"You're taller than I was thinking you'd be," Dominique said.

"Oh." Instinct drove him. He scanned the room. This part of the restaurant wasn't very crowded. There were two other couples closer to the bar, but most of the action at Wylie's would take place on the other side of it in the poolroom.

"Sorry. That was a dumb thing to say. You're taller. Like that's a compliment. Like you have anything to do with how tall you are."

"It's fine." Jake smiled. Dominique Gill had a rapid-fire way of talking that had Jake doing figure eights with his head to try to keep up.

"My father was tall," she said. "I mean, very tall. Six eight. But none of the rest of us got that gene. A couple of my cousins. But it's always been something they hated. You know. They're self-conscious about it. Oh ... not that you should be. I mean about not being that tall. You're tall enough though. I'm sorry. I'm nervous."

"Don't be," Jake said. Maybe he should have told her he was nervous, too. He was. A little. The waitress came with his ginger ale.

"Are you ready to order?"

"Oh, I am," Dominique said. "Do you need time?"

"I'll just have the bacon burger. No onions, side of fries. Dominique?"

"That sounds good. Only I'll do onion rings. We can share."

"Perfect," Jake said. He waited for her to collect the menus before turning to Dominique again.

"So, my sister says you're a nurse?" He caught her mid-sip of her water. "Sorry."

Dominique swallowed and smiled. "It's fine. Yes. I work out at Pine Grove. The nursing home. That's how I met your sister, actually. She sold my mom's house. She's a resident there now. I mean my mom. Not your sister, obviously."

"I hope she did a good job for you," Jake said.

"Oh Gemma's wonderful. She was really good with my mom. It was a hard thing ... you know ... her moving out of the house she lived in with my dad. He passed away a few years ago. Anyway, Gemma was so kind and patient with her. She made the process so smooth."

"I'm glad," Jake said. "She'll love hearing that."

"I'm worried about her though," Dominique said. "Gemma, I mean. Not my mom. I'm sure that business out at Red Sky Hill ... the Albright property. That had to have really shaken her. Do you have any leads?"

Jake took a sip of his soft drink. "I'm sorry. I can't really discuss it. Ongoing investigation and all."

"Oh sure. Sure. I'm sorry, I don't know what I was thinking. That was rude of me. I've only just met you and here I am trying to pry state secrets out of you."

"Well, I wouldn't call them state secrets exactly."

"Still. I put you in an awkward position within the first two minutes of meeting you. I'm sorry. I'm just nervous. I haven't been on a date in a really long time. Not a first date, anyway."

Jake put a hand over Dominique's. "It's fine," he said. "How about we figure this out together? I'm actually a little nervous, too."

All the tension went out of Dominique's shoulders. Her smile, which had seemed a bit forced up until now, widened, lighting her whole face. She really was pretty.

"Thanks," she said. "I'd ... I'd like that. Yes. Let's figure this out together."

Things grew instantly comfortable between them. Dominique relaxed in her chair and Jake found himself much more at ease himself. Maybe Gemma was on to something.

"So," Jake said. "How about the obligatory questions? You apparently grew up nearby?"

"Yep. Went to St. Iz. Just had my fifteen-year reunion, if you can believe that."

"I'm about to have my twentieth."

"Good. It's good you're older," she said. "I've dated younger guys. No good. And guys my age, too."

Jake hardly thought a five-year age difference made him a senior statesman, but he was afraid making that joke would set off Dominique's nerves again.

"Do you like your job?" she asked. "Sorry. Maybe that's a strange question."

"I do," he said. "It can be rewarding. But it's hard too. And it's not easy to have much of a social life."

"Well, I for one thank you for your service. I suppose you and I have similar jobs in that we work with people who aren't on their best days."

"Right. Though I'd imagine your patients are relieved when you walk in a room. I can't say that I'm a welcome sight for most people."

"Oh, I can't believe that. You? You're so, well, good-looking."

Jake laughed. "Thanks."

"I mean, except for your ear."

Dominique reached forward and ran a finger along Jake's right ear. An odd thing to do, but Jake tried not to flinch.

"Does it hurt?"

Jake touched his ear himself. As cauliflower ear went, Jake knew his was on the milder side. Just a misshapen tip and an extra fold. "Not anymore," Jake said. "It used to when I was a kid. Throbbed. Now, I barely notice it."

"I've always thought wrestling was a badass sport. I mean ... more than football. They get to wear all those pads. And basketball players, they get fouled out if they so much as touch each other."

"I suppose all sports have their pros and cons," Jake said.

"Well, Jody, my last boyfriend? He had some pretty strong opinions on wrestling. He said it was for sissies. But I never thought that though, so don't worry. I mean ...like at all. Don't worry."

"I wasn't."

The waitress came with the burgers. Jake put his napkin in his lap.

"Sorry," Dominique said. "I suppose you don't really want to hear about my ex. Lord knows I shouldn't be talking about him. Jody played football in high school. But not here. He's from Texas, originally. Which makes sense why he'd have such strong opinions about football."

"I suppose so," Jake said. His eyes went to the bar. Detective Dave Majewski had just walked up to it. He had his back to Jake so he hadn't spotted him. A moment later, he walked off with a draft pitcher and four frosted pilsner glasses.

"I bet you could take Jody down in two seconds though," Dominique said. She'd barely taken a breath. Her words came out in a steady stream. Jake noticed she'd eaten half her burger, but couldn't fathom how she managed between sentences.

"What?"

"He's taller than you. What are you? Five nine? Five ten?"

"Are we back on my height? Yes. About that," Jake said, not sure he liked where the conversation was heading.

"Is it just you?" he asked, trying to steer it to something less ... odd. "Any brothers or sisters?"

"I've got a sister. Rory. But she lives in Utah. Which is rough. She's not really around to help out with my mom. Or my dad when he got sick."

"I'm sorry to hear that."

Jake took a bite out of his burger. It was slightly overcooked but he wasn't going to be the guy to send food back on a date. Or ever, really.

"But you could though, right?"

"Could what?"

"Jody. He's six two, but he never wrestled. So, I bet you could take him down."

"Yeah. No idea."

"He's a Raiders fan. And I mean hard core. During the playoffs, it's like ... don't even talk to him."

"Who?"

"Jody!" she said. "My ex. And I mean, I get it. He's into his team. But to have a rule that I can't even talk when the game is on? That's extreme, don't you think?"

Jake shoved a fry in his mouth and gave Dominique a polite smile. She pulled at her onion rings and smiled back.

"So, do you work the day shift?" Jake asked, but started to feel like it was a lost cause.

"Four on, two off," she said. "It's not a bad schedule. But I'm on call a lot."

"Ah. That's rough."

"Jody hated it. I mean ... *hated* it. We'd get in a fight every time I had to work an extra shift. But my mortgage isn't cheap. And it's not like he ever contributed. You would, right?"

"I'm sorry?"

"If we lived together. You'd contribute to the mortgage, wouldn't you?"

Lord. Was she asking hypothetically? Please God, Jake thought. Let her only be asking hypothetically.

"Yeah. I don't think it's unreasonable for two people to contribute to household expenses, if that's what you're asking me."

"See?" Dominique reached across the table and slapped Jake on the arm.

Dominique's phone lit up. She had it resting on the table in front of her. She picked it up and rolled her eyes at whatever it said. She fired off a text and set the phone back down.

"Did Gemma help you out with your house, too?" Jake asked, desperate to find something to talk about besides the infamous Jody.

"Oh no. I bought it long before I met Gemma. But right before Jody and I started dating. So let me see. Six years ago. Gosh. That's a long time. We'd just had our five-year anniversary and the bastard dumped me. The day after. Can you believe that?"

"Wow. Sorry," Jake said. He was beginning to rethink the ginger ale. A beer would be heaven right about now.

"With a text. Can you believe that? He broke up with me with a text. I'll show you."

"You don't have to do that, really."

She did.

Dominique turned her phone screen around. She pulled up a text. The caller ID read Jody the Jackass. The text read, "This is over. I'm done."

"Sorry that happened to you," Jake said.

Dominique shook a finger at him. It went on long enough. Jake started looking to his left and right, wondering if anyone else was witnessing this.

"See," she said. "I knew you weren't like that. You'd never break up with someone by text."

"How are we doing here?" The waitress came to the table. Jake bit his tongue. He had an answer for her but knew he couldn't really say it.

"We're good," Dominique said. "You good?"

"Stellar," Jake said. As soon as the waitress walked off, Dominique turned to him.

"So let me ask you. If you were out of work, I would understand it. You know, kicking in for rent. And for the first few months, I didn't say anything. Not a word. But after four months, he wasn't even looking for a job anymore."

"Jody," Jake said, his tone withering.

"And it's not like I nagged him every day. I swear. I didn't. But when I'd see a listing for a job he might like, I would tell him. I was trying to be helpful. That's not nagging, right?"

"Dominique ... I really don't ..."

Her phone lit up again. Jake could still see the screen. It was Jody the Jackass himself. Dominique picked it up. Her eyes narrowed with anger as her fingers flew over the text keys. She hit send with a flourish and put the phone back down.

Jake opened his mouth to ask her if she liked her burger. Before he got the words out, Dominique's phone lit up again.

"If you need to answer that," he said, "I can ..."

"Oh no," she said. "Let him wait." She looked down at her phone. "You hear me? You can wait. In fact ..."

Dominique picked up her phone. She got up and came to the other side of the table. Before Jake fully knew what she was doing, Dominique sat on his lap and flipped her camera around. She pressed her cheek to Jake's and snapped a selfie. Then she stood up and fired off another text.

"There," she said. "Let him stew on that."

"I'm sorry. Did you just send a picture of me to your ex?"

"Of us," she said.

Jake's head started to pound. In his back pocket his own phone started to vibrate. Screw it, he thought. He took it out.

"How's it going?" A text from Gemma.

Jake grimaced through a smile and pocketed his phone.

"Sorry," he said. "It's nothing."

Dominique's phone actually rang. Her ringtone was a Carrie Underwood song. She waited until Carrie belted out something about scratching her name into leather seats before answering. She reached over and grabbed one of Jake's fries, popping it into her mouth.

"Yeah!" she said. "You saw that right!" She gave Jake a single thumbs-up. He plastered on a smile and gave her both thumbs-up.

"Sorry," Dominique whispered. "This should only take a minute."

Then she got up, left the table, and walked toward the front of the bar with her finger in her ear so she could better hear her phone call.

"Can I get you anything else?" the waitress materialized. "Dessert?"

Jake held up a finger. "Check, please." He pulled out a fifty-dollar bill and handed it to her. "Just keep the change."

Jake walked to the front of the restaurant. Dominique stood out on the sidewalk. Though he couldn't hear her, she carried on an animated conversation, gesturing wildly with her free hand. Aimee Piehl, the hostess, stood closest to him. She'd seen the whole thing.

"Is there a back way out of here?" he asked Aimee.

"You can go out through the alley behind the bar," she said.

Jake debated saying something to Dominique. Would she even notice that he was gone? Did he want her to?

"Dammit," he muttered. Jake decided to say goodbye. He headed for the doors. Before he got there, a loud rumble filled the air. A second later, a motorcycle rolled up to the sidewalk right in front of Dominique. The rider wasn't wearing a helmet. Jake immediately recognized him from Dominique's caller ID contact photo.

Jody the Jackass. In the flesh.

Before Jake's stunned eyes, Dominique climbed on the back of the motorcycle and the two of them sped off into the night.

"Unbelievable," Jake muttered.

"Oooh," Aimee hissed. "Tough break."

From the other end of the bar, a roar of laughter erupted. Jake's whole body tensed. He slowly turned toward the sound. There, in the back of the bar but in full view of Jake's misery, sat what looked like every off-duty member of the Worthington County Sheriff's Department.

FIFTEEN

"Tough luck, kid," Lieutenant John Beverly said. "Happens to the best of us."

"That poor girl wanted to get away from you so fast. I think they laid rubber on the street," Sargent Jeff Hammer shouted.

Jake shook his head. There was no escaping the onslaught.

"Come on," Beverly said. "Your first round's on me. You look like you could use it."

"What was it, your sparkling personality?" Deputy Chris Denning shouted from the other end of the table. Seated next to him were Deputy Matt Corbin and Birdie. Detective Gary Majewski pulled out an empty chair for Jake.

"Your winning smile?" Deputy Corbin called out. Birdie lifted her beer mug to him, winking.

Jake took a seat next to Beverly. Sergeant Hammer sat across from him. The ribbing went on for another minute or two. Jake laughed along with them. There was really nothing else to do.

"This is what I get for letting my sister set me up," Jake said. Hammer and Beverly broke into fresh laughter.

"Let Denning help you set up your online dating profile next time," Corbin said. "Ask him about his last blind date. She brought her pet hamster with her. In her purse."

Jake raised a glass to Denning. The conversation finally moved away from Jake's bad date to more mundane, work-related things.

"How's Mary Rathburn working out?" Beverly asked. "That was a surprise pick."

"Really?" Jake said. "Who else put in for Zender's spot? Landry never told me." Jake also hadn't asked.

Beverly and Hammer exchanged a look. Beverly leaned forward and whispered, "Corbin over there thought he was next in line. I gotta be honest. He would have been the more popular choice."

"Popular with who?" Jake asked. Though he had nothing against Matt Corbin, Jake wouldn't have described him as very ambitious. He was a decent deputy, but Jake had never gotten the impression he was looking for a career change.

"I'm just saying," Beverly said. "Mary was the only woman in the running."

"She was also the best choice," Jake said. "And to answer your original question. She's working out fine. She'll be ready if Zender actually does retire."

"You have your doubts?" Hammer asked.

Jake shrugged. His beer was cold and tasted good. "He's been threatening to retire for a long time. That's all I'm saying."

"How's Landry doing?" Hammer asked. "We're taking a lot of heat from that article in the *Beacon*. People are starting to ask whether she might just decide not to run for re-election."

"She'll run," Jake said. "That article was a hit piece. Probably funded by whoever's going to end up running against her."

"Any word about who that might be?" Gary Majewski asked.

"Nobody's come forward yet," Hammer said. "But that piece ... I don't know. It just doesn't sit well with me. Somebody's talking."

Beverly nodded. "Whoever it is, I'd like to wring their necks. Some of the data they reported came from the inside. They had exact numbers on some of our internal crime stats. Where'd they get that?"

"Who had access to it?" Jake asked.

"Only a couple of dozen people," Hammer answered. "Yeah, we had a closed door meeting about it the week before that exposé came out. But anybody could have leaked that after the meeting."

"If someone on the inside is trying to undermine Landry, I'd like to know about it."

"It won't come from us," Beverly said. "The command union is set to endorse her after the first of the year. I'm sure you deputies will follow suit. Landry shouldn't worry too much about that article. The *Beacon*'s had an agenda for twenty years."

"I'm glad to hear she's got command's support," Jake said. "Still, if you hear anything about who might be talking to the media behind her back ... behind *all* of our backs, I'd like to know."

Deputies Denning and Corbin got up from the table.

"Time for us to cash out," Corbin said. "My wife's been home with the kids by herself all day."

Jake, Beverly, Majewski, and Hammer said their goodbyes to
Denning and Corbin. The other end of the table was beginning to
empty.

"I don't miss those days," Beverly said. "Corbin has three kids
under five. That's the only point I was trying to make about
Rathburn over him for Zender's spot. I think his wife really wants
him off the streets."

"That's the pitch?" Jake said. "That Corbin's got more kids than
Rathburn does? If you want to make that argument, she still wins.
Mary's a single mom. Besides, what is this? 1955? That shouldn't
even be a consideration."

"I'm not saying she's not qualified," Beverly said. "Don't put
words into my mouth. I'm just saying she was a surprise pick,
that's all. You're the one working with her. If she's ready, she's
ready."

Birdie picked up her beer mug and made her way to Jake's end of
the table.

"You can have my seat," Gary Majewski said. "I've gotta get home,
too."

"See you, Gary," Birdie said.

"Thanks for your help on that convenience store break-in," Gary
said. Birdie patted him on the back as he turned to leave.

"Did I miss some excitement today?" Jake asked. "What
break-in?"

"Nothing major," Birdie said. "Somebody hit the Dollar Kart out
on County Road Fourteen. I helped Gary run down a couple of
leads. It ended up being a former employee."

"He's the one you're going to have to watch out for," Hammer
said. "I didn't want to say it in front of him, but I think Gary was

thinking he'd move over to crimes against persons once Zender cleared out."

"What?" Jake said. "Majewski's three years behind Zender in terms of retirement eligibility. And he's never once taken an interest in my caseload. Don't get me wrong. He's solid where he is. It's just complete news to me that he'd want anything to do with Zender's job."

Hammer and Beverly each ordered one more round. By the time they finished their drinks, they were ready to leave. It was past ten. As Beverly and Hammer went up to pay their tabs, it left Jake alone at the table with Birdie.

"You doing okay?" she asked.

"As well as always."

Birdie laughed. "That bad, huh? That woman ... that was Gemma's idea?"

Jake had ignored five texts from his sister since the infamous Dominique took off with Jody the Jackass.

"Lesson learned," Jake said.

"She meant well," Birdie said. "Don't come down too hard on her."

Jake gave Birdie a sideways glance. "Were you in on it? Did she tell you she was trying to fix me up?"

"She said she was worried you weren't getting out enough. That you were spending too much time at work. She doesn't think it's good for you."

"Hmmph," Jake mumbled.

"I mean ... she's not wrong. You've been eating and breathing this job over the last few months."

"I'm working a homicide," Jake said. "In case my sister hasn't noticed, the whole town's on edge because of it. Half of them think there's some boogeyman on the loose looking for his next victim."

"You sure there isn't?"

Jake set his drink down. "To be honest? No."

When the waitress came back, both Jake and Birdie passed on ordering another round. They'd both had their limit. Jake put a twenty on the table to cover his and Birdie's tab. She pulled a twenty out to cover the tip.

"Come on," Jake said. "Let me walk you to your car."

"Better luck next time!" Aimee the hostess called out to Jake as he and Birdie made their way out the front entrance. He gave her a wave.

"She seems nice," Birdie said. "I can ask around. She's probably single."

"Don't you start," Jake said. "And don't tell me you're in cahoots with my sister."

"I'm just saying she's been checking you out all evening."

Jake looked back at the front door of the bar. "She what?"

Birdie laughed. "For a detective, you can be pretty unobservant."

Jake shook his head. Birdie had parked just one block over. She drove a black Jeep Cherokee. She hit her key fob to open the doors.

"So I heard you paid a visit to an inmate at Elkton today," Birdie said. Jake stopped short.

"You heard that from where?"

Birdie shrugged. "It's a small town, Jake. An even smaller department. Do you really think the Bardos had something to do with what happened to Craig Albright?"

She opened her car door and stood in the space between it and the front seat.

"I don't know," Jake said. "I'm trying to rule that out."

Birdie whistled low. "You think there's a turf war about to go down?"

"I hope not. Hopefully in the next day or two, I'll have better answers on that too."

"What's happening in the next day or two?"

Jake paused. It wasn't that he didn't trust Birdie. He just wasn't sure he wanted anyone else to know about his conversation with King Rex. Yet.

"Jake," she said. "What's going on? You've got that look on your face."

"What look?"

"That look you get when you're hiding something."

"I'm not hiding anything. There's just very little I can say about the investigation right now."

"To who? To me? Jake. What did Rex Bardo tell you? Or better yet, what did you agree to?"

It was like she could see straight through him. "Birdie ... it's nothing. Just a lead I need to follow up on. I still need to talk to Floyd Bardo. I have information he's gone up to stay with family."

"Family," she said. "You mean he's gone up the hill? Jake, that makes his entire family liars. His daughter said he was in Vegas. Do you really think Floyd killed Albright? It just seems too ... messy for the Hilltop Boys. Not their M.O."

"I don't know. Probably not. But I need to talk to him."

"Jake ... please tell me you're not planning on going up that hill alone."

"I'm tracking down a lead. It's my job."

"You taking Rathburn with you?"

He didn't answer.

"Jake."

"Don't worry about it."

"Does Landry know you talked to Rex Bardo? Does she know you're heading up there by yourself? That was the condition, wasn't it? Rex is sending you up there alone. You trust him?"

"Birdie, stop. I know what I'm doing. I've got this handled. And I'd appreciate it if you'd keep all this under your hat."

"Will you at least promise me one thing?"

"Probably not," Jake teased.

"Jake. Promise me you won't do anything stupid. Whether he's in prison or not, Rex Bardo is dangerous."

"Luckily, he *is* in prison," Jake said. "And I told you. I've got things under control."

Birdie climbed into her vehicle, but her stern gaze never left Jake.

"Will you at least call me?" she said. "If you need help. If you're trying to do something off book, for whatever reason, I can keep my mouth shut, Jake. I hope you know that."

Jake stepped forward and leaned into her open car window. "I know that. And thanks. But I swear, you've got nothing to worry about."

Birdie pulled her seatbelt across her body. She frowned at him as she started her car. Jake stepped back and held up his hand in a wave as he watched her drive away. In the distance, as a full moon rose, he could see the outline of Red Sky Hill.

Sixteen

L og Church Pass predated the formation of the county itself. It curved in off the eastern face of Red Sky Hill, mostly overgrown now. It was little more than a two-track pass.

Jake put his grandfather's truck in low gear and cranked the windows shut to keep the branches from clawing at him as he started up the trail. Thankful for the four-wheel drive, Jake realized this path would have been impassable if it started to rain. As it was, his jaw rattled as he traveled over the rough ground. It might as well have been a jungle.

Jake wound his way up and up. The old truck was worth its weight in gold. His newer F-150 might not have made it up or would have gotten scratched and beaten to hell in the process. But Grandpa's '85 Diesel F-350 could plow through blizzards and already looked rough.

Jake made it two miles in before he hit the clearing. He was surprised to still find it. Rex had told him to drive up as far as he could go. And so he had.

Jake put the truck in park and engaged the parking brake. Even though the thickest part of the woods had cleared, he was still on an incline. He slipped his keys in his shirt pocket and stepped out of the cab.

"Hello!" he shouted. Only a chorus of locusts answered him. The trees ahead blocked out most of the sun, but it was still damn hot in the last days of September.

He reached in and grabbed his small backpack. He'd brought just a few essential supplies, not knowing what to expect when he got up here. He wore an old pair of jeans, hiking boots, and a Carhartt work shirt, thick enough to keep him from getting scraped to death by thorns.

Jake grabbed a water bottle from the passenger seat and headed toward what was left of Log Church itself. There wasn't much. Just the foundation and one cedar wall. There was a large depression in the ground where the altar had once stood. Two hundred years ago, a Jesuit priest had claimed this patch of land and commissioned the building of the church. Legend was, it lasted fifty years to the day before burning down.

When Jake was a kid, climbing up to Log Church had become somewhat of a dare. Kids would hike up and spend the night in the ruins telling ghost stories then embellishing what they saw in the middle of the night.

From the looks of the overgrowth, Jake guessed nobody had been up here to camp in years. Maybe decades. The only sign of civilization was one smashed, faded beer can under the thick brush. Jake couldn't make out the brand anymore but it had the teardrop opening of an old-fashioned pull tab.

"Hello!" Jake hollered once more. Still nothing. He pulled out his cell phone. He still had two bars here so he took that as a good sign. He dropped a pin just in case.

He walked around the standing wall. Log Church Pass picked back up there, but it wasn't drivable. Jake looked back at his truck. It was safe enough here. And yet, doubt crawled up his spine.

"Dammit," he muttered. Rex's directions had been clear. He was to drive up the trail, then keep going on foot. His kin would find Jake, not the other way around.

"Leap of faith," Jake said. He paused, then turned back to the ruins. Superstition. He pressed a hand to the wall and said a quick prayer. Couldn't hurt.

Jake repositioned his backpack and headed up the trail. He checked his smartwatch. It was ten o'clock. He wanted to make sure he had plenty of time to get up and back in broad daylight. Part of him doubted whether anyone would come to greet him at all. The woods grew ever thicker. After a half an hour of hiking, he could barely see the trail at all. He wondered if he'd managed to stray from it without realizing it. He checked the GPS on his phone. He'd been hiking in more or less a straight line.

Sweat trickled down the center of his back. Jake had a bandana in his back pocket. He took it out and wiped his brow. The water he carried had already turned warm. He had several more bottles in his pack if he needed it.

"Hello!" Jake called out. Still nothing but dense, quiet woods. He kept going. He was three miles deep now. The two that he'd driven, now a mile on foot. There was nothing here. Jake barely even saw so much as a squirrel. The knocking sound of woodpeckers high in the trees was the only real sound Jake heard.

"Dammit, Rex," he muttered. He wouldn't put it past the guy to send Jake on a wild goose chase. It would have been an easy way to stall. To give Floyd Bardo more time to disappear. Only, Jake's gut told him something different. Rex was a lot of things, but he didn't think he was an outright liar.

A small stream came in from the west. As Jake trudged on, it widened. He followed along the banks of it, having no real other options. If any of Rex's family camped up here, it would make sense for them to be close to the best water source. By the satellite images Jake pulled up before he left, he knew there was also a small lake about three miles due north of the base of Red Sky Hill. There had to be other trails too, but the trees were too thick to make anything out in the overhead images.

Old habits kicked in and Jake started to look for deer sign. With the stream running through and a marshier area up ahead, this would be good hunting ground. Years ago, he'd heard a story of a pair of hunters being run off by "wild men." Apocryphal most likely. But it served Rex's kin to keep the fear alive.

He didn't see any blinds set up anywhere, but broken branches and matted underbrush told him something had been through here recently. Something big.

Jake made his way to another small clearing. A large log had fallen and lay on a slant halfway across the stream. It seemed as good a place as any to take a rest.

Jake slid his pack off his shoulder and downed the rest of his water. He crumpled it and stuffed it into the side compartment of his backpack.

He stuck his hand into the small current of the stream. The water was ice cold. He cupped some and poured it down the back of his neck.

He closed his eyes. A breeze picked up, blowing through the trees. He could smell the sweet tang of something rotting not too far away. Probably a dead rabbit.

A branch cracked. Jake kept his eyes closed. He inhaled. The wind began to die down. Slowly, keeping his shoulders as still as he

could, he slid his hand down until it rested on the handle of
his gun.

In one fluid movement, Jake drew his weapon and twisted toward
the source of the sound.

Two men emerged from the tree line. Both wore bandanas
covering their noses and mouths. One of them was red, the other
blue. Each of them carried sawed-off shotguns and pointed them
straight at Jake.

Jake pulled up his weapon and raised his hands.

"I'm Jake Cashen," he said. "I think your cousin told you to
expect me."

They kept their weapons trained on him. "We know who you are."

Jake holstered his gun as a show of faith. Slowly, he rose to his feet,
keeping his hands up.

"Then you know why I'm here. I'm looking for Floyd. I just need
to have a conversation. I'm not officially here."

The men stepped forward. They were roughly the same height and
build. Tall. Scrawny. The one with the red bandana stepped
forward. He shared Rex Bardo's DNA all right. Ruddy skin. Gray
eyes. That dark hair. He gestured to his companion. They both
lowered their weapons.

"What do you want with Floyd?"

"I told you," Jake said. "I just need to talk to him. If you know
who I am, then you already know that too." Jake didn't want to
even fathom what network Rex had in place that could send a
message clear out here. He was just, for the moment, glad that he
could.

"You'll have to talk to Melva. She'll be the one to decide if you go any further."

"That's not the arrangement I've got with Rex."

"Rex isn't in charge out here," Red Bandana Man said. "I don't care what he told you. I don't even care who you are. You aren't going further. You aren't going back until you talk to Melva."

"Fine," Jake said. "Where's Melva?"

The men didn't answer. They merely looked at each other, then turned and started walking back the way they came.

"Hey!" Jake shouted. They didn't stop. They were on the other side of the stream and moving fast.

"Shit," Jake said. The stream was too wide to jump. He had no choice but to walk right through it, soaking his socks and boots in the process. When he reached the other side, he now made a loud squishing sound when he walked. No chance he'd be able to sneak off undetected now if the need arose.

He ran to catch up with the two men. One of them glanced over his shoulder, but said nothing. They just kept going.

It was downhill now. With his wet boots, Jake slid as he walked sideways down the steep embankment. He watched his footing, praying he wouldn't break his damn ankle.

Then he looked up.

The men were gone. He'd reached another clearing tucked at the base of Red Sky Hill. He almost didn't see it. The logs blended into the tree line. But there it was. A solid brick farmhouse. The place was rigged with solar panels, likely a recent addition. He heard a female voice singing from inside.

Jake scanned the area. Where the hell had the men disappeared to? As he got closer to the house, he could see trails leading away from it in the back. There was no way to tell where they led. The satellite images hadn't been helpful owing to how dense the woods were. He could see tire tracks though. They were all through the yard and leading away from the back of the house.

Jake came closer to the house. "Hello?" he called out. He heard a strange whistle and froze.

The two men reappeared from the other side of the house. They were joined by four other men. More Bardo kin. But none of them was Floyd.

They approached Jake. He held his arms up.

"You don't take another step without permission," Red Bandana Man said. He gestured to his companions. They approached Jake in unison.

"Check him," Red Bandana Man said.

Jake's whole body tensed as the men descended on him. "My service weapon is in its holster on my right side," Jake cautioned them.

One of the men grabbed Jake's outstretched arm and crooked it behind him. It took everything in him not to flatten the guy. But he was outgunned and outnumbered. They knew it as well as he did.

One man patted him down and another pulled his weapon out of its holster. The man patting him down ran his hand down Jake's right pants leg. He found the knife he had strapped to his leg. Pulling up his jeans, the man took that too.

"I better get those back," Jake said to Red Bandana Man. He got nothing more than a snort in reply. The man turned toward the house. He put two fingers in his mouth and let out a whistle so shrill it cleared Jake's sinuses.

The singing from inside the house stopped. The front door creaked open. A woman, short, with jet-black hair, stepped outside. She wore a blue dress with yellow flowers and a faded pink apron. She had bare feet. She wiped her hands on her apron and looked Jake up and down. She didn't smile. She didn't frown, either. She just lifted her chin, then turned and walked back into the house.

"You can go on in," Red Bandana Man said. "But we'll be right outside in case she needs us." He shoved Jake forward. Jake rounded on him, ready to throw a punch. But he got his temper in check and turned back toward the house.

It was time to go meet Melva.

SEVENTEEN

J ake walked in the front door. The house was old. Victorian. To his right was an old-fashioned parlor. Down the long hallway off the front foyer, he heard water running and dishes rattling.

"Hello?" he called out.

She had to be able to hear him. His hand went instinctively to his now empty side holster.

"Melva? I'm Jake Cashen. Your ..." He stopped. He had no idea what relation the men outside were to this woman yet.

He walked through the foyer into the kitchen. She stood at the sink, washing her hands. On the gas stove beside her was a giant silver stew pot.

"Ms ... Melva?" Jake said.

Finally, she turned to him and fixed those keen gray eyes on him. Just like Rex's. He looked exactly like her. He realized then who she must be.

"Your son sent me," Jake said. "Rex. I understand you might be able to help me find your other son, Floyd. I'd just like to talk to him."

Melva Bardo picked up a huge, sharp knife from the butcher block counter beside her. She walked over to the stew pot. Setting the knife down, she picked up a colander filled with peeled and diced potatoes and poured them in.

When she turned back to Jake, she held an old-style potato peeler in her hand. Jake stood at the edge of a kitchen island, also covered in butcher block. It was aged, weathered, bearing the scars of a thousand cuts over the years. Melva thrust the peeler at Jake. Instinct kicked in and he took it from her. Next to him was a mound of freshly washed potatoes. Melva put the colander in front of him. He set his backpack on the floor, picked up the first potato, and started to peel.

Melva stood back, arms crossed in front of her, and watched him.

"Looks like you're getting ready to feed an army," Jake said.

She tilted her head to the side. Jake guessed she had to be in her mid-seventies, at the oldest. She wore no makeup. Her skin was tanned and leathery from decades of working outside, no doubt. She had thin, sinewy arms with well-developed biceps. Rex Bardo must have gotten his size from his father's side. Melva couldn't be more than five foot one. The eyes though. They pierced through him just like Rex's. Just like Kyra's.

"What do you think you know about my family?" she finally said. Jake paused, then kept peeling.

"I know Rex is doing his best to try to keep a war from coming. I know he wants to protect you."

She took a step toward him, planting her hands on the butcher block.

"God gave me three sons. Two have already been taken from me. He gave me three grandsons. One of them has been taken from me."

Jake stopped peeling. He met her gaze. There was not so much accusation in her eyes, but judgment.

"I'm sorry about your grandson," Jake said. A year and a half ago, one of Rex's nephews had gotten caught up in a crime he couldn't control. He'd lost his life because of it. Did she hold him responsible for that?

Jake picked up the peeler and started on the next potato. No. Rex would not have sent him here if he thought his mother held a grudge against him for that.

"I'm sorry about your youngest son too," Jake said. Alton Bardo, Rex's baby brother, had been killed in action in the Persian Gulf. "But you haven't lost Rex."

"Have you come here to take my last son?"

"No, ma'am," Jake said. "It's like I said. I just want to ask him a few questions. Your son ... Rex ... believes he's been falsely accused of murdering Craig Albright. He was killed on the other side of that hill behind us. I imagine you already know that."

"Floyd had nothing to do with hurting anybody," she said. "He doesn't have that kind of thing in him."

"I hope you're right. I'm not in the business of arresting innocent men. If he is innocent, I'll be the first person trying to make sure he can prove it."

He'd gotten through a dozen potatoes as she watched him. Then, without a word, she grabbed the peeler from him. She got her knife and with the precision of a Samurai, she quartered the potatoes Jake peeled then dumped them in her pot.

"I want to thank you," Jake said. "I understand you agreed to let me look at your son Alton's letters during my last murder investigation. It was helpful. I know that must have been painful for you to dredge up."

"That boy," she said. "Now he had the heart of a killer. He was going to end badly no matter what. I always knew I was going to bury him one day."

"Still, I'm sorry for your loss."

She turned back to him. "I appreciate you getting his letters back to me."

"Of course."

"My Rex," she said. "I mean my boys' father, Rex the Third. He was no killer, either. He was soft. It fell to me to make men out of all of them. I should have taken them back up the hill after their daddy died. Floyd, at least. I don't blame you for what happened to my grandson."

She switched topics so fast, it took Jake a moment to keep up.

"I appreciate that," he said.

"But his mama might. You best steer clear of my Nyla." Nyla. She was talking about Rex's sister. The mother of the boy who had been killed a year and a half ago.

"Is she here? Nyla?"

"Oh, she's out and about somewhere. She's still in mourning."

"I'll try to stay out of her way."

Melva laughed. "If she wants to find you, she'll find you. And you won't hear her coming. Of all my children, that one's got the hill still in her."

"So it's your family, not your husband's ... not the Bardos ... who live deeper in the backwoods?"

"My children are Bardos in name only. But they're Knox through and through. I came down the hill for him." Knox, he thought. So Melva's maiden name was Knox. Floyd must have named his oldest son after her.

"Do you regret it?" Jake asked.

"You don't have children of your own," she said. He couldn't quite tell if she'd meant it as a statement or a question.

"No, ma'am."

"You don't want to risk passing your daddy's crazy on to a little boy."

Jake bristled. It had been foolish of him to think this woman didn't know who he was. Didn't know his family history. Instinct told him her line of questioning was as much a test as the potato peeling had been.

"Maybe," Jake said. "Or maybe I've just never found the right woman to settle down with."

A knowing smile lifted the corner of Melva Knox Bardo's mouth. "If the woman is right, she'll find you. You won't get much say in it. So maybe no one's found *you* worthy yet."

"You might have something there," Jake said. She wiped her hands on her apron and came to him. Jake froze. Melva's eyes searched his face. She was standing just inches from him. Then she reached for him, taking his right hand. She turned it and ran her fingers over his palm.

There was a witchy quality about Melva Bardo. Or at least she wanted him to think so. She studied his palm, her own weathered face scrunching up even more. She tapped the largest callous he had at the base of his middle finger.

"It's in you though," she said.

What was in him? His father's "crazy," as she called it? Jake had been hearing that his whole life. He had the strongest sense this woman wanted to see how far she could push him. He refused to take the bait. Refused to flinch. Refused to pull his hand from hers.

Finally, she let him go and took a step back.

"Luc will take you where you want to go," she said. Melva put her fingers to her mouth and let out a whistle. Clearly Red Bandana Man had inherited the talent from Melva's line. So they were members of the Knox family. The hill people, as the uninformed called them in town.

A moment later, Jake heard an engine rev outside.

"You'll want to get back before it's dark," she said. "You can go out the back door there." Then Melva Bardo turned her back on him and went back to stirring her stew pot.

Jake walked to the crooked screen door off the back of the kitchen.

Red Bandana Man had pulled up in a two-seater all-terrain vehicle. Jake turned back to Melva. But she'd already disappeared further into the house.

So Red Bandana Man must be Luc. Jake stepped off the porch.

"Get in," Luc said. Jake looked back at the looming hill. He had his backpack, but they'd taken his weapons. Now he was expected to hop on the four-wheeler and let Luc take him. God knew where. There were a thousand reasons why Jake knew this was a bad idea. And yet he climbed in beside Luc anyway.

Eighteen

For a second, Jake thought Luc was about to drive them straight into a tree. At the last second, he swerved the ATV and entered the woods on one of the hidden trails. As they got deeper, he saw there was a whole network of trails. "Better hold on," Luc shouted. "It gets bumpy through here."

Jake grabbed the seatbelt over his right shoulder and fumbled for the latch. Luc floored the gas pedal, navigating the rough trail at breakneck speed.

Branches whipped by, some of them close enough to scrape Jake's arm. Luc took the trail downhill until they came to a small clearing. The lake opened up to the west. Jake saw three small houses dotting the far shoreline. They were tucked so far back, he wondered if and how their inhabitants ever made it back to civilization.

But Luc kept going, entering the woods again. Another narrow dirt trail opened up. He went further south, rounding the lake shore then taking a sharp turn uphill. Jake marveled that the ATV's engine was hefty enough to get them up the hill. It did though. They left the lake behind and came to a stop on a small plateau. Three more houses tucked in together. To the north of them, Jake saw four greenhouses and several barns. Horse stables beyond that. Cows grazed in one pasture. Chickens and ducks roamed loose. He marveled at the set-up. They appeared completely self-sufficient up here, tucked away and hidden in the hills. More than ready for whatever apocalypse might come.

Luc came to a jerking stop and jumped out of the vehicle.

"Hey!" Jake called out. But Luc all but disappeared back into the woods behind the nearest house.

Jake climbed out of the ATV. He saw two others parked alongside one of the houses. The back end of one was filled with plastic water jugs. In the field beyond the greenhouses, Jake spotted a huge garden with tomatoes, cabbage, and other vegetables ready for picking. Another trail jutted off from the tomato gardens. Jake could just make out the rooftops of four more houses up the hill, plus a small mill.

The Hilltop Boys, Jake thought. Rex Bardo's family crew had gotten their name from their association with this settlement. Though as far as he knew, none of the people who ran Rex's day-to-day operations lived up here. Rumor was, his great-grandfather was the last to live in this settlement full time. The black sheep of the family who had left his roots to find wealth in the "big city" of Stanley, Ohio.

A door slammed. The noise came from the house nearest Jake. The structure was built in a Federalist-style and Jake wondered if it was original. The woods to the north of the structures had been recently logged but new trees were planted and growing.

Jake walked toward the house. He saw a shadow move across the front window, but couldn't tell if it was a man or a woman. Then, a voice called out.

"Hello!"

Jake turned. A man came around from the back of the house and walked toward Jake. Big. Burly. Jet-black hair peppered with gray.

Floyd Bardo. King Rex's only surviving brother.

"Floyd?" Jake said.

Floyd stopped. He looked back at the house with a nervous expression.

"Not here," Floyd said. "We need to take a walk."

"A walk?" Jake said, losing his patience. "Floyd, I've come a pretty long way for what should be a simple conversation."

"Not here!" Floyd insisted. He charged past Jake and headed for a small grove of pine trees. There was a firepit in the clearing beyond them with wooden chairs arranged at crooked angles around it. Floyd went to them and took a seat.

Jake let out an exasperated breath and followed the man. "You people don't make this easy."

"Easy?" Floyd said. "You think this should be easy? I think you know what happens to me if somebody besides you comes looking for me."

Jake sat in one of the chairs opposite Floyd Bardo. "Now what?"

"You're here. That's because Mama let you be. And my brother sent you. So here we are."

"I'm not in the mood for any more games. You know what I'm here to talk to you about. So let's just get to it, Floyd. You've been fingered in the murder of Craig Albright. Your brother's pretty damn insistent that you had nothing to do with it. I'm here to give you the chance to explain to me your side of it. Then, I'll decide what needs to be done."

"You're not pulling me off this hill. I'd rather die up here."

"Tell me what you know. I told your brother. If you truly had nothing to do with what happened to Craig, I'm gonna be the first one in line making sure you don't go down for it. I just want the truth."

Floyd shook his head. "The truth is, I'm the dumbest son of a bitch that ever lived."

"You and Craig. You were mixed up with the cartel. It went sideways."

Floyd shook his head. "You could say that."

"You need to say it. All of it."

Floyd Bardo dropped his head. He buried his face in his hands and his shoulders shook.

Christ, Jake thought. The man broke completely down. He sobbed for a full minute before finally lifting his head and meeting Jake's eyes.

"Rex told you to talk to me. That's why I'm here. He knows it's your best play. And I know he wouldn't have given me this kind of access if he thought you were guilty. So let me help you if I can, Floyd. But you know it's gotta start with the truth."

"Yeah. Okay? Yeah. You've got it right. Me and Craig had a side business with the cartel. They moved their product into town. I distributed it for them. But I'm not saying a damn word about what happened to Craig unless I have your word that arrangement doesn't come back to bite me. Because it's over. Finished. I've got nothing to do with the cartel anymore. We ended it. There's nothing you can prove on that without my say-so. So your word. You can't come after me for the drug shit. None of it. That's gotta be the deal or I'm gone. I can go even deeper into those woods, Cashen."

"I'm sure you can. I'm trying to catch a killer, Floyd. That's my interest right now. So yes. You have my word."

Floyd sighed. "It was fine. It was handled. Craig? He owed us. That farm? The land? It belonged to my mother's kin. Seventy years ago, my great-grandpa Knox let his cousin, Craig's old man, take it. But there was a condition. If we ever needed it back. Or if we needed something in return, the Albrights had to deliver."

"So when the cartel approached you ... you figured out a way to collect."

"A meeting place. That's all it was. Craig didn't have to do a damn thing but make his place available to us. He got paid well for doing nothing. Opening his doors and closing his mouth. That's it."

"So you had a lucrative little side hustle. The cartel came calling as soon as King Rex got locked up, didn't they?"

Floyd didn't answer, but the set of his jaw spoke volumes.

"You did this without your brother's endorsement?" Jake asked.

"It was handled," Floyd said. "For seven years, there were no problems. Like I told you. All Craig had to do was keep his mouth shut. He did that. Then ... last year ... the cartel started trying to move in shit I don't like. Fentanyl. That stuff's a killer. I know what it does. So did Craig. He'd been talking about wanting to retire. Move to Florida. Get out of the business."

"That caused a problem for you," Jake said.

"It caused a problem for them! But even so ... Craig thought he figured out a way to handle it. Craig was gonna turn everything over to his brother-in-law. It wasn't my idea. He went behind my back and tried to broker a new arrangement."

"That's not how these people work," Jake said. "You don't retire from that kind of thing."

"I told him that. I warned him. I begged him to just sit tight. Let me try and figure something out. I was working on it. I knew if Rex found out about what they were trying to move into town, things would get ugly fast. No way my brother would get on board with that kind of thing. It's not what we do. Well, one night, I got paid a visit. They pulled me right out of my bed. Threw a pillowcase over my head and stuffed me in the trunk of a car. They told me there was going to be a new arrangement. One that put me in charge for good."

Jake's head spun. "Wait, a minute ... you're telling me ..."

"The cartel wants Rex eliminated. They said they'd let Craig out of our arrangement, but only if I was head of the family once and for all. They wanted information. My brother's work detail on the inside. Who his closest confidants are."

"They wanted to kill him," Jake said, his tone sober.

"I was between a rock and a hard place. If I didn't cooperate, they'd kill me. If I *did* cooperate, they'd kill my brother. Then Craig's out there making plans of his own. Giving sensitive information to his idiot brother-in-law. The cartel was getting twitchy, to say the least. So I told him. If he tried to make trouble, it wasn't gonna end well for him."

"You threatened him? Craig?" It tracked with what Drew Harter had said. He'd used those exact words in his statement. Floyd had told Craig things weren't going to end well for him.

"I suppose he might have taken it like that. I was trying to protect my interests. I was trying to not get dead. But I didn't kill him."

"Who was your contact with the cartel?" Jake asked.

"It changed over time. But lately, they sent in one of their heavies. This guy? Let's just say he had a specialty and the cartel wanted to make sure I knew it. He came into town. This guy ... you don't understand. He might as well be a ghost. I knew if I had dealings with him, I'd be a liability too."

"This hitman. You met with him?"

"I met with him."

"I need a name. A description. I need to know everything that was said."

"Big guy. Beefy. Dark hair slicked back. Jacked, you know? Wore a lot of rings. Big gold ones. Diamonds. Covered in tats but I couldn't read 'em. Wasn't trying to. Tribal stuff. You know. On his fingers too. Some letters, but they were half covered up with the rings. I was trying *not* to pay too close attention. I just wanted to get out of there."

"Write it all down, Floyd," Jake said. "Names. Dates." It's the one thing Jake kept on him. He had a small notepad and pencil in his back pocket. He handed it to Floyd. Floyd took it and started writing. He was left-handed. A small thing, but Jake knew from Craig Albright's autopsy that the bruises on his face were likely made by a right-hander.

"You gotta understand," Floyd said. "He was talking about how easy it was gonna be to get rid of Rex for me. That they were gonna make sure I got to run things my way with no more interference. He was acting like it was my lucky day."

"A name, Floyd," Jake said, impatient.

"I didn't know what to do!" Floyd said. "I was afraid to try and get word to Rex. I didn't know who I could trust. It was a line too far. They wanted me to turn on my own family. I won't do that. Then ... Craig winds up dead. And not just dead ... I know what they did to him. When they couldn't get me to cooperate, they sent me a message through Craig. So I had no choice. I had to disappear. I came here. Hid out. I figured if they couldn't find me, they wouldn't be able to finish their plan to off my brother."

"Floyd, I need a name. I need to know everything you know about this guy the cartel hired to take out your brother."

Floyd kept writing. When he was finished, he handed the notebook to Jake.

"Alvaro Fox. That's the name he gave me. He could have been lying. It's not like I was in a position to ask to see his ID. I just have a phone number and a name. I told you. I only met him once. Then after, when I had the information they wanted about my brother, I was supposed to call this number. Wait for more instructions."

Jake knew the phone number Fox gave Floyd was likely a burner, but there was a chance Jake could get somewhere with it.

"You understand," Floyd said, "that right there is the kind of thing that could end me. I'm not coming down off this hill."

"What about your kids?" Jake asked. "You don't think the cartel is going to start knocking on your door the same way I did?"

"They had nothing to do with any of this. Besides … there's too much heat in Blackhand Hills right now. That's the thing I don't get. Craig's murder was big and messy. It drew attention the cartel doesn't usually want."

"Floyd, I need to know where you were the night Craig Albright was killed."

Floyd frowned. "I told you. I didn't have anything to do with what happened to him."

"Oh, you had something to do with it. But I believe you that you weren't the one to slit his throat. Still, I need your alibi. And it better check out."

"That Thursday night, I was in Lancaster. I had a consultation on a big job for a new medical center they're putting in."

"Who'd you meet with? Who saw you?"

"I stayed at the Motel Five off 22. Checked in around five p.m. Thursday night, checked out Friday at nine in the morning. Paid with the company credit card."

Floyd reached into his pocket and pulled out his wallet. He handed a blue credit card to Jake. "Take it. Call them. Thursday evening, I had dinner at the bar right across the street from the motel. It's called Digby's. My waitress's name was Reva. She's the daughter of the owner. I know that because we had a whole conversation. She'll remember me. She thought my first name was amusing. I hit on her. She gave me her damn phone number. She wrote it on my receipt. I used my credit card there too."

Floyd handed Jake a crumpled white piece of paper. There was indeed a phone number scrawled on the bottom.

"Call her too. I didn't do this. I didn't kill Craig. He's dead because he didn't listen to me. If he'd have just laid low for a while, I would have figured out a way to get him out. To get us all out of this. Rex was working on it. I told you. My brother wanted no part of bringing that poison into Blackhand Hills."

Rage poured through Jake. He had the urge to slap Floyd Bardo. Did he honestly think he was tough enough, smart enough to keep the cartel in check? He also knew that once they'd begun to move product into the region, they'd keep trying.

"I'm no killer," Floyd said. "I swear to God. You have to help me."

"Have to?" Jake said.

"You said you're out here to catch a killer. So catch him."

Floyd pointed to the piece of paper with the burner number on it.

"This guy is the devil, Jake. You saw what he did. He's gonna do it again. We both know it."

It seemed Floyd Bardo was waiting for Jake to say thank you. He took a breath and tried to let his rage subside.

It was getting late. In another hour, the sun would set. And Jake had a long way to go to get off this damned hill.

NINETEEN

"Looks like you're not leaving," Floyd said as they walked back up the small hill toward the biggest white house. In the distance, Luc and two of the other bandana men came out of the faded red barn in the northwest quarter of the property.

"What?" Jake turned to Floyd. His fingers itched to rest on the handle of his gun. He regretted handing it over. Did Luc and the others think they could just shoot him and not expect every cop in the state up here within twenty-four hours?

From across the yard, Luc gestured to Floyd, making a circle with his index finger around his head.

"Come on," Floyd said. "She gets angry when we're late."

"She?"

Floyd strode past Jake and climbed into one of the ATVs parked in between the houses. Luc and the others headed for their vehicles.

"Son of a ..." Jake was good and tired of the Knox/Bardo family's shorthand. Grumbling, he climbed in beside Floyd.

"I'm gonna warn you," Floyd said. "My sister would like to see you dead. Maybe don't give her another reason to kill you."

"Your sister?" Instead of answering, Floyd jammed the four-wheeler into gear and lurched forward hard enough Jake nearly spilled out the side. He grabbed the bar above him as Floyd hit the gas and barreled down the hill.

The others fell into formation behind and beside them. Five ATVs. A dozen other men. They'd come from everywhere and nowhere.

A ten-minute hellish ride down the hill and back through the woods and Floyd burst through the clearing in Melva Bardo's front yard.

"What is this?" Jake asked.

Floyd slid out of the driver's seat. He was halfway up the yard before he turned and called out to Jake. "Dinner!"

Jake squeezed his fists and his eyes shut. At the same time, his stomach growled loud enough that Luc heard it as he climbed out of his vehicle.

"Go around back," Luc told him. "Wash your hands at the pump or she'll brain you with her skillet."

"Naturally," Jake said through gritted teeth. He followed the other men. They each lined up at a wrought iron hand pump, passing a bar of soap between them. In the southwest corner of the yard, Jake spotted five long wooden picnic tables. They'd been set with red-and-white-checkered tablecloths and mason jars filled with silverware. Beside each plate were more mason jars filled with what looked like lemonade.

"Sit there," Floyd said. "Mama wants you close enough she can hear you. Her ears aren't what they once were."

Jake doubted that. From what he observed, Melva Bardo missed nothing.

The back screen door swung open. A woman came bursting out. Black hair. Fierce eyes. But it wasn't Melva.

"Be nice, Nyla!" Floyd called out. "He's a guest."

Nyla held Melva's huge stew pot in her oven-mitt-covered hands. She scowled at Jake in a way only Bardos could.

Nyla. This must be Rex and Floyd's sister. The one who blamed him for the death of her good-for-nothing son. Jake was sure that if he'd been standing closer, Nyla would have heaved the steaming contents of that pot right at him.

Melva came out behind Nyla. She carried a ladle in one hand. In the other, she balanced a large basket of biscuits against her hip. She whispered something to her daughter. Nyla's scowl didn't lessen, but she came forward and slammed the pot on the nearest table.

"You can serve yourselves," she called out. Melva put the biscuits and the ladle beside the stewpot. The men lined up as they were told, bowls in hand. One by one, they spooned out heaping bowls of whatever gruel Melva had made.

Floyd nudged Jake with his shoulder. "She won't bite you. You're on grace."

Jake grabbed the nearest bowl and made his way to the stew pot and Nyla Bardo. That's when the scent of Melva's concoction hit him. It was heaven. Though it looked awful, like some sort of whitish-yellow lumpy paste with flecks of pepper in it.

Nyla glowered at Jake. He kept her gaze and spooned out the stew. The stuff was heavy and roughly the consistency of wall spackle.

That's when Nyla Bardo struck. Like a feral cat, she curved one hand, one-inch painted-red nails out like a claw. Jake set his bowl down and readied himself for the first blow. It never came. Melva Bardo moved faster than Jake would have guessed. She grabbed her daughter by the wrist and shoved her backward hard enough the younger woman lost her balance and landed hard on her rear end. "I told you to behave," Melva snarled.

"You know what he is!" Nyla shouted. "You all know what he did. He's going to destroy us all if you let him! Kill him now before he kills another one of us!"

"That's not your call to make," Melva said, her voice calm and low. "Go back up the hill, Nyla. Until you're fit to be around people again."

That was it. Melva had spoken. Nyla spit on the ground. If the woman were a witch, Jake was pretty sure she'd just cursed him with something awful. But she stood up, dusted herself off, and stormed off, disappearing around the front of the house.

"Eat," Melva demanded. Jake picked up his bowl and found an empty seat near the head of the table. Melva sat at the end on Jake's right.

He stirred his bowl, took a spoonful, and blew across it. Then, he tested the soup.

It shouldn't have been as good as it was. There was nothing to it. Just potatoes, onions, and some sort of unstructured dumpling.

"Irish Potato Soup," Floyd explained.

"It's delicious," Jake said through a full mouth. Then he dipped one of Melva's homemade biscuits into the mix.

"I should warn you," Melva said. "I can keep that girl under control here. But only here. You see her in town, you steer clear."

"I'll keep that in mind," Jake said. "And thank you for this. For dinner."

"We know our manners, Detective," Melva said. "I know what you've heard about my family."

Jake put his spoon down. "And I know not to put too much stock in rumors."

"We mind our own business," she said. "As long as others mind theirs, you'll never have a problem with anyone with Knox blood in them."

No problem, Jake thought. Only side deals with the cartel that might put poison in his town. Jake ate a few more heavenly spoonfuls.

"Did you get the answers you wanted?" Melva asked him. She stared directly at her son, Floyd.

For a moment, Jake wasn't sure she was talking to him or to Floyd. "I just wanted the truth," he said. "We'll see if I got it."

"Did you tell him the truth?" Melva asked her son.

"Yes," he said.

"Then you got the answers you wanted," she said. "So I don't expect you'll have cause to ever come up here again."

Jake set his spoon down. "Others will. It depends on how you do business."

It was foolish, maybe. Not a threat by any means. But Jake wondered how much Melva knew about Floyd's arrangement with the cartel. By the keen look in her gray eyes, he expected she knew everything.

"We. Mind. Our. Business," she said.

"Your business," he repeated. "As long as your business doesn't hurt the people I'm sworn to protect."

"Your people?" she said. "Seems to me maybe you're forgetting some of who your people are, Detective."

He looked at her. Melva sat back with her arms folded across her chest. It was then Jake noticed she wasn't eating. She hadn't even poured herself a bowl. Melva Bardo was chewing on something entirely different. Jake.

"Your people came from this hill too," she said.

Jake smiled. "You mean my grandmother's people?"

"Ava," Melva said.

"I've heard that. My great-great something grandmother? Three or four generations back. You're talking over a hundred years ago or something." He'd heard those rumors his whole life. His grandmother never really admitted to it. It was just something his grandfather used to tease her about.

"Or something. Your great-great grandmother was a Knox, too. We don't forget our people. But only if they don't forget us."

"My people are also down there," Jake said, pointing toward Red Sky Hill. "And they are the ones who stand to get hurt by things your son has brought to that town."

"It's over," Floyd said. "I told you."

"You've sat at my table," Melva said. "You've broken bread."

Jake picked up the remnants of one of his biscuits. "So I have. But I won't watch another kid die from something that your business brought in, Floyd."

"You made me a promise," Floyd shouted.

"I keep my promises. I expect you to."

There was new tension through the group. Melva had served dinner to two dozen men, including Jake. He knew there were likely twice that number or more still deeper in the backwoods. A small army if she needed them. Strong. Capable. And this was the perfect place to make someone or something disappear.

A sharp whistle cut through the air. Then Melva's army mobilized. The men sprang up from their seats. At least four of them drew guns they had holstered to their sides.

Four other men moved to Melva's side as she rose from the table. They formed a circle of threat around her.

"What the hell is going on?" Jake asked. He rose from his seat and once again went for a weapon he no longer had.

Luc and a few of the others ran to the front of the house, shouting. He heard an engine rev. Jake ran after them.

Something had happened. Something bad.

Then, he heard a woman's voice. A shout. And Jake's heart went right down to his shoes.

Luc had Birdie Wayne by one arm. Two of the other men tried to grab the other. She delivered a deadly kick to one of the men's chest, knocking the wind straight out of him.

Then she yanked against Luc's grasp.

"Stop!" Jake shouted. "Stop! She's with me. She's a friendly." Though Birdie looked anything but. She was a wild woman, blonde hair flying. She'd gotten to her weapon and drew down on Luc. In an instant, four Knox men had weapons trained right at her.

"Stop!" Jake said, running toward her.

Melva had finally made her way around the house.

"She's a cop!" Jake shouted. "She's a friend of mine."

"She comes to my front door armed?" Melva asked.

"Jake," Birdie gasped. "Are you okay?"

"I'm fine," he said. "And I'm leaving. Just as soon as you give me back what's mine." He directed his command to Luc.

"Then leave," Melva shouted. "And don't come back without an invitation."

"I was invited this time," Jake said. "And you know why."

Melva lifted her chin at him. Then she glanced at Luc. All at once, Luc and the others lowered their weapons. Luc tucked his gun in the back of his waistband and went to the front porch. He came back with Jake's backpack, service weapon, and knife.

Jake jerked them out of Luc's grasp. Behind him, Birdie stood there, her weapons still drawn.

"It's okay," he told her. "You can put that away. We're walking out of here."

"I told you," Melva said. "We know our manners around here. Luc? Take them down. Remember what you learned here today, Jake? Remember who your people are."

Jake took Birdie by the arm. Luc walked over to the largest ATV. This one had a back seat.

"Come on," Luc said. "Before it's full night if you want to make it back. It gets dangerous after dark."

"Dangerous," Birdie said. "Jake ..."

"Just ... don't," Jake said. He led her over to the ATV and had her climb in the back. As he climbed into the passenger seat, he couldn't take his eyes off Melva Bardo. The King's mother.

Then Luc sped away and drove Jake and Birdie off the hill. Jake just hoped Nyla wasn't out there somewhere, waiting to pick him off.

TWENTY

Birdie would barely talk to him after Luc dropped them off in the clearing next to the Log Church. She fumed. Her lips had turned white and all but disappeared. For the first time, Jake realized how much she looked like Ben, her dead brother and his best friend. In her rage, her face had gone colorless just like Ben's used to, save for two red dots in the center of her cheeks. He used to tease Ben, calling him Raggedy Andy like the rag doll his mother had.

"Birdie," he said as she stormed to the driver's-side door of her Jeep.

"What if something had happened to you?" she said.

"It didn't."

She just stared at him, those two red dots in her cheeks growing.

"Birdie."

"Nobody heard from you. You weren't answering your phone. All day."

"There's not much of a signal out here."

"Exactly! And there are about a thousand ways for those people up there to make you disappear if they wanted to. You let them disarm you?"

"It's ... complicated," he said, not knowing how to explain any of it to her that didn't prove her point.

"It's not. It's simple. Let me ask you something. If I'd have come to you ... or if you had caught wind of some plan of mine to go looking for Floyd Bardo up that hill by myself, what would you have done?"

He grumbled. "It's not the same thing."

"It's exactly the same thing. And you didn't answer my question. What would you have done?"

"Tried to stop you," he sighed.

"Right. I was worried. You made me swear not to tell anyone what you were up to. If something had happened to you ..."

"It didn't. I had it under control."

"Didn't look like it. Looked like they had you under control, Jake."

"I'm sorry."

Birdie took a breath as if she were going to launch into another tirade. Then she stopped. "What?"

"I said I'm sorry. You're right. It could have ended badly. Only it didn't and I knew it wouldn't."

"Because you trust Rex Bardo?"

"To a point, yes. On this? Yes."

"You're still an idiot. And you put me in a tough spot. If you didn't come down ... what was I supposed to tell Gemma? Or Landry?"

"Birdie ..."

"Don't. I'm mad at you. I'm gonna stay mad at you for a while. You deserve it."

He couldn't come up with an effective counter-argument. "Birdie ..."

She put a hand up in a stopping gesture. Then she climbed behind her wheel and turned the ignition.

"Birdie!" he said again, walking around the front of her car. In response, she revved her engine to drown him out.

"I'm sorry," he said again, but there was no way she could hear him. She pivoted, putting one arm on the back of the passenger seat as she looked behind her and backed down the hill.

The next morning, Jake got much the same from Sheriff Landry as he debriefed her on what he'd learned from Floyd Bardo.

"Something could have happened to you, Jake," she said. He sat at the table in the war room having just put Floyd Bardo's picture up with an arrow drawn in dry erase marker between him and Craig Albright.

"Nothing happened to me. Nothing was going to happen to me. These people ... it's hard to explain."

"Try," Landry said. "You're telling me the Hilltop Boys have been distributing cartel product throughout Worthington County for years. Right under our noses. Craig Albright had been using All-Brite Electrical as a front?"

"Not the business itself. As far as I can tell, there was no commingling of funds or laundering going on. Though, if he were running a cash business, I wouldn't have put that past him. No. Bardo … Floyd Bardo says Albright was just providing the Hilltop Boys and the cartel with a meeting place on his property. Albright's great-grandfather was kin to the Knoxes. That's Rex Bardo's family on his mother's side. They gave the elder Albright the farming land and the house at the base of Red Sky Hill seventy years ago. But there was always the understanding that if the Knoxes wanted to reclaim it, or needed a favor, the Albrights had an obligation."

"So this was the Bardos coming to collect on that promise."

"Apparently."

Landry paced, keeping her hands on her hips. "And then what, you're saying Craig Albright was dumb enough to think he could just retire … walk away when he was ready to snowbird south?"

"Floyd's saying that. Yes. It tracks with Drew Harter's story. Craig's brother-in-law."

"But he's not a Bardo or a Knox. They were never gonna let him off. How do we know Floyd Bardo didn't hand deliver Craig to the cartel's hitman? Seems to me that would have solved a problem for him."

"Floyd wanted out too," Jake said. "Or more importantly, Rex wanted Floyd out. In their minds, things were going along fine until the cartel started moving more dangerous product through. Fentanyl."

"Poison," she said.

"They have a code," Jake said. "I'm not saying it makes them noble or anything. Or heroes. But Rex isn't stupid, Sheriff. He knows having that crap running rampant through town is bad for business. His business. It got out of hand. I think the cartel figured they could bully Floyd. And they can. So Rex had to flex his muscle."

"And the cartel didn't like that."

"They did not," Jake said. "They approached Floyd. Told him they wanted to stay in business with him. Give him an even bigger cut. In exchange for intel on Rex that Floyd could provide. They were gonna take him out and prop Floyd up as the de facto leader of the Hilltop Boys. Killing Albright was part of that. It sent Floyd a pretty strong message. Here's what happens if you decide to cross us. And here's what happens if you try to get out."

"How was it supposed to work?"

Mary Rathburn walked quietly into the room and shut the door behind her. She had a yellow sticky note dangling from her finger. She taped it to the table while Jake answered Meg's question.

"He got a code name and a burner phone number," Jake said. "Floyd was supposed to provide info on Rex's work detail on the inside. Names of Rex's closest soldiers and confidants. When he had the information they wanted, he was to call this number and wait for more instructions. When Albright turned up dead, Floyd got spooked. He literally ran for the hills. Floyd's a lot of things. He's in over his head and has been for years. Never mind the cartel, Floyd can't handle running the Hilltop Boys on his own. He's weak. Rex knows it. I think even Floyd knows it. The cartel overplayed their hand with him. Whatever else he is, Floyd's loyal to his brother. He wasn't gonna hand over information that would get Rex killed."

Landry sat down in the nearest chair with a thud.

"How do we prove all of this? How do we shut this down?" she asked.

"We don't," Jake said. "For now, we don't have to. The cartel overplayed their hand with Albright's murder, too. It has ended up drawing way too much attention. Too much heat. And it's about to get way hotter now that I know about Floyd's contact."

"Jake. How?" Meg said.

"I'm gonna find him. I'm gonna use the intel Floyd Bardo gave me and I'm gonna bring him in. He's going to face charges for killing Craig Albright. I've got a message of my own to send to the cartel and to the Hilltop Boys. This won't stand. None of it. Not in our town."

Jake couldn't be sure, but it seemed as if Meg Landry's hair had new gray running through it. He understood the weight this put on her shoulders. It didn't matter that Floyd Bardo and Craig Albright were the ones to bring the cartel to her back door. Fentanyl came into Worthington County under her watch. That would be the headline. That would be the noose by which her political detractors would hang her.

"I still have at least one person I can trust in the Bureau," Jake said. "Let me find out what I can about this contact of Floyd's. If he's our man, we'll go from there."

"How do you know Floyd Bardo isn't stringing you along?" Landry asked. "How do you know the Hilltop Boys aren't using the cartel to take you out instead of the other way around?"

Jake knew his answer wouldn't please her. He knew how it sounded when he tried to explain it to Birdie when she finally answered her phone last night.

"Rex Bardo trusts me in his own way," Jake said. "And it's gone beyond just words, Sheriff. His mother invited me to sit at her table and break bread with her. That means something."

Both Mary and Landry stared at Jake in a way he knew meant they weren't convinced.

"Melva Bardo also invoked our family connection."

"You're related to the Bardos?" Mary said.

"Not exactly. We have a common cousin three or four generations back. Through my great-great grandmother on my Grandma Ava's side."

"You're kidding," Landry said. "Jake ... half the people in this town are probably related if you go back far enough."

"Maybe so. It's just ... a feeling I got when I sat with her. I know what it sounds like. And I'm not an idiot. I know I have to watch my back."

"Fine," Landry said. "You've proven yourself to me more than once, Jake. I trust you. But I do not trust anyone with the last name Bardo. Through marriage or blood. No more solo trips up that hill. In fact, no more trips up that hill at all unless you take the SWAT team with you. Do you understand? And I still don't think I believe a word Floyd Bardo says."

"Actually ..." Beside him, Mary picked up the sticky note she'd taped to the table. "Jake. I ran down that alibi information you gave me on Floyd like you asked. I spoke to Reva, the waitress at Digby's in Oakton. Floyd's bank is going to email me his credit card statement. But his story checks out. He was in Oakton the evening Craig Albright was murdered. The waitress remembered him. She admitted she wrote her phone number down on his receipt. She gave me a physical description and picked him out of a photo array I sent her.

They also have security camera footage that records who comes in and out. Floyd's on it. She said she's willing to testify if it comes to it. His alibi is tight. So he told you the truth, at least about that much."

Jake met Landry's eyes and shrugged. "It's something."

"It is," Mary agreed. "Only I don't understand why he wouldn't have just come forward with all of this from the beginning."

"Because Floyd Bardo is more scared of what the cartel might do to him versus the state of Ohio. For the moment, I don't blame him."

"You should bring him in anyway," Landry said. "Get him in protective custody. If he decides to disappear, then we've got nothing."

"He's safest where he is," Jake said. "His family on that hill can protect him better than I can. That's the other thing I'm certain Rex Bardo wanted me to see. It's one of the reasons why he gave me permission to go up there. That and so I know what they're capable of if we try to root them all out. We can't. Not without a lot of people getting hurt or killed for no good reason."

"Jake, I hope you're right," Landry said. "I hope you know what you're doing."

Jake bit his tongue. It was in him to answer her, "So do I." But it meant something that she put her trust in him. The weight of it seemed to settle over his shoulders.

"Good work on the alibi rundown," Landry said to Mary. "Keep her close, Jake. Rathburn's officially your partner on this from here on out. I'll get Lieutenant Beverly to start expediting the paperwork."

Mary made a sharp intake of breath. She suppressed a giddy smile. Jake patted her on the back. He meant to follow Landry out in the hallway. Instead, his phone rang. Puzzled by the caller ID, he decided to take it across the hall in his office and away from Landry and Rathburn.

"Cashen," he answered.

"Hey, Jake. Bill Nutter."

Jake had known Bill Nutter for a few years. He'd retired as the property crimes detective years ago and now frequented the local Papa's Diner every Tuesday morning with a group of other retired cops who called themselves the Wise Men, though no one else would.

"Hey, Bill. What can I do for you?"

"Nothing for me. It's only ... is it too early for you to break for lunch?" Jake pulled the phone away from his ear and checked the time. It was just after eleven.

"Not too early, no."

"Well, I'm sorry to be so clandestine, but there's something I think you need to see. And you need to hurry. How quickly can you make it out to the Black Star Grille out on Jefferson Road? Do you know where it is?"

"Ah ... fifteen, maybe twenty minutes?"

"Good. That should be enough time. I'm here now. I'm sending you a picture. It's blurry. I didn't want to risk getting too close that either of them would recognize me. I think it'll explain everything. Just ... get here. Quick if you can. I'll wait in the parking lot."

Nutter clicked off. A moment later, a picture text came through. Jake had to expand it with his fingers before he recognized the people in it. When he did, he swore under his breath and made a beeline for the parking lot.

TWENTY-ONE

Bill Nutter met Jake in the parking lot of the Black Star Grille. The place was just over the county line and hard to find if you'd never been there. Most GPS apps would have you take a right turn into the lake if you plugged the address in. That's just how the locals and the proprietors wanted it. As such, it was the perfect place to grab lunch if you didn't want to be found.

"They're still in there?" Jake asked Nutter as he walked up to him.

"Yeah. Got here about ten minutes after I did. Grabbed a booth in the very back. I was walking out of the john or else they would have walked right past my table. I don't know. It just gave me a real bad vibe from the get-go so I asked my waitress if I could move to a table out on the patio. You can see them from there but they can't see you. Come on. I'll show you."

Jake followed Bill around the back of the restaurant. There was a large enclosed patio built right along the shoreline. Nutter opened the screen door and led Jake to his prime, hidden viewing spot of the corner booth in question.

Ed Zender sat with his back to them. He was gesturing with his hands but Jake couldn't make out what he was saying. His companion listened with rapt attention. Anger heated Jake's blood. Zender was dining with none other than Rhett Pierson, an investigative reporter for the *Daily Beacon*. The man who had written the three-part exposé/hit piece on the Worthington County Sheriff's Department and Meg Landry in particular. "Have you been able to make out any of their conversation?" Jake asked.

"Just a word here and there. No context. But Zender gave him a file folder when they first sat down."

Jake wanted to punch the wall. "He's the leak. He's the frigging leak. Pierson published internal crime stats and other information he could have only gotten from somebody on the inside."

"Yeah. That's what I'm figuring. That's why I called you."

"You didn't confront him? You're sure neither of them know you've seen them?"

"I'm sure. I snapped a couple of pictures with my phone, but they didn't come out so great. The light's bad. The thing is. And this is just a hunch. But from their body language this isn't the first time they've met. They didn't wait to be seated, Jake. They marched over to that booth like they've got some standing reservation."

"I want to wring his damn neck," Jake muttered.

"I know. I don't get it. Them having lunch together doesn't prove anything by itself. Only, Pierson's the enemy. He's always had it in for the department. It's been an unspoken rule for years not to talk to him. So what's Zender's angle? He's getting ready to retire so why's he trying to burn the house down just as he leaves it?"

"Spite? Revenge?"

"You really believe that's all it is?"

"No," Jake said. "But there are a few people in the department who aren't too thrilled with Landry's pick for his replacement."

"The girl," Nutter said.

"Bill ..."

"Sorry. Sorry. I'm an old man. Deputy Rathburn. Never had the pleasure of working with her. You sure she's not too young?"

"She's over thirty, Bill. She's probably older than you were when you made detective."

"Damn. No need to make me feel even older."

One of the servers approached Pierson and Zender's booth. She wasn't alone. On instinct, Jake and Nutter faded back into the shadows. A third man walked up to the table. The server gestured to him and handed him a menu.

"Jake," Nutter said. "Is that ..."

"What the hell is going on?" Jake whispered. Rhett Pierson rose from his seat and shook hands with their new lunch companion. Zender scooted over to make room for him.

"Tim Brouchard," Jake said. Brouchard was dressed casually. Jeans. Motorcycle boots. A tee shirt. He had his hair in his now signature ponytail. Brouchard and Zender looked far too familiar with each other. Jake felt Nutter's instincts were spot on. Whatever was going on, this wasn't a chance meeting. And it wasn't the first one.

Brouchard waved off the server when she came back. He leaned forward, whispering something to Pierson. Pierson's face lit up with a conspiratorial smile.

"I'm gonna kill him," Jake said.

"That's one sinister trio there," Nutter added. "Though I hate to see it. I'd say both Brouchard and Zender have gone over to the dark side, Jake."

Tim Brouchard threw his head back and let out a hearty, probably fake laugh. Pierson took a pen out and started writing something on a notepad. He picked up the file folder Nutter saw Zender give him and took out a sheet of paper. Brouchard looked at it and nodded his head furiously. Then Zender moved. Brouchard got out of the booth to make way for him. Zender scooted out and headed for the men's room.

"Screw this," Jake said.

"Jake," Nutter called after him. But Jake was far too angry to take the high road. He waited until Zender rounded the corner, then went into the men's room after him.

"Meet some new friends, did you?" Jake shouted. With his back to him, Zender jumped. Jake did a quick check under the one stall. They were alone.

"Did you follow me?" Zender asked, his face a mask of rage.

"You've been leaking information to the *Beacon*? To Pierson? You, of all people, should know how many lies that weasel has published over the years. And you're sitting there having lunch with him?"

"You're spying on me? Cashen, you're way out of line here. Who I chose to have lunch with on my days off is my business. I don't owe you any explanations."

"I think you do. And I think you owe Meg Landry even more."

"You gonna go squealing to Mommy?" Zender said, his face contorted with contempt. It had always been there. Ever since Landry pinned a detective's badge on him, Jake knew Zender resented him for it.

"You've been out to get her since the day Sherriff O'Neal hired her," Jake said. "O'Neal let you slide. Landry actually expected you to do your job."

"You think you're some hotshot. I know who you are, Jake. I know what you are. It's only a matter of time before you snap, just like your old man. Your own family doesn't want to have anything to do with you. If it were up to the county commissioners, you'd never even have been let on the department. O'Neal only hired you because he felt sorry for you. Because he felt sorry for your grandfather. You didn't earn your spot, Jake. Don't think for a second that you did."

Jake curled his fists. He wanted to punch Ed Zender right in the throat.

"You're on your way out, Ed," Jake said. "What's the point of all of this? Meg Landry's never done anything to you. I've never done anything to you."

The door swung open behind Jake. Tim Brouchard walked in. His face fell when he saw Jake, then turned red with anger.

"He bothering you, Ed?"

"What are you gonna do about it if I am?" Jake said, his jaw clenched. He found himself hoping Tim Brouchard would take a swing at him.

"I don't think my client has anything more to say to you," Brouchard said.

"Your client?"

"You can save your opinion for the voting booth," Brouchard said, puffing out his chest.

"The voting booth," Jake repeated. He looked at Ed. "The voting booth. You? You're planning to run for sheriff against Landry.

That's what this is all about. You're using Brouchard for opposition research? And Pierson to plant bogus hit pieces in the press."

It made perfect sense. Brouchard would fight dirty. No way Zender would have been shrewd enough to come up with this plan on his own. "I'm done talking to you," Zender said. "You can read my statement to the press when I make it."

Tim Brouchard held the door open and made a sweeping gesture, as if to usher Jake out.

"You two deserve each other," Jake said. He stormed out and practically ran into Bill Nutter coming from the other direction.

"You okay?" Nutter asked. He kept up with Jake's stride as he made his way back out to the parking lot.

"He's planning to run against Landry," Jake explained. "I think Brouchard's put him up to it."

"Talking to Pierson was his idea," Nutter said, catching up quickly. "Zender wouldn't have come up with that all by his lonesome. Man. You think he's got a real chance of beating her?"

"I don't think the command or deputy's unions will go for it."

Nutter looked unsure. "I don't know, Jake. Some of them might think Zender's one of their own. Landry's still considered an outsider by a lot of the old-timers."

Jake shook his head. "I can't even think about this now. I've got a damn murder to solve. Of which Zender's fully aware. For him to pull this right now ..."

"Sounds exactly like something Tim Brouchard would do," Nutter said.

Jake couldn't argue the point. He also wondered whether Brouchard's representation of Drew Harter wasn't some part of his strategy as well.

"I'm sorry," Nutter said. "I didn't mean to pull you away or distract you. I know you've got a lot on your plate."

"No. I'm glad you did. You were right. I needed to see this for myself. It's better I know than be blindsided."

"You gonna tell Landry?"

"I'm gonna have to. But not today. I've got another lead to try to run down."

"Anything you need help with? Or another set of ears?"

Jake put a hand on Bill Nutter's shoulder. "Not this time. I sure do appreciate the offer though."

The two men said their goodbyes. Jake didn't want to be around when Brouchard and Zender came out of the restaurant. He couldn't trust himself not to haul off on one of them again. What he said to Nutter was true. He had to pull his focus back to Craig Albright's murder.

He got behind the wheel and started the twenty-minute drive back to Stanley and the office. Two minutes in, his phone rang. An old friend returning a call.

"Special Agent West," Jake said, smiling. He worked with Gable West for years before he left the Bureau. He was the one man Jake still trusted from those days.

"Hey, Jake. Sorry I missed your call. It sounded important. What'd you get yourself into this time?"

"I need a favor."

"Of course you do. I heard a rumor you've got a bit of a mess going on down there. Another murder. Why do I feel I'm going to regret asking what I can do for you?"

"I've got an informant who thinks there might be a cartel connection to what happened at Red Sky Hill."

Jake gave Gable the highlights of Floyd Bardo's story and the details of Craig Albright's murder.

"Christ, Jake," Gable said. "That sure sounds like you've got the cartel's attention. What do you need from me?"

"Floyd Bardo gave me a name and a cell phone number. A burner, I'm sure. I need to see if you can make anything from it. I wanna get this guy if I can."

"Sure," Gable said. "Only you realize your tab is getting pretty steep, Jake."

Jake laughed. "I thought it was the other way around, Gabe."

"Send me what you got," Gable sighed. "I'll see what I can scare up."

"I appreciate it," Jake said. He'd just pulled into the parking lot of the sheriff's department. Thankfully, he noticed Meg Landry's car was long gone. It meant he could at least avoid ruining her day until tomorrow. Until he could figure out what, if anything, could be done about Ed Zender and Tim Brouchard.

TWENTY-TWO

The next morning, Craig Albright was finally laid to rest. Rachel had opted for a small service at Nowak's Funeral Home. They had a reception hall on the property and Spiros and Tessa Papatonis catered the event. Jake sat with Mary in the back of the main viewing room, trying to blend into the wall.

"I cannot believe she opted for an open casket," Mary whispered. Jake couldn't either. Dale Nowak did magic, but there was no denying that Craig Albright had died a violent death. Dale had been left with no option but to fit a neck brace on the body to conceal his fatal injury. He'd put white gloves on Craig's hands to conceal what had been burned and mangled.

"I don't know," Jake said. "For some people, it's still a comfort."

Jake and Mary came to pay their respects, but also to observe. He recognized most of the people who filed into the room on their way to the casket. Almost every local business owner. Rachel Harter's extended family. Craig's customers. Friends.

Drew Harter stood vigil next to the casket. Rachel seemed too distraught to meet the mourners. She sat in a chair in the corner, her closest friends closing ranks around her.

For Jake's money, Drew Harter seemed far too jovial for the occasion. Laughing. Joking. Glad-handing and slapping backs.

"He's working the room," Mary whispered. "Trying to make sure he's got Craig's customers shored up."

"Looks that way." A few times, Drew glanced nervously over at Jake. Tim Brouchard had made a brief appearance. He'd whispered something lengthy into Drew's ear. Jake guessed he instructed him not to say a word about the murder investigation. And not to go anywhere near Jake himself. That was fine with him.

Gemma came alone. Jake hung back as she made her way to the front of the room. His sister knelt before the casket and said a quick prayer. When she rose and turned, her face had gone sheet white. Jake went to her.

"Hey," he said, putting an arm around her. "You okay? You didn't have to do this. Nobody would think twice if you skipped today."

"I had to come," she said, her voice sounding distant. Foreign. She was on autopilot. "I had to pay my respects. And I thought ... I don't know. It's stupid. I thought maybe seeing him would drive away these visions I've been getting. Of seeing him the last time."

"Did it work?"

Gemma shook her head. "No. It was a bad idea. But I want to at least pay my respects to Rachel. But she's just ... gone. She barely recognized me."

"Are you going to be okay? I can leave with you. I can take you home."

"No. It's okay. You should stay. I know you're working. I'll be all right. We can catch up later. You still have to tell me how your date went."

"My date?" With all the excitement over the past couple of days, he hadn't circled back with Gemma and regaled her with the disaster that was his date with Dominique Gill. Now certainly didn't seem like the time.

"We'll talk later," she said as more people filed into the room. "I just need to get out of here."

"Call me if you need anything," he said. "I'll check in after work."

Gemma kissed Jake on the cheek and made her way to the lobby. He was worried about her. She was tough. She could handle anything. But she didn't look like she'd been eating much or sleeping well.

Mourners went by the casket in groups. Many of them passed by Jake and Mary.

"You've gotta catch the bastards who did this." Jake heard that sentiment at least a dozen times. He could only give a quiet nod. A few people tried to pry and get him to answer whether he had any leads. After about the tenth time, he knew it was time for him and Mary to come up with an exit strategy.

That's when Mick Harter and his granddaughter made their way to the back of the room. Mick leaned heavily on his cane. Alexis held on to the older man's arm. Jake rose to his feet. Mick had a permanent scowl on his face. Jake half expected the man to raise that cane and jab it into his chest as angry as he looked. Instead, Mick Harter stopped and straightened as much as he could, matching Jake's height.

"I didn't think you'd show up," Mick said, his voice thick and gravelly.

"I wanted to pay my respects."

"You wanted to case the joint," Mick said.

"Grandpa," Alexis whispered. The girl looked haggard. She wore piles of makeup, but it couldn't hide the dark circles under her eyes. Jake knew all too well what she must be feeling. He'd buried his own parents under violent circumstances once upon a time. There was shock. Anger. The sense that it was all just a horrible nightmare but you can't wake up. Then a thousand what-ifs. He knew Alexis Albright would likely have those thoughts for the rest of her life. Jake still did. His worry for Gemma grew. This whole thing with Craig might have stirred up ancient history they rarely talked about.

"Yes," Jake said. "I'm still doing my job, Mr. Harter."

"But whoever did this to my family is still out there somewhere. I need to know that my daughter and granddaughter will be safe. You understand me?"

"I understand you," Jake said.

"We're doing everything we can, Mr. Harter," Mary interjected. "I know how difficult this must be for you. But we are using every available resource. As soon as we have something to tell you, we will."

"She won't listen to me," Harter said. He gestured behind him to where Rachel Albright sat staring into space as people tried to talk to her. Tried to hug her. Tried to get any reaction out of her at all. Most simply smiled and moved on. Many murmured as they left, commenting on how bad a shape Rachel was in.

"She won't listen to anyone," Mick continued. "She just sits in a chair all day. Just like that. Crying. Moaning. I don't know if she's ever going to come out of it."

"She'll come out of it," Alexis said. "She just needs time. We all need time, Grandpa."

"You should go back to school, Lexie," Harter said. "You shouldn't throw your life over because of all of this."

"We can talk about all of that later. Let's just ... let's just get through the day, all right?"

Mick Harter jerked his arm away from his granddaughter. Her shoulders dropped and Jake got the sense the girl had been trying to manage the old man's anger as well as her mother's grief. He wondered if Alexis had had much time to deal with her own.

"Mick?"

Another older man broke through the crowd. Relief flooded Alexis's face. The man wore a Vietnam veteran's baseball cap. He threw his arms wide and embraced Mick Harter. The two men were soon lost in hushed conversation. They moved away, leaving Alexis standing with Jake and Mary.

"He's just worried," Alexis said. "He feels helpless. My grandfather is of a generation that thinks women need men to take care of them. He thinks my mother is his responsibility now. That I am."

"What about your uncle?" Jake asked.

Alexis's expression soured. She looked back at her Uncle Drew, still working the crowd at the front of the room.

"Uncle Drew's good at taking care of Uncle Drew." Her words came out so quickly. A moment later, she blushed as if she could take them back.

"I'm sorry," she said. "I don't mean to sound ... I don't know ... petty. We're all just under a lot of strain."

"Of course you are," Jake said. "And you don't have to apologize to me. I know what you're going through."

Alexis froze. "Oh. My gosh. Yes. I suppose you do." Her eyes instantly welled with tears. Then she rushed forward, throwing her arms around Jake. She clung to him in a vice-like grip. It took Jake by surprise.

"It's going to be okay," Jake found himself whispering. He remembered people telling him that over and over again when he was a kid after he buried both his parents. He'd wanted to ask how. How did they know? By the look in Alexis Albright's eyes, she was asking the same question.

"You're strong," Jake said to her. "It's going to take time. Maybe a lot of it. But you learn to live with it all. Just don't … try not to let her suck you under."

Alexis looked back at her mother.

"She won't live very long without him, I don't think," Alexis said. She straightened and let Jake go. "I think she's going to go next. Not that she'd take her own life. Just … do you think people can really die of a broken heart?"

"I don't know," he said.

"I'm sorry. I don't know why I just dumped all of that on you. You've got enough on your plate. We're all counting on you. I know you'll find who did this."

"It's okay. You can reach out to me if you need anything."

"When you find out who did this," Alexis said, "do you think you can call me first? Do you think you could maybe let me be the one to break it to my mother?"

"Yes," Jake said. "I think I can do that. I promise I'll stay in touch."

Alexis nodded. A new group of mourners came in through the back. She smiled and excused herself.

"That was rough," Mary said. "You were good with her. I don't know how you do that."

"You'll have to learn," Jake said. "I'm afraid it's part of the job they don't really train you for. In my case ... I've just had some experience being where she is. And that was pretty mild."

Mary nodded. "I know there are a lot of people who don't think I'm going to be able to handle this job."

"No, there aren't. And even if there were, don't worry about that. Just do what you have to do. Trust your gut. You'll be fine. Now ... let's see if we can make that clean getaway."

Mary was right on his heels as they slipped through the coat room and were about to go out a side door. Most of the people had started to make their way to the reception hall. Though Jake's stomach growled, he'd eat at home.

He could see the lobby through the hallway. The front doors were wide open and a black Mercedes pulled up. The back door opened. Floyd Bardo's two oldest children stepped out, Knox and Kyra Bardo. Kyra looked ... expensive, dressed in a sharp black suit, white pearls and black high heels. Her makeup looked professionally done.

"What are they doing here?" Mary asked.

"I have no idea," Jake said. He stayed out of Kyra's line of sight, ducking back into the coat room. He wanted to observe her without getting drawn into another confrontation. Knox was cleaned up today too, with his hair slicked back, wearing a suit and tie. His was crumpled though. As if he'd pulled the thing off the floor in the back of some closet. Even from here, Jake could sense Kyra's annoyance with her brother. He trailed behind her as the pair of them walked through the lobby and to Craig Albright's viewing room.

"What do you make of it?" Mary asked.

"Not sure yet. If I had to guess, it's a show of force for Drew Harter. Floyd might not be here, but Rex will want Drew to know the Bardos are still watching."

"So are we," Mary said.

"Yes. Come on. Let's get out of here."

Jake walked Mary to her car, then got behind the wheel of his own. He was tempted to stay a bit and wait for the Bardos to make their way back out.

As Mary drove off, Jake got a text. He looked down. It was Gable West.

"Got a hit on that burner number you sent me. You've got yourself a jackpot, Jake. How soon can we meet?"

Three people walked out of the front of the funeral home together. Kyra and Knox Bardo along with Drew Harter. They'd come out to talk away from the rest of the crowd perhaps. Kyra had her hand on Drew's arm. He stared at her, looking nervous, then breaking into a smile.

"You name the time and place and I'll be there," he texted Gable West.

Kyra kissed Drew on each cheek. Jake couldn't help but wonder if it was a figurative kiss of death.

Twenty-Three

West didn't want to meet in public. Instead, he picked a rest stop thirty miles north of Columbus and pulled into an empty spot way in the back near the dog trails. Jake parked alongside him and stepped out of the car.

There was no one out here. Just a few random travelers stopping to take their kids in for a pit stop. This wasn't one of the fancy plazas. They were lucky to find stale snacks in an ancient vending machine in the lobby. Jake slid on his sunglasses and opened the passenger-side door of West's car.

"Thanks for coming so quickly," West said, whispering it. He was still on a call and held his cell phone up to his ear.

"I'll tell him. He just got here. I appreciate the heads-up. Let me know if anything changes. Copy that."

Gable hung up and stuck his phone on a magnetized holder clipped to his dashboard. He had a file folder perched on the console between them.

"Whatta you got for me?" Jake asked.

West picked up the file folder. "Well, your guy ... Floyd Bardo. I'd say he's telling you the truth."

The air went out of Jake's lungs. Until that moment, he hadn't realized how badly he wanted that to be true. There were a thousand reasons not to trust anyone with the last name Bardo. It meant something to chalk one into the win column.

"The physical description, the tattoos on his fingers. They fit a man we believe whose real name is Matteo Torres."

"Torres. Not Fox?"

"Alvaro Fox comes back as a known alias for Matteo Torres. But nobody calls him that except maybe his mother. He's known in most circles as El Carnicero or El Carnicero Oscuro."

Jake was able to recall enough of his high school Spanish for a loose translation.

"Butcher. The Dark Butcher."

"That's the one. He's about as bad as they come, Jake. This guy's a known sicario for the cartel. He's suspected of carrying out dozens of hits. Nobody's ever been able to catch him though. He disappears into the ether."

West opened the file folder and handed Jake an 8x10 photograph. As much as Jake had seen in his career, the image made him wince. The body depicted was nearly unrecognizable as human but for the fact it had hands and feet.

West put another photograph in front of him. This body was half buried, its fingers sliced off. His cheeks bulged out, his lips were sewn shut.

"He fed his fingers to him like sausages," West explained. "The M.E. found them stuffed in his mouth." Jake put the photographs face down.

"How'd you put all this together?" Jake asked.

"The number. The burner phone. It's still live. Which tells me this guy has no idea Floyd Bardo or anyone else is talking. I hope you've got him stashed someplace safe. You ask me, he's got an expiration date."

"He's safe enough," Jake said. "He's got kin up in the hills. They'll never rat him out."

"Good. I gotta be honest. I don't even know that I'd trust his safety in protective custody."

"Neither would I."

"Anyway, the number came up on a wire. Part of an operation being run by the Columbus Metro Drug Task Force. The thing lit up like a Christmas tree in the last few days."

"They're actively surveilling him?" Jake asked.

"Bet your ass. He's holed up in a motel just outside of Columbus. About twenty-five miles north of us. They've been sitting on him for the last twenty-four hours. Federal judge in the Southern District came through with the warrant in record time. A real stand-up guy. They got lucky."

"What are they hearing?"

"All kinds of stuff. Torres has been busy. A whole hive. Dates. Times. Deals. This wire's produced a list of potential targets as long as your arm. They've got enough to go in and they're antsy to pull the trigger. Just before you got here, my contact in Columbus called. That's who I was on the phone with. Torres is getting ready to move. They want to go in within the hour."

"I'd like to be there when they do," Jake said. "You think you can arrange that?"

"Already done. I can get you there inside of a half an hour."

"Do we know if he's armed? A guy like this isn't gonna wanna be taken alive, Gabe."

"They're operating under that assumption. They're assembling a full team. The goal is to get this guy alive. They're just waiting on search warrants for the guy's car and motel room. By the time we get there, they should have them in hand. Then it's go time."

"Yeah. I'd like to watch the show."

"I can get you a front-row seat. Leave your car here. We can come back for it later."

Jake nodded. "I'm ready." He was more than ready. Jake's brain buzzed. His fingers started to tingle. It would take every ounce of resolve not to jump out of the car as soon as they got close.

Gable's phone rang again. He hit the speaker button as he answered.

"Tell me you're on the road already," Gable's caller said.

"Lieutenant Peters, I've got you on speaker with Detective Cashen." As he said it, Gable put his car in reverse, then floored it as he turned and hit the on-ramp.

"Hey, Cashen," Peters said. "There are a lot of people down here that are gonna want to shake your hand."

"You don't have your man just yet," Jake said. "Don't jinx it. We'll be there in twenty minutes." West kept pressing the accelerator. Jake watched as the odometer hit eighty-five.

"Fifteen," Jake said. "If West doesn't kill us on the way."

"He drives like a mad man. I've had the pleasure. West, try not to blow our cover by squealing into the parking lot, idiot."

A maniacal smile lit Gable West's face. He edged the car up to ninety miles an hour. Jake checked his seat belt and hung on for the ride.

Twenty-Four

The Tall Pines Motel was in the middle of nowhere. What it was not was anywhere near pine trees. Gable got word when they were just a few minutes out to pull into a nearby gas station across the street. Lieutenant Nick Peters from the Columbus P.D. met them there.

"You're just in time," Peters said. "He's about to move. My people are getting in place."

Jake took a position behind Peters's SUV. Two more plain clothes cops stood beside him. Peters was up on his radio.

"Units 819 and 820 are in the lot, plain clothes near the suspect's car."

Two tan Chevy sedans pulled into the parking lot of the motel across the street.

"Suspect's in Unit 102 on the ground floor," Peters explained. "He's been there since early this morning. He just got instructions to be at the airport in Covington within three hours. He's got a ticket to fly down to Mexico City this afternoon."

"You have eyes on him?" Jake asked. Gable came around to the side of Peters's car. He'd pulled a pair of binoculars out of his truck.

"There's a small gap in the curtains," Peters said. "He's packing a bag. We know he's armed. We're hoping to make as little fuss as possible."

A pit formed in Jake's stomach. Peters's team would have the element of surprise, but they were dealing with a trained sicario.

"You better go in heavy," West said, reading Jake's thoughts.

Peters was getting something from his radio. He wore a Bluetooth earpiece and pulled the mic closer to his mouth.

"Copy that," he said. "Hold your positions."

Peters turned to Jake and Gable. "He's gone into the bathroom."

"What's behind him?" Jake asked. "We sure he can't jump out a window or something?"

"We're sure," another of the men said. "We've got two units in position at the back of the building. There's a sandwich shop back there that shares an alley with the motel. We've got it cleared out and a unit standing by in the kitchen. If he tries to slip out that way, we'll be ready."

Jake felt that familiar twinge of adrenaline. It had been a long time since he'd done a takedown of a high-risk target.

"He's moving!"

The sound shot through Peters's earpiece, loud enough for Jake to hear it. All four men moved around Peters's car for a better line of sight.

"Go!" Peters commanded. "Go. Go. Go!"

Gable handed Jake his binoculars. Jake focused on the door to room 102. It was cracked open. He could see a figure moving inside. He wore a white tee shirt. Tanned, muscled biceps filled out the sleeves. He slung a bag over one shoulder and carried another in his left hand. Jake zoned in. He could just make out the spider web tattoos on the guy's fingers, just like Floyd Bardo described.

"That's him all right," Jake said.

Torres walked out of his motel room and slid on a pair of mirrored sunglasses. He paused for a moment, surveying the parking lot.

"Everyone in position," Peters commanded through his mic. Torres started walking toward a blue Chevy only twenty yards away.

"Take him, take him, take him!" Peters shouted. "Do not let him make it to that vehicle!"

Three unmarked sedans poured into the parking lot, stopping at tactical angles, blocking the exit to the street. Torres froze.

"He knows," Jake said. "He's spotted you."

More vehicles squealed into position. At least a dozen officers ran from the vehicles, weapons drawn and charging toward Torres.

"Gun!" someone shouted through the radio. "Gun! Gun!"

Every muscle in Jake's body tensed. He wanted to run. He wanted to draw down. He wanted to be in the mix. Beside him, he could feel the buzz go through Gable West as well. But this wasn't their operation. There was nothing they could do but stay out of the way and watch it play out.

"Freeze!" Even without the radios, from across the street, Jake could hear the officer's command to Torres. He faked left, then right, but there was nowhere to go.

Jake found himself saying a silent prayer. "Go down without a fight."

Three officers moved in. Within seconds, they had Torres splayed out over the trunk of his blue Chevy. The man went rigid, but didn't resist.

Spots swam in front of Jake's eyes and he realized he'd been holding his breath the whole time.

"Suspect is in custody! Suspect is in custody!"

"Let's go," Peters said. Jake ran with Gable and slid into the passenger seat. He barely got the door shut before Gable peeled out and raced across the street. It took all of thirty seconds to get there. Gable parked and Jake ran out. He wanted to look in Torres's eyes at least once before they hauled him away.

"You Cashen?" A short detective with red hair met him as Jake walked up to Torres. Another plain clothes detective was busy reading Torres his Miranda rights.

Torres had gone glassy-eyed. He was calm. Smirking. When a squad car pulled up alongside him, he actually shot Jake a wink as they helped him into the back of it.

"I'm Hal Sobel," the detective said.

"This is your operation?" Jake asked. Sobel nodded.

"Wait here," Sobel said. He walked over to the two uniformed officers and gave them instructions. Then he slapped the truck of the squad car and came back over to Jake.

"You got your search warrants in place?" Jake asked.

Sobel nodded. "Everything. Hotel room. Car. We're on it."

"Good. Good," Jake said. Another officer had already taken Torres's two bags.

"I want to thank you," Sobel said. "We've been hoping for a break in this case for months. We knew the cartel was planning something big, but our sources were starting to dry up. With what we've gotten from this wire, Torres is looking at heavy charges."

"He won't talk," West said. "He's not going to give you anything about his associates."

"Hopefully it won't matter," Sobel said. "Torres's been pretty chatty over the last twenty-four hours. We've got drop points, numbers, aliases. It's a treasure trove, just from the wire itself. I don't care if he doesn't say a word."

"You don't have a lot of time," Jake said. "As soon as his associates figure out Torres is sitting in a jail cell, they're gonna go to ground."

"We're serving ten other warrants today," Sobel said. "This is big, Cashen. A career maker."

"I'm glad," Jake said. "You know I want him for a murder in Worthington County."

"As soon as he's booked, he's all yours. I'll have my people set him up in an interview room for you."

"He's not gonna talk," West said.

"I appreciate it," Jake told Sobel. The man didn't have to do it. Not this soon. Torres was his collar on his turf.

Another detective came forward. She was still wearing her blue gloves. "We've found some interesting things already. Come take a look."

Sobel caught Jake's eye. The two of them walked over to Torres's vehicle. His luggage lay open on the pavement.

"Whatcha got, Bieman?" Sobel asked. Detective Bieman leaned down and opened the small black duffel Torres had carried over his shoulder. Jake peered inside.

"Looks like five burner phones," she said. She pulled out an inner leather bag and laid it on the ground. Slowly, she unzipped it.

"Christ," Sobel muttered.

Jake peered over the man's shoulder. Bieman pulled a few items out.

"Jumper cables, a pack of drill bits. Looks like clamps. He's got what looks like a dentist's drill in here, too."

"Careful," Jake said. Next to the drill bits, he spotted a baggie filled with syringes. Bieman dropped the bag.

"He was planning something," Sobel said. "We've got lots of chatter about a job he was here to do. I think that's where he was headed next."

"You just made someone's day," West said. "Any idea who his next victim was?"

"Not yet," Sobel said. "We might never know. I just hope whoever it is gets smart and gets lost."

The two uniformed officers got behind the wheel of the cruiser. Torres was in the back, cuffed, and staring straight at Jake. Jake couldn't help himself. He walked right up to the vehicle. Sobel put a hand up, signaling to the two officers to hold up.

There was nothing sinister about the man just then. He looked about as disinterested as if he were waiting in a fast-food drive-through. He shot Jake a wide smile.

"Get him out of here," Jake said. Sobel gave the signal. The squad car carrying Matteo Torres, El Carnicero Oscuro pulled out of the parking lot headed for the Columbus Police Department. Jake would be just ten minutes behind it.

TWENTY-FIVE

"He's in here," Sobel said. The Columbus Division of Police Central Headquarters was a massive building. It could fit ten of the Worthington County Public Safety buildings within it. Matteo Torres had been taken to a holding room. He sat with his hands cuffed through a metal loop on the table. He had just enough slack to sip the water he'd asked for from a red plastic cup. Other than the chains, his posture was casual. Almost as if he were sitting waiting for a takeout order, rather than the litany of drug charges piling up before Jake even got to him.

"Thanks," Jake said to Sobel.

"Take your time. It'll be a little while before the feds get here. So far, he hasn't made a peep all through booking. I don't think you're gonna get anything out of him."

"Probably not."

Jake walked into the room. Torres looked up. No expression. Maybe just the slightest narrowing of his eyes. Jake took a seat opposite him and slapped his file folder on the table.

"Matteo Torres," he said. "Alvaro Fox. Alonzo Meija. Peter Boles. Ricardo Lupe. John Torrance. Who are you today, Torres?"

Torres met Jake's stare. He was a handsome man, or could have been if it weren't for the scars cutting through his brow and upper lip. Hard, rugged lines framed his eyes. He had a thick head of black hair. Too black. It was dyed.

Jake opened the file folder and laid out the Albright crime scene photos as if he were dealing a hand of poker. In a way, he was.

Torres looked at them. He tilted his head to the side. Reaching for one of the more grisly shots, he slid it closer and picked it up.

"You gonna tell me that's not your handiwork?" Jake asked.

"You seem to think you've got it all figured out already," Torres said, setting the picture down. "You think you're smart? Think you're some big man? I know who you are. Couldn't cut it with the Federales. Now you're driving around in your little shit water town making what, twenty bucks an hour?"

Jake ignored Torres's attempt at an insult. He had more pictures in his file folder, ones Gable West had sent him of more of Torres's alleged victims.

"It's an art form, isn't it?" Jake said. "I can see that. A sculpture. Or a piece of music. You take your time to make them suffer how you want them to."

Torres smiled. "You're a sick bastard if you think like that."

"The thing is, these aren't innocent victims. I know that. These are bad men who knew what they were getting into when they got into bed with the cartel. Cost of doing business. Criminals. All of them. Even him."

Jake tapped Craig Albright's picture. "He broke the rules. Tried to rewrite them to serve his own ends. I know he was given plenty of warnings. I bet when you showed up, he wasn't even surprised."

"That's a good story," Torres said. "But you got nothing on me. No physical evidence."

"I know you're not scared of me. And you're not even scared of going to prison. You figured it was only a matter of time, right? But I bet you hate how this went down. You were thinking it'd be some blaze of glory. Live by the sword, die by the sword. Blood in and blood out. It wasn't supposed to be this cop from a crappy little backwater town in Ohio, right?"

Torres shoved the crime scene photos closer to Jake.

"A bunch of inbred hicks from the hills. That's gotta stick in your gut, doesn't it? These people have barely gone more than twenty miles from the shacks they were born in. You know that, right? You figured this one was gonna be easy. Fish in a barrel. How's it feel to be outsmarted by the likes of Floyd Bardo? And me with my twenty bucks an hour?"

Torres snarled. Jake watched every muscle in his upper body go rigid. Yeah. It bothered him.

"You're a craftsman, aren't you? A specialist. A maestro. And look at you. About to go down for picking off a nobody."

"You. Got. Nothing," Torres said.

"Not exactly a denial. You know, I think when the day comes, when they put the needle in your arm for killing Craig Albright, I'm gonna be there. I'm gonna watch and you'll know exactly what I'm thinking. You got sloppy. Took one too many chances."

Torres was angry. A vein popped out in his neck. Jake knew if he kept pushing, the guy would snap. He wasn't dumb enough to admit anything, but maybe he was dumb enough to let some small detail slip.

There was a quick knock at the door and Sobel poked his head in. "You got a sec, Cashen?"

"I've got all day." Jake stood up and turned his back on Matteo Torres. He followed Sobel across the hall. They'd set up a room with tables. The contents of Torres's car, luggage, and hotel room drawers were spread out and in the process of being tagged and photographed.

Jake went to the nearest table. "Those look like sculpting tools." They were. Jake spotted a wooden-handled fettling knife. A chill went through him as he realized what he'd said to Torres was accurate. Torture was an art form for this monster.

"He's got a bag full of wooden dowels too," Sobel said. "Probably had his victims bite down on them to help them bear some of the pain if he wasn't ready to kill them yet. You see anything here he might have used in your homicide?"

Jake kept looking. There were a pair of blow torches at the end of one table. "These," he said. "My victim's toes were burned one by one. And the pliers. A couple of his fingernails were ripped out."

"You need to take a look at this," Sobel said. "We finished combing through Torres's car. One of my people found some receipts crumpled under the mat on the front passenger side." Sobel held up a baggie containing the receipts. He handed it to Jake.

One was from the fast-food place right next to the Tall Pines Motel. But another was from a gas station in Stanley. Jake's blood ran cold. He filled his own tank there at least once a month. It was no more than a mile from Craig Albright's farm. He squinted, trying to make out the date. The register ink had faded. He held the paper up to the light. His blood turned to ice as he finally made out the date and time.

"I don't even know how this is real," he said. "The idiot got gas in town two hours before killing Craig Albright. This puts him a couple of miles from the crime scene."

"We found this too," Sobel said, his tone flat. He handed Jake another baggie. This one was filled with business cards.

"They were in his glove box."

Jake didn't even have to read it. He recognized the All-Brite Electrical logo with the smiling yellow light bulb.

"You got enough with this?" Gable West came into the room.

"Yeah," Jake said. "I've got enough with this. How about you?"

As if her ears were burning, Jake's cell phone rang. He checked the caller ID. It was Sheriff Landry. He sent her a quick text in response.

"Talk later. I'll have some news. Stand by."

He set the baggies down on the table and took a picture of them with his phone.

"I'll be back in a second."

Jake went back to the interrogation room where Matteo Torres sat. He was done playing games.

He put his phone on the table and pulled up the image he'd just snapped.

"You're dumber than I thought you were, Torres, El Carnicero Oscuro. They're gonna have to start calling you El Carnicero Tonto."

Torres looked at the photograph. His face didn't change.

"You got nothing, asshole. Nothing."

"I've got enough. You're under arrest for the murder of Craig Albright. They're gonna hold you without bond. Today was the last bit of blue sky you'll ever see if I have a say, butcher."

Torres shoved Jake's phone back across the table. "I got nothing to say to you. I'll be calling my lawyer now."

Jake smiled. "Yeah. I bet you will. But you're mine, Torres. What'd you call me? Hillbilly cop? Yeah. That's me. I'm gonna enjoy being the last face you see when they stick the needle in your arm while they're paying me my twenty bucks an hour."

Matteo Torres lost his cool. He swore at Jake in Spanish as Jake turned his back on him and shut the door.

TWENTY-SIX

"I'm gonna need you standing beside me, Jake," Landry said. He stood on the back porch, looking out at the dense woods that formed the southwest corner of his grandfather's property. It went two hundred acres deep through rolling hills, the top of which was the big house. A nearly three-thousand-square-feet colonial-style building with five bedrooms built for the large family his Grandma Ava had wanted. The house came to fruition, even though the big family never did. There had just been Jake's father and an unspeakable tragedy after that.

"I'll try to be there in an hour," Jake said. "I need to talk to Craig's family in person. They need to hear what's about to happen from me. I made them a promise."

"Of course," she said. "Please convey my condolences to them. And take your time. I can hold off the hounds until you get here."

"Thanks," Jake said, then clicked off. He took another long sip of nearly cold coffee. Then he punched Rachel Albright's cell phone number. He wasn't surprised when she didn't answer. Since the funeral, no one had seen her around town. She'd withdrawn into herself, her daughter said. Disassociated. Jake wondered whether his news would help her or make it even worse. He left a voicemail but thirty seconds later, his phone rang. Mick Harter.

"Detective," Harter said. "I see you tried to call my daughter. She's not up for a phone call right now."

"I understand that, sir," Jake said. "I have some news that needs to be delivered in person. It's not something that can wait. I tried to get a hold of your granddaughter too."

"She's not here. I sent her back to school. She can't put her life on hold anymore."

"I see," Jake said. "Well, I need to talk to your daughter. And you. Can I come over? Will you be there with her?"

"Always," Harter said, then erupted into a round of coughs.

"All right. Give me twenty minutes and I'll be there." Jake clicked off and finished his coffee.

Mick Harter was waiting for Jake as he pulled up the long, winding gravel drive on Mansfield Road in Durris Township in the westernmost part of the county. Harter lived in a seventies-era ranch house. The kind they don't build anymore. Jake knew developers had come in trying to get him to sell on more than one occasion. Harter's property sat right in front of a new condo subdivision, sticking out like a sore thumb. He had an old Chevy truck up on blocks in the front yard. Two pole barns. A bathtub Virgin Mary plus other assorted lawn art displayed on the front lawn. It made Jake smile. He wondered if the old man decorated his front yard just to make the neighbors with their HOA angry. It was the kind of thing his own grandfather would have done.

"Thanks for meeting me," Jake said. "Sorry about the short notice. Is Rachel inside?"

"She is," Mick said. "But why don't you tell me what you've come to tell her first?"

Mick sat on a white, wrought-iron bench. He rested both hands on the top of his cane. The front door was open. Jake noticed a tear in Harter's screen door. It had to be letting the flies in. The lawn itself was in need of a mow.

"The rider's on the fritz," Harter said, following Jake's line of sight. "It's hard for me to get under it and tinker these days."

"Maybe I can take a look at it after I get off work," Jake said.

"I'll get to it," came Harter's gruff response. Jake put a hand up in surrender. He reminded him of his own grandfather in more ways than one.

"Dad?" came the call from inside the house. "Are you talking to someone? I told you I don't want to see anybody. Tell them to go away."

Mick Harter let out a groan and tried to get to his feet. He didn't quite make it. Jake lurched forward and put a hand under the old man's arm, gently lifting as he tried again. "I'm fine," Harter said. "Once I'm up, I'm fine. Don't get old, kid. That's my best advice for you."

"I'll keep it in mind."

"Come on," Mick said. "She'll bitch, but she's sitting in the family room at the back of the house watching game shows. She's been there for days. I can barely get her to eat."

"When's Lexie coming back?"

"She's not if I have anything to say about it. She's better off in Boulder. She's got a job there. She's thinking of taking a leave of absence but she's gotta straighten some things out with her boss first. I think it's a bad idea. Craig wouldn't want that for her. Nobody wants her to put her life on hold except for Rachel."

Jake opened the screen door and held it for Mick. The older man grabbed the door frame, took a breath, then heaved himself over the threshold.

Jake followed him through the living room and kitchen toward the back of the house. There, he had a sunken family room. It was just two steps down. He took them sideways. Rachel Albright sat in an overstuffed recliner, a pink and white Afghan pulled up to her chin. She clicked off the television and glared at Jake.

"I told you I don't want to see anybody," she said.

Jake made sure Mick was settled on the couch then he went to Rachel. He took a chair from the roll-top desk in the corner and placed it near Rachel so they could sit and talk.

"I have news," he said. "We've made an arrest in Craig's murder."

Rachel blinked. For a moment, Jake couldn't tell if she'd heard him. Then, a single tear fell down her left cheek.

"His name is Matteo Torres," Jake continued. "We believe your husband was the victim of a contract killing carried out by a drug cartel. Torres is a hitman, Mrs. Albright."

She shook her head.

Harter's den was connected to a screened-in sunroom at the very back of the house. Drew Harter came in that way. He didn't look at all surprised to see Jake. Jake figured his father must have given him a heads-up.

"Drew," Rachel said, her voice small. "Detective Cashen said they caught the man who killed Craigie. A hitman. Why would a hitman want to hurt someone in my family?"

Jake saw Drew exchange a look with his father and wondered how much he'd told him. Mick's face hardened.

"There are a lot of details in the investigation I won't be able to talk to you about just yet," Jake said. "But I wanted you to know we got the guy. If he's indicted, he'll probably face the death penalty. Though that won't be my call to make, you understand?"

Rachel Albright finally met Jake's eyes. "Good," she said, surprising him. "I want him to. For what he did to us. He shouldn't be allowed to live. He's a monster."

"Yes. Yes, he is," Jake said. "There's going to be a press conference in about an hour. I have to be there but you don't. I'm going to send a patrol car out here just in case any media members want to try to get a statement from you. You don't have to talk to them, okay?"

She nodded. "Okay. I have to tell Lex. I have to call her. Daddy? Can you find my phone for me?"

"I'll find it," Drew said.

"I'll help you," Jake said, rising. He walked over to Mick and leaned down to whisper in his ear.

"Is she going to be okay?"

Mick nodded. "You go do what you gotta do. I can take care of my own."

Jake patted Mick on the shoulder. The old man's knees might not be solid, but his back seemed to be. Jake followed Drew to the front of the house.

"Outside," he ordered Drew. Drew paused. He looked ready to argue, then thought the better of it.

"I want to thank you," Drew said, extending his hand to shake Jake's. Jake didn't take it.

"This is what happens when you get mixed up with the people Craig brought into your family's life. You understand?"

Drew stood there for a moment, holding his hand out. Then his face fell and he dropped his arm to his side.

"I think maybe you need to talk to my lawyer from now on."

"Yeah," Jake said. "I'm sure I do. Doesn't mean I won't stop checking in on you, Drew. Your sister's been through enough. Your father has been through enough. It's time you started thinking about someone besides yourself. You get me?"

"It's time for you to leave. My family doesn't need you here. This is private property and your invitation has just been revoked."

"It's your father's property," Jake said. "Look around. He needs help. Cut the damn grass for him. Fix that screen door. It's letting the bugs in. Be a man, Drew. For once in your life."

Jake turned his back on Drew Harter. He couldn't stand the sight of him any longer.

One hour later, Jake stood in front of a bank of microphones beside Sheriff Landry. She faced a barrage of questions. None of that fazed her, or Jake. But one reporter took up residence right in the front. Rhett Pierson from the *Daily Beacon*.

"Sheriff, the people of this town will demand answers. My sources tell me Matteo Torres is a known sicario for the Mexican drug cartel. What was he doing carrying out a hit in Blackhand Hills?"

"And you know that's the kind of question I won't be able to answer right now. Mr. Torres is, of course, innocent until proven guilty. I'm confident our criminal justice system has and will continue to work the way it's supposed to. What's important here today is that the public is made aware that there is no ongoing threat. We believe the murder of Craig Albright has been solved. The rest is going to have to play out in the courts as it should."

"I think the citizens of the Blackhand Hills region deserve to know why illicit drugs have been funneled into town under your watch, Sheriff. And what you're going to do about it."

Jake bristled beside her. To her credit, Meg didn't take the bait.

"I believe we've answered all the questions we can regarding the suspect involved in the Albright murder. If and when there is more to tell you, I know where to find you. That is all."

Sheriff Landry gathered her notes and stepped away from the lectern. In the back of the room, Tim Brouchard stood with a smirk on his face. No doubt his client, Drew Harter, had already filled him in on Jake's visit to his father's residence. As the press began to disperse, Brouchard pushed himself off the wall and made his way toward Jake.

Jake knew he should have just followed Landry through the door and out of the press room. He should have slammed the thing in Tim Brouchard's face.

"Good work, Detective," Brouchard said. "El Carnicero Oscura. That's going to be a hell of a feather in your cap. I'm expecting a statement to follow completely exonerating my client of any wrongdoing."

"Not happening. And I never gave his name to the press. If he keeps his nose clean, he's got nothing to worry about. Though I doubt he will. Your client's hands are dirty in this. Let's not pretend otherwise."

"My client has a full immunity deal."

"Which isn't the same as being innocent, Brouchard. You might want to be careful of the company you keep."

"Is that a threat?" Brouchard said. He took a step closer to Jake, getting in his face.

Jake squared his shoulders. "You bet your ass that's a threat," he said. Then he turned and slammed the door in Tim Brouchard's face after all.

TWENTY-SEVEN

"I'm sorry," Gemma said. She stood in the kitchen holding a basket heaped with warm, homemade rolls. "I already softened the butter for you."

Jake looked back into the living room. His nephews, Ryan and Aiden, put their heads quickly back in their phones. He'd get no help from either of them.

Jake walked to his sister and grabbed a roll, and took a bite. Flaky and still piping hot, the bread melted on his tongue. As apologies went, it was a good one. He only had a single question.

"Which thing are you apologizing for? Past or future?"

"I called Dominique Gill," she said.

In the chaos of the last few days, Jake barely had time to think about this ill-fated blind date. Or he'd blocked it out of his mind. Bringing it up at Craig Albright's funeral didn't seem right either.

"She's so sorry, Jake," Gemma said. "She had a really bad day at work. Her mother was on her case. She wasn't herself."

"Is that what she told you?" Jake said, grabbing another roll. This time, Gemma snatched them away.

"You'll fill your stomach up on bread. Gramps made venison stew."

Grandpa Max reached up and pulled the bowls off the shelf. "Buffet style!" he called out. "Boys, wash your hands before you even think about grabbing a spoon."

Jake knew in Grandpa's mind, he still qualified as one of the boys. He went to the sink and did as he was told.

"Gemma," he said. "The woman took off with her boyfriend before the check came. She wasn't having an off day. It was a disaster. But hopefully that'll cure you of trying to get in the middle of my personal life."

Behind him, Ryan and Aiden burst into laughter. Jake lobbed a wet sponge at Ryan, hitting him square in the chest.

"It's not my fault," Gemma said. "Dominique just wasn't right for you. But we've got a new receptionist at the office. Her name is Shayla and she is exactly your type."

"I have a type?"

"Well, she's single. So she's your type."

Jake rolled his eyes. "Work on your own love life for a while, Gem. I'm too busy anyway."

Ryan and Aiden took their places at the table. Jake filled a bowl with Grandpa's delicious, warm stew.

"That's that eight-point Ryan shot last fall," Grandpa said. "I knew he'd be a good eater."

Jake slid into his chair and waited for his stew to cool a bit before taking a bite. Younger and less wise, Aiden shoveled a spoonful into his mouth then had to promptly spit it back into the bowl after scalding the roof of his mouth.

"I saw the press conference," Gemma said. "You really think you caught the guy who ... did that?"

Gemma's voice faltered. Suddenly, he felt like a first-class jerk. He'd been so worried about making sure Rachel Albright got the news in person, he hadn't remembered about his own sister. The whole thing had set a bomb off in her life, too.

"I'm sorry," he said. "I should have called you beforehand."

Gemma put a hand up. "Don't. I understand. I'm just glad you made an arrest. It's been ... well ... everyone in the office has been kind of skittish about showing houses. We're doing them in tandem now. Nobody's been willing to go out alone."

"You don't have to be scared anymore," Jake said. "We caught the guy. I can't get into the details, you know that. But this was an isolated situation. You don't have anything to worry about."

"Not a bad idea to have a buddy system when you're showing houses though anyway," Grandpa said. Jake couldn't argue that point. He just hated that his sister ever had to feel scared.

"Do you have any idea when the Albrights' house will be turned back over to the family?" she asked.

"Mom," Ryan said. "Gross. Who's going to want to buy that house now? They'll have to burn the thing down. Even then, people are gonna think it's haunted."

"I'm not asking for myself," Gemma said. "Well, not entirely. I'm asking because ... well, I don't know. I'm worried about Rachel. I've been hearing things."

"What things?" Jake asked.

"People are starting to talk. You know how it is in this town. It's just ... well ... You know my friend Brenda Fraley. From back when I used to work at the salon. Rachel still goes there. Brenda said the last time she came in ... her daughter brought her. Thought maybe having her hair done would cheer her up. Or at least make her feel more normal. Anyway, Brenda said Rachel looked like a ghost herself. That she was talking to herself. She had some kind of breakdown and her daughter had to get her out of there before Brenda had a chance to dry her hair. I'm just worried. How did she take the news when you told her? If you can tell me that."

Jake's stew was finally cool enough to eat. Aiden watched him take a spoonful, then got brave enough to dig into his own again.

"She seemed pretty withdrawn," Jake said. "Checked out. I think she might be medicated. Maybe that's not such a bad thing for now. Her daughter went back to Colorado, at least temporarily."

"How awful," Gemma said. "Do you think it would be okay if I went over there? Brought some pre-made dinners or something?"

"I think you can try," Jake said.

"She won't go back to the house," Gemma said. "She already told me that. Honestly, I got the impression she wouldn't mind if the thing did just burn to the ground. I'm hoping Alexis can maybe take over some of this for her when she gets back into town."

"It's rough," Jake said. "She's staying with Mick, which I think he's glad about. But Mick's not in the best shape himself. I didn't like what I saw when I went over there. In fact ... Ryan, I was actually going to talk to you about that."

"What'd I do?" Ryan asked with a mouthful of stew that earned him a stern look from his great-grandfather.

"Mick Harter has a large property out on Mansfield Road. Do you know it?"

"Sure," Ryan said. "A couple of guys on the team live in that subdivision right behind it. Their parents aren't too happy about how much crap he's got in the front yard."

"Oh, it's an eyesore," Gemma said. "I sold a condo back there last year. It's the first thing anyone sees when they come into the sub from that road. If I'm showing there, I always take my clients the back way in from County Road Nine."

"Well," Jake continued. "Mick's got a few things that need doing. His lawn's overgrown. Weeding and edging. His screen door needs replacing. Nothing major. But Ryan, I was thinking maybe you and a couple of the guys from the team could go over there and help him out."

Ryan frowned. "He's mean, Uncle Jake."

"I know he's mean. That doesn't mean he doesn't deserve help. He's more stubborn than mean."

"It's tough getting old," Grandpa said.

"Well, he's not meaner than you," Ryan said.

"There you go," Jake said. "So you'll be an expert. If you grab three or four guys and head over after conditioning, you could knock his chores out in an hour. In fact, I'll take you myself. Make the introductions."

"Where's Drew Harter in all this?" Gemma asked, though her tone dripped with sarcasm.

"Well, to be fair. He claims he's busy dealing with Craig's business. I think he figures that's his contribution. Also, I kind of get the impression Mick doesn't mind if he stays away."

"That kid's always been trouble," Grandpa said. "I still say if Craig got mixed up in something he shouldn't, that boy probably led him to it. From the day he could talk, that kid always had some kind of scheme. Some get-rich-quick. Mick was real happy when Rachel married Craig. He built something for himself. He was never afraid of hard work. I think Mick was hoping it'd rub off on his son."

"Rachel said Craig took her brother on as a favor to their father," Gemma said. "Let's just hope he can step up. Make up for all the years of grief he's caused his old man."

"Sure, Uncle Jake," Ryan said. "I'll round up some of the underclassmen and we'll go on over there whenever you say."

"Good," Jake said. "I appreciate it. And Mick will too, whether he says it or not."

"Tell him you get credit for it for service hours or something," Grandpa said. "Make it seem like he's the one helping you out. That's how I'd approach it."

"It's a good idea," Jake agreed.

"It's a damn shame," Grandpa said. "Mick Harter was one of the strongest sons of bitches I ever met. Took no crap from anyone. He was a good friend to have and a nightmare of an enemy if you got on his bad side."

Jake smiled. "Sounds like what they say about you."

Grandpa waved him off. "I'm just saying. Mick was one of the good ones once you got to know him. But one tough bastard. I once watched him take out three guys. Came into Wylie's Bar one night. Thugs from Cincinnati. Came in spoiling for it. One of 'em got a little rough with Louanne. Back then, she was one of the best waitresses they had. Backed her into a wall. Well, Mick came out swinging. Took that guy by the neck and flung him halfway across the bar. Then made quick work of the other two before they even knew what happened. Knocked all three of them out cold. Mick barely broke a sweat. Just sat down and sipped his beer. That was probably two months after he got back from Saigon. His buzz cut hadn't even had a chance to grow out yet. Nowadays, they're teaching you kids not to fight for yourselves. Not to defend someone else who's weaker than you. Kicking you out of school. I fear for this country, I really do. And now he needs help to mow his own lawn. Don't get old, kids. That's my advice."

Ryan and Aiden's eyes were already glazed over. A common occurrence when Grandpa Max went off on one of his tangents about the old days. Someday, Jake knew they'd appreciate it. He just hoped it wouldn't come too late. Grandpa Max had a thousand stories to tell. He'd heard most of them. The old man's eyes were clouded now. He could only see in the brightest of light. His hands were gnarled. His back bent. It scared Jake to think someday soon he might not be around. That Ryan and Aiden would likely live most of their lives without Max in it. But today, he was here and his stew tasted just as delicious as always. Maybe better.

TWENTY-EIGHT

Worthington County Prosecutor Corey Ansel was nervous. No. Not so much nervous, more manic. Jake sat at the end of a long table. The war room at the sheriff's department had been mostly dismantled and moved over to Ansel's office across the street. In three days, Matteo Torres, one of the most brutal contract killers on the planet, would appear before the grand jury in rural southern Ohio, of all places. Ansel understood the weight of it. But he was new to the job. Green in a lot of ways. Jake couldn't believe he was thinking it, but he wondered if the Torres case might be better served under the last prosecutor.

"It's solid," Ansel said. He kept sitting, then bouncing up, practically sprinting to the front of the room where he kept a giant easel notepad with Torres's picture taped to the top of it. "But run it through again."

Across the table, Mark Ramirez muttered something in Spanish under his breath. It wasn't flattering. If Jake were close enough, he would have kicked him. Jake knew Ramirez felt like Ansel was wasting his time. That this was a meeting that could have been a phone call or an email. Dr. Stone sat on Jake's right, displaying the patience of a statue. Ansel was at least the seventh prosecutor the doctor had worked with during his tenure as M.E. Mary Rathburn sat at the end of the table taking notes.

"I want Floyd Bardo here," Ansel said. "I want to be able to pick up a phone and call him at a moment's notice. And I need assurances that he'll show up when he's supposed to. I need him to establish probable cause. I'd prefer he was in our custody."

"He won't agree to it," Jake said. "Not yet. And I'm telling you. He's safer where he is."

"Which you won't tell me," Ansel snapped. This had been a bone of contention between them.

"I've told you what you need to know. You have a cell phone number. Bardo knows when and where he's supposed to report. When the time comes, it won't be a problem. And I'm telling you, he won't break his word to me."

"His word. You keep saying that. You're putting a lot of faith in this man's word."

"He also doesn't want to go to prison on federal drug charges, Corey. He doesn't want to spend the rest of his life in hiding if he can avoid it. But you're going to have to trust me for the time being that Floyd is safest where he is. I'm not gonna pretend this isn't a precarious deal, but it's a solid one. You wrote the proffers yourself."

He hadn't meant it as sarcasm. But the moment he uttered the words, Ansel stopped pacing and glared at Jake. He *had* written the proffer when it came to Floyd Bardo, but not Drew Harter. The specter of Tim Brouchard still hung heavy in the room it seemed.

"Where are we on the DNA?" Ansel asked Ramirez.

"You won't have it," Mark said. "Torres is way too smart not to have wiped down his implements after killing Craig Albright. You've got the preliminary reports."

Dr. Stone had the most disturbing crime scene photos in front of him. In addition to the Albright murders, Ramirez had brought photos from one of Torres's kills in Texas. When Jake first saw them, he had a hard time distinguishing them from Craig Albright's. The burns to the toes. The injuries to the victim's fingers. They were exactly the same.

"He was a mule," Ramirez said. "Tried to turn state's evidence against the cartel. Torres has been used to send an increasingly violent message to rats."

"He's escalated," Dr. Stone said. "I swear, this guy has figured out a way to make a career out of being a serial killer."

"You're not worried about Drew Harter?" Ansel asked Jake.

"Not in the slightest. Drew's an idiot, but he's not stupid, you know? And neither is his lawyer. To be honest, of all your witnesses, Harter's the one I'm most confident in."

Ansel's face fell. Jake found a smile for him. This wasn't the first or last time he'd have to hold the hand of a jumpy prosecutor.

"Floyd Bardo is solid," Jake said.

"This is solid," Ramirez said, tossing one of the worst photos toward Ansel. It showed a close-up of Craig's bruised and battered face. "I don't have DNA, but Dr. Stone can testify that these implements were of the type used to make those injuries. Plus Bardo. Plus Harter. Plus the fruits of Jake's search warrant down in Columbus when they picked up Torres. I think the words you're looking for are thank you. Thank you for handing me a low-flying goose egg of a softball right over the plate. Relax, Ansel. Five years from now, you'll be able to use this case to springboard your entry into state-wide politics. Everybody at this table knows that's where you're headed."

Ansel smiled. The bastard actually blushed. Then his face fell and he began pacing again. "Jake, you're sure Floyd will show up for the grand jury? He knows he's under a subpoena."

"Everyone knows their jobs, Corey," Jake said. It was a pointed comment. He glared at the man when he made it. Unbelievably, Ansel didn't seem to grasp the dig. Jake let out a hard breath. For the second time, he wondered if this wouldn't be easier if Brouchard were handling it. The devil you know, and all that.

Ansel's cell phone rang. He kept right on pacing as he answered. "Be right there," he said, then clicked off.

"I've got another small fire to put out. Do you gentlemen ... um ... and lady mind waiting for me for a few minutes?"

Dr. Stone waved him off. Ramirez was less charitable. "Sure," he said. "I've got all the time in the world."

As soon as Ansel shut the door and disappeared into the bowels of the building, Ramirez turned to Jake.

"Can he handle this?"

"He's going to have to," was Jake's answer.

"He'll handle it," Dr. Stone said. "I'll walk him through it when I get on the stand. Once the grand jury hears what was done to this poor bastard, they'll be primed and ready to indict. And your case is solid."

"At least he'll have the good sense to put you on first," Jake said. "If this thing gets to a regular jury trial, he should do the same."

"Is your sister going to testify?" Ramirez asked.

"Not for the grand jury. Ansel won't need her. To be honest, I think he's issued subpoenas for more people than he needs. I don't know why he's calling Harter."

"I think maybe it wasn't Ansel's idea to have Harter be there," Mary said. "Has it occurred to you that Brouchard wants a reason to be there? There will be media coverage."

"She's probably right," Ramirez said. "I don't trust that guy as far as I could kick him."

"Which guy?" Stone asked. "Ansel or Brouchard?"

Jake guessed it was on the tip of Ramirez's tongue to say either one. He clammed up instead.

"Gemma's doing okay though?" Mary asked. She reached across the table and pulled the picture currently in front of Dr. Stone closer to her.

"She's doing okay," Jake answered. "She's skittish about showing houses by herself. I'm hoping this indictment will help calm her down. That it will calm everyone down."

"Still," Ramirez said. "I'm not getting the strongest vibe of confidence in Ansel. I'm sorry. He might get past the grand jury, but if he doesn't figure out how to grow a pair, you think he's got a shot at a conviction?"

"This guy can't walk, Jake," Mary said. "Craig's murder is bad enough. But this. All of this?"

She gestured toward the span of photographs laid out on the table.

"I'm sorry," Stone said. "From a medical standpoint, it's impressive. This one here in San Antonio. M.E. there says he kept his victim alive for two days. Shot him full of adrenaline when he started to fade. Wanted him awake for the worst of the torture. Albright got lucky. I never found any trace of adrenaline in his system."

"He didn't give you anything?" Ramriez said. "Torres? I don't know. I would have thought he'd want to gloat. Proud of his handiwork and all that."

"Oh, he gloated. Just not in a specific way. He's too smart for that."

Jake picked up the photo Mary had been looking at. Craig Albright's bulging, sightless eyes stared up at him. Stone's words echoed in his mind. Torres liked his victims awake for the worst of it.

"He cut him first," Stone said. "That wound across his cheek. He might not have used adrenaline, but Craig's injuries ... most of them anyway ... were superficial. Survivable. Would have been painful as hell. But I don't think any of them alone would have rendered Albright unconscious. That's the story I'll play up for the jury. How deliberate and intentional this all was. Designed for maximum pain. Like this guy."

He picked up another photograph. The victim was a low level coyote. His body was found in a ditch just over the border in Tijuana. The lacerations. The burn marks. This man's ears had been cut off. One eye removed. The autopsy report from that killing indicated the victim had been alive and likely conscious for all of it. As Stone said, the poor soul's body had been pumped with adrenaline to ensure it.

"How sure are the feds? They're gonna be able to make the drug charges against him stick?"

"Why does that matter?" Mary asked.

"I'm just ... It'd make me feel better knowing no matter how much Ansel might fumble around on the Albright case, I need to be able to sleep at night. You know? Give me the fairytale ending that this guy is never ever gonna see the light of day again, no matter what we do here."

"It's out of my hands," Jake said. "I trust Gable West. I trust the team in Columbus."

"But they're saying the same thing about us," Ramirez said.

"Yeah," Jake said. "They're saying the same thing about us."

"Almost makes you wish Brouchard had waited to screw his life up until after this case," Ramirez said. Then he quickly cleared his throat. "Sorry, Jake. I know that case was personal for you."

"They're all personal for me," Jake said under his breath.

"Jake," Mary said. "I've been meaning to ask you about this. I'm starting to hear some rumors that Tim Brouchard might be looking to involve himself in the next sheriff's election."

"As a candidate?" Dr. Stone said. "He's not qualified."

Jake had not yet told anyone about his confrontation with Tim Brouchard. He hadn't even told Landry he knew the source of the interdepartmental leak. Ed Zender still hadn't come back to the office as he burned through vacation days. But he knew he owed Landry the truth.

"He's up to something," Jake said. "But I don't feel comfortable getting into it until I've had a chance to talk to Landry directly."

"You sure that's smart?" Stone said. "I like Meg Landry. Don't get me wrong. But she's vulnerable in the next election. We all know it. She's not a lock by any means. So the doomsday scenario, Jake, is you get a new boss. And you've already made an enemy out of them before they take office."

"I'm not gonna count Landry out," Jake said. "The command and deputy's unions will come out in support of her."

Mary bristled. "Jake, I'm not sure that's true. I've been hearing rumors about that too. Some of the rank and file are worried about the same things Dr. Stone just brought up."

Jake felt his blood start to simmer. "Somebody's gotta grow a backbone in this town. I'm tired of people waiting to see which way the wind blows instead of sticking up for the person who we all know is best for the job."

"I'm sorry," Mary said. "I'm not trying to make you mad. I'm just ... look. I know I'm not a lock, either. I know what people say about me. I know I'm not the popular choice to replace Ed. What I'm asking you ... if you hear something. I'll understand if Landry has to make another choice. A safer one. I'd just like a heads-up. You know?"

Jake thumped a fist on the table. "Landry's got your back, and so do I. You can count on it. Quit listening to rumors. Are we clear?"

Mary put her hands up in surrender. The climate in the room had turned to ice.

"Well, I can't wait around for Ansel," Ramriez said. "I'm already an hour late for a crime scene down in Zanesville. You tell him he can call or email me if he needs more information ahead of the grand jury. And tell him I know how to do my job."

Ramirez excused himself. Dr. Stone wasn't far behind. When it was just Jake and Mary alone, he put a hand on her shoulder.

"I meant what I said," he told her. "Landry knows how to do her job and she's not afraid of the rank and file or gossip."

Mary smiled up at him. She trusted him. Jake realized how much that mattered to him. And he knew it was time to have a difficult conversation with Meg Landry.

Twenty-Nine

"Give me good news, Jake," Landry said as he walked into her office early the next morning. She looked haggard. Puffy around the eyes. Her hair wasn't quite right, though Jake knew better than to mention any of it.

"Rough night?" he asked.

"Raising a teenage girl in the twenty twenties. One star. Do not recommend."

Jake laughed and took a seat in front of her desk. "What'd you do this time, Mom? Nag?"

"Breathe," she answered without missing a beat. "She only comes out of her room when there's food on the table and half the time she won't eat it. She scowls at me. Occasionally talks to her dad."

"I hear it gets better," Jake said.

"Sorry. I don't mean to unload. What do you have for me? And please. I'm not kidding. Something good. I know you met with Corey Ansel yesterday. Does he have the Torres case locked up tight for the grand jury?"

"I think so." Jake hesitated, not wanting to burden her with the doubts Ramirez and Stone expressed about Ansel's competence. Jake truly did believe the kid would settle into his role. Plus, Ethan Stone was a beast on the stand. Juries loved him.

"If he screws this thing up ..."

"He won't. We're not going to let him. This is the grand jury. It should be like falling off a log. Even for Corey Ansel."

"You know, you'll kill me for saying this, but there's a part of me that wishes Tim Brouchard were around for this one. Like he couldn't have waited until the next election cycle to blow up his life and everyone around him?"

She must have seen something in Jake's face. Or maybe it was just his silence after the comment. But Landry slowly sat back in her chair.

"What is it?" she said.

"It's nothing. It's probably nothing. But I probably should have come to talk to you about this sooner. There's been a lot going on ..."

"Don't tell me you're leaving me," she said. "If you try to hand in your resignation, I swear I'm going to make you eat it. You're one of the few people helping me hold this place together right now."

Jake smiled. "I appreciate the compliment. No. I'm not resigning. Where would I go?"

"You're right. Nobody else would have you."

Jake wanted to argue the point, but wondered if she wasn't right. He'd burned a lot of bridges before winding up back in his hometown. He liked to think it turned out okay for both him and Meg Landry. What he didn't like to think about was the prospect of a new sheriff behind that desk.

"Listen," he said. "You mentioned Brouchard. There's a thing you need to know. Your instincts were right on that hit piece Rhett Pierson published about the department."

"Department? It wasn't about the department, Jake. It was about me. Me personally."

"Well, I think I might know who leaked our internal numbers. I got a call from Bill Nutter. He was out having a drink at Digby's. He called me over. Pierson was sharing a booth with Ed Zender. They were passing documents back and forth. Then Brouchard showed up."

It took a moment for Jake's words to register for her. Landry blinked wide. "Zender," she said. "Ed Zender. You're telling me he's my mole? He's sharing drinks with Rhett Pierson?"

"Yeah. We had a bit of a confrontation in the men's room over it. I probably shouldn't have lost my temper ..."

"No. I hope you went apeshit, Jake. I hope you slammed him into a wall. This was Zender?" She rose from her chair and walked around her desk. She started picking up steam as she paced the length of the room.

"Sheriff ..."

She whipped around. "Zender's been pissed since the day I brought you up from field ops. The day I made his job easier. Allowed him to warm a chair and collect a paycheck. This is how he gets revenge? By hanging me out to Rhett Pierson and the *Daily Beacon*? Christ, Jake. Pierson is a snake. Sheriff O'Neal warned me about him. In this very room. Zender was sitting in the same chair you're in right now. Zender was no fan of Pierson's either. Why? Why is he doing this?"

"It seems Ed's not without his own ambitions."

"What are you talking about?"

"Meg, Ed's going to announce. Probably after the first of the year, when he's officially retired. But I think he's gonna make a run for sheriff."

Meg Landry erupted in a laugh. "That's a joke, right?"

"It's not a joke. I don't know what he's thinking. I don't know if he's been put up to it. I kind of suspect that's the case. If so, it's Tim Brouchard blowing the smoke up his rear end. I'm pretty sure Brouchard's aiming to run Zender's campaign against you."

"Double whammy. Brouchard can control somebody like Ed. He tries taking me out. As a nice little bonus, he gets to make your life miserable, too."

"I think that about sums it up, yeah."

Landry went back to her seat and took it. "You know, if I weren't so pissed, I might actually enjoy this. I can wipe the floor with Zender in any debate."

"I'm sure you can. If it were just about who was better for this job, it wouldn't be an issue."

"Am I going to lose the endorsement of the unions? Jake ... I'm not an idiot. I know whatever respect I have around here is tenuous. The second some of these bozos think they can put one of their own in this office ... they might take it."

"I haven't heard anything like that yet," Jake said. "Plus, I don't care how shrewd Tim Brouchard is, Ed is Ed. Given enough time, he'll figure out a way to trip over his own two feet. Besides, your job is work. Actual work. Or at least it's supposed to be."

Meg put her fingers to her temples and started to make circles. "You know what this is going to come down to? Lord. This is exactly why Tim Brouchard offered his services to Drew Harter when he was your prime suspect in the Albright killing. He's gonna come after you, too. He's gonna figure out a way to claim credit for solving this case for you through Drew Harter."

"Probably. I'm not worried about it. I'm too busy actually doing my job."

"Good. Good. Jake ... thank you. I know you're looking out for me."

"I've got your six, boss. Always."

Jake rose.

"I'm sorry," she said. "I know how much that has cost you ... or could cost you."

"I told you. I'm not worried."

Meg Landry leveled a hard stare at him. "Good. Just make sure Matteo Torres fries and maybe we'll both come out the other side of this."

"Copy that," Jake said. She gave him a weak smile, but he knew how much he'd just ruined her day.

THIRTY

Saturday morning at seven a.m. Jake stood in the driveway of his sister's house, staring at a motley group of bleary-eyed teenage boys. At Jake's request, Ryan had rounded up four of his teammates ready to do whatever work needed doing at the Harter place. Jake had no idea what to expect when they got there. His calls to Rachel had gone unanswered. At this point, he figured if they showed up unannounced ready to work, Mick might be hard-pressed to turn them away.

Gemma came out in a robe and flip-flops, carrying a travel mug full of coffee.

"Figured you could use this," she said.

"I knew there was a reason I liked you." Jake took the cup from her and took a sip. He scrunched his nose. She'd made it how she liked it, loaded with flavored oat milk creamer and stevia or whatever sweetener she was using these days. Still, it was coffee and he sorely needed it.

"Do they know you're coming?" Gemma asked.

Jake turned to his nephew. "Grab a couple of rakes from the shed. Some lawn bags. Oh, and the trimmer and edger. The old man's probably got all that out there, but we'll divide and conquer."

He turned back to his sister. "Rachel hasn't returned my calls. It's a nice day. The nicest one we're gonna have on a weekend for a while. I figure the worst that'll happen is the old man will throw us off the property."

He was kidding about the last bit. His sister's worried expression told him she didn't care for the joke. "I just hope they're all right. It's good you're going out there. Somebody needs to be checking on Rachel. I wish her daughter would hurry up and come back from Boulder."

"She's not answering your texts, either?"

"No. It makes me sad. We weren't close friends. But we were friends. Now, I think she just associates me with what happened. Which I can understand. It just sucks."

"I'll tell her you're worried."

"When's your grand jury?"

"Tuesday morning. I'm hoping it doesn't go beyond one day. That's another thing I want to talk to Rachel about. She needs to know what to expect. She doesn't have to be there."

"I'm glad I don't either. I don't know if I'm ready to talk about all of that yet."

Jake put a hand on his sister's shoulder. "You okay?"

She shrugged. "I'm not the one who suffered some tragedy here, Jake."

"Not this time," he said under his breath. His sister had found enough murdered bodies in her life. He wished he could take the trauma of that away from her. She was strong though. Maybe stronger than all of them.

"We ready, Uncle Jake?" Ryan asked.

"Yeah. Load up."

He watched as three of the boys piled into the backseat of his truck. Ryan and Travis Wayne got in the front with Travis in the middle. He was the smallest of the boys. For now.

"He looks more and more like his dad every day," Gemma said. "It takes my breath away sometimes."

In a few weeks, Travis would endure the first anniversary of his father's death. So would Jake.

"I'll give you a call when they're finishing up. I'll bring them all back here."

"Finish your coffee," she said, smiling. "You look like crap."

Jake shot her a look, then climbed into the driver's seat. He honked his horn as a goodbye while he backed out.

It was just a fifteen-minute drive out to the Harter place. The boys filled it with typical teenage banter. They felt comfortable enough to let loose some language that would have curdled his grandmother's blood. Somehow, they must have thought the driver's seat had made Jake deaf. He just smiled and let them talk.

Travis laughed beside him, the butt of a few of the older boys' jokes. He launched some zingers back at them that would have made his father, Ben, pretty proud.

As they pulled up Mick Harter's long driveway, Jake stiffened. The front lawn still hadn't been cut since the last time he was here. He'd been hoping this trip would turn out to be a waste of time.

That Drew Harter would have manned up and taken care of his father like Jake asked him to.

Jake parked in front of the house. The boys piled out but hung back as Jake made his way to the front door. He pressed the doorbell and waited.

He checked his phone. He'd texted Rachel last evening, telling her he'd be coming with the boys. She didn't respond but the message had been read. He decided to take that as acquiescence.

"Rachel?" he called out. Still nothing. "Mick?"

"There are cars in the garage," Travis called out. He peered through the small windows of the garage door. If worse came to worst, Jake had thrown a push mower into the bed of his truck. It would be a lot of lawn to cut without the tractor-mower Jake knew Mick Harter had. But it would get the job done.

Jake knocked. Still nothing.

"Ryan," he said. "Why don't you go around back, see if you can find anyone?"

Ryan gave him a look as if he'd just asked him to swallow nails. But he did as he was told.

"Rachel?" Jake called out. "It's Jake Cashen. I've got some kids out here to help out with yard work. I just wanted to let you know and see if you'll open the garage for us. Then we'll leave you alone."

Still nothing. Though Jake swore he heard footsteps coming from inside.

"Maybe they don't want us here," Travis said, hopeful.

"Pull my mower out of the truck. That'll be your job. Keegan, Randy, I've got blowers back there. When Travis is done, you can clear off the porch and the driveway. I'll have Ryan do the edging.

Ian, you're with me. We're gonna see about fixing this screen door. I've got tools in the back."

"Uncle Jake?" Ryan said. He'd just come back around to the front of the house.

"See anyone?"

"Uh ... yeah. Maybe you can take a look."

Puzzled, Jake stepped off the porch and followed his nephew around the back of the house.

Mick Harter had a pole barn about a hundred and fifty yards in the northwest quadrant of the property beyond a shed he kept closer to the house.

"Is that him?" Ryan asked. "The old man?"

Jake got closer. The shed blocked the view of anyone looking toward this part of the house, but Jake and Ryan had a clear shot of the side of the pole barn. Mick Harter's truck was pulled up alongside the barn with the tailgate open. A man stood in front of it with his back to Jake and Ryan. Fifty-pound feed bags were stacked to the top of the truck bed. The man stood rod straight, then pulled one bag out, threw it over his shoulder as if it weighed nothing, and stacked it on a pile just inside the barn.

It was Mick Harter. His cane was nowhere to be found. His limp was nowhere to be seen. Jake watched as the man hauled another bag off the truck bed, hoisted it on his shoulder, then stacked it with the others. His steps were sure. His grip was strong. He hauled and stacked the bags one by one with quick, fluid motions. At one point, he easily hopped into the bed of the truck to pull out a bag that had shifted to the far end. Bending over, he slid the bag to the end of the truck bed, hopped down, then hoisted the bag over his shoulder.

"I thought you said he was having trouble walking," Ryan said.

"I did. I mean ... he was." They were too far away for Mick Harter to hear them. Mick's truck radio was also blaring seventies southern rock.

"Coach Cashen!" Travis called out to him. Mick Harter seemed oblivious to everything going on up at the house. His radio drowned everything out.

"Coach Cashen," Travis said again. "Mrs. Albright's on the front porch. She wants to talk to you."

"Come on," Jake said to Ryan, pulling him away from the shed. Though he didn't know why, Jake decided he didn't want Mick to know he was there just yet. He wasn't sure what to make of what he'd seen.

They went around to the front of the house. Rachel Albright stood on the porch. She looked thin and gaunt. Her stick legs poked out from under a denim dress.

"Mrs. Albright," he said. "I didn't know if you got my message. I brought some of the kids I coach to do some work for your dad if he needs it."

"He's not available right now," she said. "He went to lie down a little while ago. I didn't have a chance to ask him."

Ryan opened his mouth to say something. Jake put a hand on him to keep him quiet.

"That's all right," he said. "Do you think he'd mind if we borrowed his riding mower in the garage? I'll get the boys started."

"I think you better not," she said. "Dad likes to do things a certain way. He's stubborn. Won't let Drew help him, either."

"The grass is a foot high," Travis said.

"Is it?" Rachel said, sounding out of it. Maybe overmedicated.

"Guys," Jake said. "Just go wait in my truck for a minute."

All five boys scattered, leaving Jake a moment alone to talk to Rachel Albright.

"We've been worried about you, Rachel," Jake said. "I know my sister's been trying to get a hold of you."

Rachel chewed her bottom lip. She seemed on the verge of tears.

"I've just been busy. Getting ready to move."

"Move?"

"We've decided to go ahead with the plan to move to Florida. The house is almost ready. I can't stay here in Ohio. Too many bad memories. I've finally talked my dad into coming with us. It'll be good for him. He can't take another harsh winter here."

"Sure," Jake said. "I can imagine that's gotta be tough on him with his trouble walking. When are you leaving?"

"Tuesday morning," she said. "Dad booked us on an eleven o'clock flight. Lexie is gonna meet us there on Wednesday. She's such a good kid. She's taking a leave from work. She might end up transferring to Destin permanently so she can be close. Tell your sister I'm sorry. I know she wants answers about the house."

"I don't think that's Gemma's main concern, Rachel."

"Well, I can't go back to that house. Ever. You can tell her Lexie will be in touch with her. In a few weeks, once things settle, she'll fly back here and pack up what she wants. I told her I don't want a thing from it. She can donate the rest. As far as the house ... I don't know. I'm going to have to explore my options for the quickest way to unload it. I don't even care about the money anymore."

"Well, if you need any help with that, there are plenty of people in the community who would be glad to. Gemma included. You know ... Torres will be facing the grand jury that morning."

Rachel's face went white. "You said I didn't have to be here for that."

"You don't. I'm just letting you know. I'll be there. There's nothing you need to do for now. But I'll be sure and get a hold of you once it's finished. And you know you can call me on my cell whenever you like."

"Okay. Thank you. Now, if you don't mind, I'd like to go back inside. I'm not feeling all that well. And I need to check on my dad. He's on medication he's supposed to take at certain times. I was about to fix him a snack."

"Rachel?" a voice shouted from inside. "Somebody out there?"

"It's just Detective Cashen, Dad. It's okay. You don't have to get up."

Behind him, the boys had gathered around the truck. Ryan caught Jake's eye and his jaw dropped. Jake made a gesture, waving downward. Rachel moved to the side of the door, giving Jake a better view inside. Mick Harter came down the hall, bent-backed and leaning on his cane.

"Mr. Harter," Jake said. His brain buzzed. He had a thousand questions. Instinct made him still. Not now. Not yet. Mick Harter seemed to have no idea that he and Ryan had seen him able-bodied just five minutes ago.

"Mr. Harter, I brought some boys with me. I thought I could have them help you with some chores around the house."

"Don't need 'em," Mick shouted. "I take care of my own."

"Dad," Rachel said. "They're trying to help. Maybe you should let them."

"Go on home," Mick said. "I won't say it again."

Rachel gave Jake a pained look and mouthed the words, "I'm sorry."

"No trouble at all," Jake said, finding a smile. "Sorry to bother you. Rachel, I'll be in touch probably Tuesday afternoon. Can I trust you'll answer your phone?"

"Sure," she said. Rachel opened the broken screen door and stepped back inside. Mick Harter stood there, glaring at him. Then Rachel shut the door in his face.

Stunned, Jake stepped off the porch and rounded up the boys. As he got into the truck, Ryan finally turned to him.

"What the heck is going on with that guy?" he asked.

Jake started the ignition. "I don't know." But he knew the real answer was nothing good.

THIRTY-ONE

"**I**s it true what they're saying about Ed?"

Mary Rathburn got to the office a half an hour before Jake did Monday morning. Over the last few weeks, he'd managed to create a small space for her in his corner of the office. It wasn't much. An old desk and a computer that currently wouldn't play nice with the network so Jake let her use his when he wasn't.

"Which thing?" Jake asked. He had a tray of coffee in one hand, his overstuffed backpack in the other. He put them both down, then handed Mary one of the coffees. She thanked him.

"That he's going to run against Landry."

Jake sat down. "It's worse than that. I need this to not leave this room for the time being. Landry's still trying to figure out what to do with it. But Ed along with Tim Brouchard are probably the ones responsible for leaking internal information to Rhett Pierson at the *Daily Beacon*. He's behind that hit piece against the sheriff."

Mary set her mug down. "Wow. I guess that tracks. Jake, that's shady as hell. And unethical. Is it a fireable offense?"

"I don't know. I think it's probably gonna be more complicated than that. If Landry goes after him with IA, it might look like she's trying to use her office to undercut a political opponent."

"Which is what he's doing!"

"I know. It's just ... complicated."

"I don't know what he's thinking. I'm sorry. I suppose I shouldn't say any of this. Not here in the office anyway. But I can't think of a worse person for the job than Ed Zender."

Jake couldn't argue the point. But it was a fire that would have to simmer for a little while longer. He had to deal with the one in front of him.

"I don't disagree. But I need to focus on what I can control for the time being. You should too. Corey Ansel isn't going to call you in front of the grand jury tomorrow, but I'd like you to be there."

"Absolutely. Are you ready? Do you need anything from me?"

Jake paused. He hadn't realized he'd been staring off into space until Mary snapped her fingers, drawing his attention.

"You okay?" she asked. "You look ... well ... like you haven't gotten any sleep."

"I haven't," he admitted. "It's just ... I paid a visit to Rachel Albright this weekend."

"I heard she wasn't doing well. You know, my next-door neighbor is a nurse at Dr. Finley's office. She's kind of a gossip. She asked me the other day if I've seen Rachel. I got the impression Finley's worried about her. My neighbor didn't come out and say that. She knows it would be a privacy violation. She just ... well ... people are worried."

"Me too. Only ... Rachel wasn't the problem. There was ... look. Do you know if Mick Harter sees Dr. Finley too?"

"You know, I never asked," Mary said. "I assume so. He sees half the people in town."

"You suppose you could get your neighbor to casually gossip about him?"

"Jake, what's going on?"

Jake scratched his chin. "I don't know. Nothing. Probably. Only ... you've seen Mick, right? Physically, how would you describe him?"

"He's a mess. That day when he came in after Craig's body was found, I thought he was going to die on me. Seriously. I was scared. Actually, now that you bring that up. I *do* remember the EMTs asking him about who his doctor was. He said Finley. Jake, what's all this about?"

"I told you, I was out there this weekend. I took my nephew and some of the wrestlers I coach out there to see if Mick would let them do his yard work. Just like you, I've been worried about him. About both of them. Well, I saw Mick. He didn't know I was there. I'd texted Rachel but she never responded. So Mick wasn't expecting me, you know?"

"Okay?"

"Mary, he was hearty. What I saw. The guy was lifting fifty-pound feed bags onto his shoulder and stacking them in his pole barn like they weighed nothing."

"He can barely walk. How is that possible?"

"Right," Jake said. "That's exactly it. Anyway, that alone maybe wouldn't have made me think too much about it. But I went back up to the house to talk to Rachel. A few minutes later, Mick walks in through the back. Now he knows I'm there. He's shuffling. Leaning on his cane. Acting like he's having trouble breathing."

"It's an act?" she said.

"I think so."

"Why? What are you thinking?"

"I don't know. Maybe he's running some scam with his insurance company. Or collecting disability when he shouldn't be. I just don't know."

"But it bothered you," Mary said. "So much so you haven't slept. You said Rachel was home. Do you think she knows?"

"I'm not sure. She seems pretty out of it. Overmedicated. When I first showed up, she told me her dad was taking a nap in the back room. Obviously, that wasn't true. So either she lied to my face or she didn't really know where Mick was and what he was doing."

"That's hard to believe. They live in the same house."

"True. But like I said, she's checked out. Doped up. And her daughter is back in Boulder. I just don't think Rachel's all that interested in what's going on with her father. Or the planet, for that matter."

"It's odd. Do you think it'll be a problem? In terms of Craig Albright's murder case?"

"Mick's not a witness to anything. There's no reason for anybody to put him on the stand."

"That's good. You gonna tell Ansel about all this?"

"I think Ansel's got enough on his plate without me confusing him. And I don't know what it means. It might not mean anything."

"Well, if he was faking his near heart attack that day ... he's scarily good at it. I mean, he was sweating, his face seemed gray. All of it."

"Yeah. It's just ... strange."

"Give me a day," she said. "My neighbor? Carly? If I ply her with a vodka spritzer and get her talking, she tends not to shut up. I'll see if she knows anything."

"I don't want to get her into trouble."

"She gets herself into trouble. She says more to me than she should because she thinks it's safe because I'm a cop. Like you can't be breaking privacy laws if you're talking to law enforcement."

"Ah," Jake said. "Remind me never to go to Dr. Finley's office."

"You're not kidding. I take my son all the way to Oakton for that very reason. I'd rather drive an extra twenty minutes instead of dealing with gossip."

Jake's cell phone rang. He pulled it out. Gable West's number popped up on the screen.

"I'll let you take that," Mary said, rising.

"No. I think maybe I want you on this call."

Mary sat back down. Jake put the phone on speaker as he answered.

"Morning," Jake said. "I didn't think you fed types got into the office before eleven."

"You were one of us fed types, Jake," West said. "Don't assume I share your bad habits."

"Don't remind me. I'd like to say I'm in recovery."

"Hey, you got a second to talk?"

Jake bristled. He knew Gabe well enough to know this wouldn't be good news.

"Sure thing," Jake said. "Do you mind if I keep you on speaker? My partner's here. I don't know if you've met Mary Rathburn."

"Partner? It's about time they sent someone to pick up your slack. Yeah, that's fine. Nice to meet you, Mary."

"Hello, Agent West," she said.

"Call him Gabe," Jake said. "He'll get cocky."

"Hey, listen," West said. "I just wanted to touch base on the Torres matter. You're headed before the grand jury tomorrow?"

"We are," Jake answered.

"How are you feeling about it?"

"Why are you asking?"

There was a longer pause than Jake liked before West answered.

"Look, I just got off the phone with the U.S. Attorney's office. They're giving some pushback on the federal drug charges against him."

"For what reason?" Jake asked.

"It's a lot of bullshit, if you want my honest opinion. They're not happy with everything Torres said on the wire. Or rather, what he didn't say."

"Are you telling me they're gonna punt?" Jake asked.

"They're not saying that. Not flat out. But you know these people as well as I do. They wanted the Columbus guys to put everything on a silver platter. Look, I've heard the wire. I've seen what they have. It's a solid case for money laundering, fentanyl trafficking, and weapons charges, in my opinion. Only I'm not the one with the power to do anything about it. I just thought I'd call and give you a heads-up."

"A heads-up," Jake said. "You mean you want to make sure things are buttoned down here in case the feds won't do their job?"

"Honestly? Yeah. So give me your gut. Do you have enough to fry this monster?"

"It's a good case," Jake said. "We've got a new prosecutor. He's green. But between me, Mark Ramirez, and our medical examiner, I'm confident. They'll indict."

"Good. Good. It'll be a relief. We need to keep this guy locked up forever, Jake. He's as bad as they come. I've seen a few other kills the DEA thinks Torres committed. He's escalating. Each victim ... it's like he's perfecting his skill. He can't ever see the light of day again. That's all I know."

"Well, I appreciate you calling and piling on the pressure," Jake said.

Gable laughed. "Yeah. I'm sorry. But you know what I'm dealing with over here."

"I do. But if you're telling me the U.S. Attorney is going soft because they expect us to win this murder case, I don't know if I like that. They need to go after their end just as hard."

"That's what I told them. Believe me. Just ... keep me in the loop, all right? Call me as soon as the grand jury comes back."

"Sure," Jake said. "Hey ... as long as I've got your ear. I need you to do me a favor."

"Another one?"

Jake locked eyes with Mary. She looked puzzled. He gestured for her to shut the office door to ensure no one passing by could hear this part of the conversation. She did.

"Listen, I need you to look into someone for me. Michael Harter. Date of birth October 19,1944. Current address 840 Mansfield Street. Durris Township. He's a Vietnam vet. Army. I don't know the years he served. Probably between '68 and '72."

"You wanna tell me why?" Gable asked.

"He's the father-in-law of my victim, Craig Albright."

"Jake," Gable said, his tone suspicious.

"It's nothing. It's probably nothing. I just need to know his background. What did he do in-country? Whether he's got any associations I need to know about."

"Seems simple enough," West said. "Why do I know it won't be?"

"It's a minor favor," Jake said. "Barely a blip."

"That's what you always say. Rathburn? You still there?"

"I am indeed," Mary said.

"Let this be your first lesson on partnering with this lunkhead. You watch. This is going to be more than just a blip."

"Drama," Jake mouthed to Mary. Then to Gable, "Good talking to you, man! So sorry, I'm making you do some actual work today."

West responded with a few colorful phrases that made Jake laugh.

"All right," West said. "Give me twenty-four hours. I'll see what I can dig up. In the meantime, you do your job and come back with an indictment."

"That's the plan," Jake said. "And thank you. I owe you one."

"You owe me ninety-seven," West said, then hung up the phone.

"He's a good guy," Jake told Mary. "Deeply unfunny, but a good guy."

"Is it wrong that I hope he doesn't find anything?" she said.

"No. I hope he doesn't either."

"Twenty-four hours," she repeated. "Give me that long as well on my end. I'll invite Carly over for a Monday-night cocktail."

Jake thanked her. Just like West, he hoped Mary couldn't find anything, either. He hoped in twenty-four hours, he could hand Meg Landry a win from the grand jury.

THIRTY-TWO

Tuesday morning, at nine a.m., Corey Ansel was set to put his case against Matteo Torres, El Carnicero Oscuro in front of the grand jury. Twelve members of Worthington County would decide whether he could establish probable cause that a crime had been committed. It would take only a majority vote to indict. Neither Torres himself nor his attorney would appear. Only Ansel would get to call witnesses and present his arguments to the jury. They too could ask questions of the witnesses if they felt the need.

It should be simple. A formality. But as Jake took his seat in the hallway, he had his first inkling that something was wrong. Floyd Bardo had stopped answering his phone.

Mark Ramirez and Dr. Stone had already arrived. Jake took a seat on the bench beside them.

"Your boy Ansel was fifteen minutes late," Ramirez said. "Judge wasn't happy. He just called the responding deputy."

"Denning's in there now?" Jake asked.

"Just went in about a minute ago," Ramirez confirmed.

"How'd he look?" Jake asked Ramirez.

"Denning?"

"No. Ansel."

"Frazzled. Like a deer in headlights."

"It'll be okay," Ethan Stone said. "He'll find his footing. This is cake."

"He doesn't know what he's doing," Ramirez said through gritted teeth. "He's got a list of witnesses as long as my arm. This is just the grand jury. There's no need for this big a show. He's wasting everyone's time including the judge's. It's a bad look. We all know Torres is gonna bring out some hired gun paid for by the cartel if this thing goes to trial."

"*When* this thing goes to trial," Stone said. "Don't worry. It's gonna be fine."

"I had a call from Gable West yesterday," Jake said. "The U.S. Attorney is balking a little on the federal drug charges against Torres. They're waiting to see what happens here before they get their hands dirty."

"Typical," Ramirez said. "This guy needs to be killed twice, Jake. You know what's gonna happen if he ever gets out of a jail cell?"

"He's gonna disappear," Jake said, not wanting to think about it.

"Ansel is gonna be fine," Stone said. "Have a little faith."

The elevator doors opened. Tim Brouchard walked out, motorcycle boots and all. Drew Harter trailed behind him wearing a suit jacket that was too big on him. He shot Jake a nervous look.

"You don't have to sit out here with them," Brouchard said, giving Jake a glare of contempt. Brouchard went further down the hall and spoke to one of the bailiffs.

"How's your sister?" Jake asked Harter.

"Brouchard says I don't have to talk to you."

Jake shrugged. "Suit yourself."

"She's gone," Harter said, talking to Jake anyway. "She's leaving for Florida this morning."

"Ah. Well, hopefully that will be good for her. I understand she's still pretty traumatized."

"Yeah? Well, so am I. But you don't care about that, do you?"

"Drew?" Brouchard said, practically shouting it. "This way." He put a strong arm on his client and ushered Drew into an empty conference room across the hall.

"Weasel," Ramirez said under his breath. "You are not gonna convince me that that little putz isn't mostly responsible for what happened in that barn. Now he's just gonna pick up where he left off. Not a care in the world. What's he even doing here? He's not necessary for this. See? This is what I mean. Ansel's all over the place."

"I think Brouchard likes being here more than anything else," Stone said. "There's a bank of reporters out there. Tim's gonna love strutting past them. You watch. He's gonna figure out a way to take credit for all of this when the jury votes to indict."

"Weasel," Ramirez repeated. "Drew Harter's hands are as dirty as anyone's. I feel bad for the sister. You think that jerk-off is gonna be able to run that business by himself?"

"He won't make it," Jake said. "I predict within a year all of Craig's customers are going to go elsewhere for their electrical needs."

"Serves him right," Ramirez said. "You think he'll at least do the right thing in the courtroom today?"

"Brouchard's an ass, but he's not stupid. He's gonna make sure Harter doesn't screw up his immunity deal. It's enough of a feather in his cap, too. Like Stone says, it'll give him the chance to strut out there in front of the news cameras as soon as they're done here."

Stone got up and walked to the end of the hall. He peered out the second-floor window. They were at the front of the building. He had a clear shot of the main courthouse steps.

"Oh, they're out there all right," Stone said. "More than when I got here. Couple of live trucks."

"I wouldn't be surprised if Tim arranged for half of them," Jake said. He hadn't filled in Stone or Ramirez on Brouchard's next trick, trying to install Ed Zender as sheriff. They all had enough on their plates for the day.

Stone came back and took his seat beside Jake. Jake checked his phone. He had three unanswered texts to Floyd Bardo. He'd checked with the deputies downstairs. Floyd had yet to arrive. He was supposed to have been here over an hour ago.

"You okay?" Stone asked Jake. "You look worried."

"Not worried. Yet."

Jake got up and walked down the hall out of earshot of the others. He punched in Floyd's number. It went straight to voicemail. He called Mary. She picked up right away.

"I was just about to call you," she said. " I wanted to tell you about what my neighbor ..."

"Hey, Rathburn," he said, cutting her off. "I'm getting a little concerned that Floyd Bardo hasn't shown up at the courthouse yet. Who'd you send to escort him here?"

"One second," she said. "Let me put you on hold."

She did. The county's infuriating canned music played in his ear. He waited two full minutes before Mary came back on the line.

"So, Jake. Matt Corbin went to the house to pick Floyd up. Behind his excavating business. They were supposed to meet at eight. Corbin says Floyd's kid answered the door and told Corbin his dad had made other arrangements to get to the courthouse."

"He what?" Jake fumed.

"He's not there yet?" Mary asked.

"No sign of him yet."

"Do you think something happened?"

"I don't know."

"What if he doesn't show?"

Jake wanted to answer that he'd wring Floyd's neck. He agreed with Ramirez that Floyd probably wasn't even a necessary witness for this phase. The more he showed up in public, the more dangerous it could be for him.

"He'll show," Jake said, hoping to manifest it. "Just keep your phone on you."

"Always," Mary promised. Jake clicked off and went back to the bench with Stone and Ramirez.

"Christ," Ramirez said. "It's been almost an hour since Denning took the stand. What the hell is Ansel doing with him? It's not like he'll be cross-examined. I'm supposed to be in Lima in a couple of hours. At this rate, we'll be here well past lunchtime."

"We may have a bigger problem," Jake said. "Floyd Bardo might be AWOL. He ditched the escort I arranged for him."

"I wish I could say that surprised me," Ramirez started. He launched into another rant but Jake didn't listen. His attention went to the elevator doors as they opened.

This time, Floyd Bardo walked out. Jake felt equal parts relief and rage. Floyd was flanked by all three of his children. Knox, Kyle, and Kyra. They filed out of the elevator. Both boys and their father wore black suits. Kyra wore a bright-blue dress and five-inch heels. She put a hand on her father's shoulder. He leaned down while she whispered something in his ear. All the while, she kept her eyes locked on Jake's.

"Save my seat," Jake whispered to Ramirez and Stone. He got up and went to Floyd.

"Cutting it a little close, aren't you?" Jake said. "You were supposed to let Deputy Corbin bring you in. Wasn't too smart you traveling on your own."

"We're used to taking care of our own, Detective," Kyra said.

Floyd looked around nervously. "I don't want to be here. I told the prosecutor that. It's too open."

"Open is your friend right now," Jake said. "But while you're here, you do exactly what I tell you. Got it?" Jake gestured to two deputies stationed further down the hall.

"Wait here," Jake told the Bardos. He met the deputies. They were Nate Sheffield and Patrick Foreman.

"I need you to do me a favor. Keep yourself glued to that man." He pointed to Bardo. "And I mean glued. If he goes to take a leak, one of you goes with him."

"For how long?" Foreman asked.

"Until he heads back up to Red Sky Hill," Jake said. "He shouldn't have come down by himself."

Sheffield was staring at Kyra Bardo, his jaw practically on the floor. If he were a cartoon, Jake imagined he'd have hearts for eyes.

"You clear on what I asked you?" Jake barked at Sheffield, snapping him back to attention.

Sheffield cleared his throat. "Um. Clear. We'll stick to him like glue."

"Good." Jake went back to Floyd. Jake agreed with Ramirez that having Floyd here was an unnecessary risk. Torres was tucked safely away in federal lockup. But the cartel could have eyes anywhere and everywhere.

"Come here," Jake said. There was another open conference room down the hall, around the corner from where Brouchard sat with Drew Harter.

The Bardos, along with Deputies Sheffield and Foreman, followed Jake into the conference room. Jake turned to Floyd. "Did you just march through the front entrance?"

"We went through security," Kyra answered.

"You drove here in your car?"

"How else would we get here?" Kyra said.

"You were supposed to have a sheriff's escort. You were supposed to wait for them to pick you up."

"We got tired of waiting," Floyd said. "I'm getting tired of all of this."

"Until you're finished testifying, you need to do what I say. I'm trying to keep you alive. For now, you don't go anywhere without one of these deputies going with you. Is that clear?"

"We take care of our own," Floyd said, parroting his daughter's words.

"Right," Jake said. "Like you took care of Craig Albright."

"My dad is doing you a favor, Detective." Knox Bardo pushed his way between Floyd and Jake, getting in Jake's face. "You need to mind your manners."

"Knox!" Kyra shouted. "Sit down."

Knox glared at his sister. Jake went rigid, feeling his fists begin to curl. Waiting ... hoping Knox would get physical. But Kyra seemed to know how to keep her brother on his leash. Knox dropped his shoulders and went to sit at the table as she told him to. His brother Kyle went with him.

"This shouldn't take long today," Jake said. "I don't know what order Ansel is planning on calling his witnesses. I'll make sure he knows you're in here. But I need you to stay in here. If you need something, you ask the deputies. I don't want you talking to anyone else, okay?"

"Whatever you say, Detective," Floyd said, though his voice dripped with contempt.

"Jake?" Mark Ramirez came to the door. "Deputy Denning just walked out. Not sure if you're next or what."

"Just ... stay put," Jake said to the Bardos. He gave a sharp look to Deputy Sheffield to make sure the man understood his job. Then he went to join Ramirez in the hall.

"Man just waltzed right in here from the front entrance," Jake muttered. "Not a care in the world. It's like he wants to have his head blown off by the cartel."

"You think they'd be that bold?"

"I think until Floyd testifies, anything could happen. I'll feel a lot better when he disappears back up that hill."

Chris Denning stood further down the hall. He looked hot. He caught Jake's eye and rushed toward him.

"How'd it go?" Jake asked Denning.

"A little rough," Denning said. "Ansel's pretty nervous and it's showing. Took him a minute to get into a groove. And that's only after I pretty much had to guide him toward what to ask me. He'll probably manage to fumble his way through it today, but, man. If this thing goes to trial, he's gonna get his ass handed to him by a good defense attorney."

"We'll burn that bridge when we get there," Jake said. "What's the hold-up?"

Denning looked back toward the closed doors. "I don't know. Some procedural issue the judge needed to clear up. Ansel told me to tell you he's gonna call you in next."

"Thanks."

Jake went back to the bench where Ramirez and Stone sat. He was about to take his seat when his cell phone rang. He would have ignored it. Only it was Gable West.

"I gotta take this," he told Ramirez and Stone. "I'll just be down the hall. If Ansel pokes his head out, let me know."

Ramirez gave Jake a joking salute. As his phone rang a third time, Jake rounded the corner down the hall. He reached a small alcove where a pay phone used to be and answered.

"Your timing stinks," Jake said. "I'm about two minutes from heading into the grand jury room."

"Copy that. Listen. I wanted to get this info to you as soon as possible. I don't know what it means yet and I'm hoping you do. I got the intel you wanted on your witness, Michael Harter. Do you want to call me back later?"

"No," Jake said. "I've got a minute, I think. What did you find out?"

"Jake, this guy ... Harter? Why did you ask me to look into him?" He'd known Gabe West for a long time. His tone had dropped an octave. Jake knew that meant trouble.

"Gabe ... what did you find?"

"You were right about most of the broad strokes. Guy did two tours in Vietnam. Enlisted just out of high school. Army. Special ops. But Jake, most of his record was classified."

"Okay ... But you were able to find out, weren't you?"

West let out a sigh. "Yeah. Jake, if you were going to throw me a hot potato, you could have warned me."

"West, level with me."

"This guy? Harter? He was part of an elite unit. The Phoenix Program. Jake, this is one of those things the Army tends not to want to acknowledge even exists or answer questions about."

Jake's head started to pound. His pulse raced as Gable continued.

"This program? They were into some bad shit, Jake. Counter-terrorism against the Viet Cong. Run by the CIA. Your guy Harter was a master interrogator. They'd send him in whenever we had senior Viet Cong in custody. Look, I don't know exactly what he was into, but I can guess, if you know what I mean."

"Torture," Jake said.

"I didn't say that. The Army sure as hell isn't going to say that. But this guy is radioactive. I'm pretty sure I'm going to get a call from a certain Alphabet agency just for asking the questions I did. A heads-up would have been nice."

"I didn't know," Jake said.

"You knew something or you wouldn't have asked. Anyway, I'm sending over what I have. Do with it what you need to. I'll take the heat."

"I appreciate that, Gabe."

"I know."

"I owe you."

"I know that too. I just hope I don't come to regret it."

Gable hung up. A second later, a photo text came through from him. Jake opened the screen.

"Jake?" Corey Ansel came down the hall, his face flushed. The kid was sweating through his dress shirt and fanning himself.

"Christ," Jake said. "Are you sick?" Jake looked back at his phone, quickly scanning the military records West had sent through. There was a photo of Mick Harter taken more than fifty years ago in his military uniform. Young. Stony-eyed. A master interrogator. Likely skilled in methods of torture.

Jake looked up. Ansel was talking but Jake couldn't focus on what he was saying. It was nine forty-five.

"Call Ramirez," Jake said. "Or put Stone on the stand. I have to go."

"What?" Ansel said. "You can't ..."

"Just ... stall ..." Jake said. He was already running toward the stairwell. He just prayed he wasn't too late.

THIRTY-THREE

It was crazy. Ridiculous, maybe. Only Jake knew in his gut it wasn't. He was right. As he slid behind the wheel and peeled out of the courthouse parking lot, he called Mary using his Bluetooth voice command.

She answered on the third ring.

"Your ears must be burning," she said. "So listen. I was just getting ready to text you. How'd the grand jury go?"

"It's still going," Jake said. He made a sharp right turn, heading for the highway on-ramp. Going eighty, it would take him at least forty minutes to get to the airport, assuming he hit no traffic snarls.

"It's still going. Listen, I need you to …"

"I wanted to tell you. I talked to my neighbor," Mary interjected. "You know the one I told you works for Dr. Finley?"

"Yeah," Jake said, that feeling in his gut starting to tingle again.

"I asked her about Mick Harter. I mean, not directly. I was smooth about it. Anyway, I think your instincts are right. There's something going on. Carly wouldn't come out and tell me. There were a lot of, 'oh the things I could tell you if it weren't for HIPAA laws.' But I said a lot of things like how sorry I felt for him, how hard a time he's having getting around. Well, Carly rolled her eyes a lot. At one point, she told me not to let Mick fool me. Jake, whatever's going on with him, it's been going on for a while. Carly and Dr. Finley are bound by confidentiality. But I bet if you could subpoena his medical records, they'd paint a different story than what he's portraying. So why?"

"Mary," Jake said. "That's great. We may very well need that subpoena, depending on how the rest of my day goes. In the meantime, I need a favor. I know you've got a full plate ..."

"Name it," she said.

"Harter and his daughter are supposed to be getting on a plane as we speak. I need to know which one. They're flying out of Rickenbacker and into Destin. Rachel made mention of it being an eleven a.m. flight. Can you track it down for me? I need to know what gate they're at. I need to try to stop them."

"Give me a few minutes. Do you know what airline?"

"I don't. Just that it's flying out of Rickenbacker. I don't even know if it's non-stop. Hopefully, there won't be that many outgoing flights to choose from."

"I've got my laptop open. Just give me a sec ..." Jake could hear her clacking away on a keyboard. He hit almost ninety miles an hour. With rush hour long past, the roads were pretty clear. If he didn't make it, he'd have to figure out a way to intercept Mick Harter when he landed.

"I think I've got it," Mary said. "You're in luck. There's actually only one flight out this morning headed to Tampa. It boards at eleven fifty. Gate 19. You'll be cutting it close. Do you want me to try to give airport police the heads-up you're coming?"

"Yes. You're a godsend."

"If I leave now, I can meet you there," she said.

"No time. I'll call you when I'm headed back to Stanley. I may want you to meet me at the station."

"Whatever you need. Jake, be careful."

"Always," he said, clicking off.

The next forty minutes were torture. His phone blew up with calls from Corey Ansel, Mark Ramirez, and finally Landry. He had time for none of them.

At eleven thirty, he screeched to a halt along the curb for the drop-off lane for domestic flights. He flashed his badge when the porter gave him an angry look.

Running at top speed, he followed the signs to Gate 19, praying Mary got through to the airport police and they'd already detained Mick Harter for him.

Two police officers met him at the TSA checkpoint for domestic flights. Once again, Jake showed his badge. They'd been expecting him. "We'll walk you to the gate," the female officer said. "Your partner explained the situation. We thought it best not to try to spook your witness by calling for him over the PA. He's checked in, but so far, nobody matching his description is anywhere near the waiting area at Gate 19."

He could be anywhere, Jake thought.

"You're sure he didn't leave?"

"No," the female officer said. Her male counterpart sprinted alongside them as they made their way down the long corridor to the domestic gates. Luckily, Gate 19 was on the nearest end. Flight 1384 had already begun to board first-class passengers.

Jake scanned the waiting areas. He couldn't see Rachel Albright or Mick Harter anywhere.

"It'll take us a little while to check security footage," the female officer said. She quickly introduced herself as Theresa McCormack. Her partner was Jeremy Lindoff.

"No time for that," Jake said. "He's gotta be here somewhere. Did he ask for priority boarding? Do we know? He might be walking with a cane."

Lindoff and McCormack trailed behind Jake as he made his way to the ticket agent assisting the passengers waiting to board. Jake pulled up Mick Harter's photo and showed it to her.

"Has this man checked in yet?" Jake said. "Have you seen him? He's traveling with his daughter." Jake showed her a picture of Rachel.

"Um ... I saw them. I think. She had some kind of episode. Crying. They might have gone to get some coffee or something. I'm not sure."

"Where?" Jake asked.

"Over there." She pointed to a small coffee shop between a sandwich place and a gift shop.

"Wait here," Jake said to Lindoff and McCormack. "If you see them, sit on them."

Jake ran toward the coffee shop. There was one customer in line, a young mother holding a squirming toddler on her hip. Jake turned, scanning the crowd. There was a men's room just across from him. He headed there while gesturing for Officer McCormack. She hustled to his side.

"Can you check the women's?" He showed her Rachel Albright's photo again.

"Sure thing," she said.

Jake made it to the entrance. The exit door beside it opened. Mick Harter walked out. He froze, seeing Jake. The man was bent over, leaning on his cane.

"To the last," Jake said. "You're committed, I'll give you that."

Mick Harter looked nervously to his left and right. From the corner of his eye, Jake saw Officer Lindoff running toward him. He must have seen Mick Harter about the same time Jake did.

"We need to talk, Mick," Jake said.

"I've got nothing to say to you, Detective."

"You've been lying about your mobility, Mick. You've been lying about a lot of things. You know I can prove it."

Mick didn't straighten. If anything, he leaned on his cane harder. Jake saw him with new eyes, almost as if the military ID he'd seen from Mick's youth superimposed itself on the man standing before him today. Jake saw the hard glint in Mick's eyes. Eyes that had seen and known horrors Jake could only imagine. Mick's gnarled hand rested on the knob of his cane. He was wearing a large ring. Jake had seen it before, but hadn't really noted it. He did now though. It had a large emerald in the center with a sword and two arrows crossed over it. He could just make out the phrase *de oppresso liber* engraved on one side.

To free the oppressed.

"I don't have to talk to you," Mick said. "I know my rights."

"Sure you do. But you're not getting on that plane today, Mick. You're coming back to Stanley with me. And we're going to talk. You know I'm going to follow you wherever you go until we work this out. It's going to go much better if you just come willingly."

"Daddy?" Rachel Albright had just come out of the women's restroom. Officer McCormack was at her side.

"Final boarding call for Flight 1384. Will passengers with tickets for Zone Three please check in at the gate."

"Daddy, that's us," Rachel said, though she was already crying. Did she know? Did she suspect?

"It's all right, honey," Mick Harter said, though he never let his gaze fall from Jake's. "You just get on that plane. I'll fly out another day. Right now, Detective Cashen and I need to have a talk."

"I don't understand," Rachel said. If she were acting, she was good at it.

"Mick," Jake said. "You know how this goes."

He could swear there was a twinkle in Mick Harter's eyes as Jake said the words he knew by heart. "You have the right to remain silent ..."

"Daddy?"

"Shh," Mick said to his daughter. "Everything's going to be all right."

Then to Jake. "My daughter's getting on that plane, isn't she?"

"Yes," Jake said.

Rachel kept sobbing, but did as she was told. As soon as she was out of earshot, Mick turned back to Jake. "After you, Detective."

They started the long walk back to Jake's car. With each step he took, Mick's posture straightened and his gait became more sure. Just before they left the concourse, Mick passed a garbage can. He paused and threw his cane into it.

THIRTY-FOUR

"You've been lying a long time, Mick," Jake said. The man sat across from him, straight-backed. Gone was the enfeebled old man with the bent spine. Here was the skilled Army master interrogator. The man with nothing left to lose, perhaps. He said nothing. For two hours, he simply sat in that chair, only asking for a glass of water at the outset. His glass sat full in front of him; he'd yet to take a single sip.

Jake's cell phone was on the table in front of him. A text came through. The one Mick Harter had been waiting for since the moment they left the airport.

"Rachel's flight has landed safely," Jake said. "You can relax. You got what you wanted. What I promised you. Now, tell me about Craig, Mick."

Jake was alone. That had been Mick's condition. No one in the observation room next door. No cameras. No recording devices. Whether Mick truly trusted Jake didn't matter. He was a man of his word.

"See, it bothered me for a long time," Jake said. "Matteo Torres is as evil as they come. The way he tortures his victims. Burned feet. Fingernails plucked out one by one. Drills. Hammers. Torches. But there were certain things. He uses adrenaline to keep them going. Keep them talking. But there's no trace of that in Craig's system. And the location. There's no sense to it. El Carnicero doesn't kill his victims in their own homes. He wants them found though. I'll give him that. He sends a message. Here's what happens if you mess with the cartel. If you try to get away."

Nothing. Just a cold stare.

"Craig was stupid," Jake said. "You knew that, didn't you? He talked a big game. Thought he could simply retire from his dealings with the cartel. Put his trust in the likes of Floyd Bardo. That was probably his first mistake, wasn't it? No. That came even earlier. The day his old man took over that farm at the foot of Red Sky Hill. It wasn't his. It will always belong to the people on the other side of that hill, won't it? There was always going to come a day when they'd come to collect."

Harter shifted in his seat but kept Jake's eyes.

"But it was good for a while. A long while. And he thought he had it easy. All he had to do was provide the meeting place. It's not like Craig ever got his hands really dirty. He just ... looked the other way and kept their secrets. The Hilltop Boys and the cartel. For his silence and his space, they paid him very well. Millions. Enough to renovate the barn, the house, Alexis's college education, then finally Rachel's Florida dream house. He probably thought it was like winning the lottery.

"Only ... he wasn't *that* smart, was he? All those extravagant purchases. Somebody was bound to notice and start asking questions. Is that what caught your attention?"

For the first time, Mick reached for his glass of water. With a rock steady hand, he took a sip.

"Did you warn him? Tell him not to do anything too flashy? Well, if you did, he didn't listen. That was his problem, wasn't it? He never listened. And Rachel never questioned. She's used to having men take care of her, isn't she? The way you raised her."

"Rachel has nothing to do with this," Mick said.

Jake narrowed his eyes. With that one sentence, just seven little words, Mick Harter had just said nothing and everything.

"She's profited from it. The house. The cars. She's wanted for nothing. Did the things she's always done? Looked pretty. That's her one job, right?"

"Careful, boy," Mick said. "You might just hurt my one feeling."

"You don't quit the cartel," Jake said. "Not unless it's in a body bag. You know these people. I know these people. Craig only thought he did. Isn't that right? He must have told you. Must have tried to reassure you. When was it? A year ago? Two? He had a plan. An exit strategy that you knew wouldn't work."

Jake had a small evidence bag sitting on the table. In it were Mick Harter's personal effects. There wasn't much there. His wallet contained only a hundred dollars in cash. His Army Special Forces ring. His keychain. Jake picked up the bag and held its contents up to the light.

"It was a clean crime scene," Jake said. "I mean, Craig himself ... well ... that was a mess. But they never found any clothing fibers that shouldn't have been there. No hair or blood or anything that wasn't Craig's or people who had business being there. Only ... there was this."

Jake opened the file he kept with the crime scene photos. He pulled out a close-up of Craig's face, showing the worst of his bruising.

"The medical examiner theorizes Craig was punched in the face more than once. No defensive wounds. His hands were zip tied to his chair. This here ... where the skin broke. We think his tormentor was wearing a ring. That's new. El Carnicero never did that. A blow that hard? I bet it would have torn the glove the killer was wearing. Don't you think? You can clean up a lot. But did you think to clean the ring? It's been a long time since you've sat across a table like this, hasn't it, Mick? When I turn this ring over to BCI and have their lab do their thing ... I think I might find something. What do you think?"

A snarl. The first real reaction from the man.

"You think you've got it all figured out," Mick said. "You like to tell stories. So tell me another one, Detective."

Jake set the baggie down. "Okay. I think I will. I think it goes like this. You knew something was going on. The purchases. The extravagant lifestyle. The rumors about Craig's family connections. I bet you had reservations when Rachel came home telling you she was gonna marry that man."

"They disowned him," Harter said.

Jake smiled. "The people up that hill. You had to know they could be just as bad as the cartel. They take care of their own. But they'll also eat their young to protect themselves."

Mick Harter glowered at Jake. "What makes you think I won't?"

"And so you have. That's what this is, isn't it? This whole thing? Are you going to tell me what you did, you did for her? For Rachel?"

Harter didn't answer.

"Craig wouldn't listen. I'm sure you warned him. Told him what happens to people that run afoul of both the Bardos and the cartel. God. He was bold enough ... stupid enough to think he could manage it all."

"My son-in-law had a mind of his own," Mick said.

"Sure. Probably told you he was gonna take care of Rachel. All the spending. That was his way of doing it, wasn't it? The very thing that ended up blowing up in his face."

Mick took another sip of water.

"You knew full well how the cartel was gonna deal with people who caused problems for them. You did your research. And you bided your time. I'm gonna pull your medical records, Mick. When I do, I think it's gonna show me you started using that cane what, a year ago? Two? So no one would suspect this doddering old man of carrying out such a brutal attack. Such a physical attack. But see ... what I want to know is ... Rachel. For the last few weeks, she's been living under your roof. I saw you. You didn't know that. But that day I came out to the house with my nephew, that's when I knew you'd been lying. In the last twenty-four hours, I've gotten quite an education in all things Michael Harter. Lieutenant Michael Harter. You want to tell me about the Phoenix Program? They gave you a pretty name. What was it? Part of the Provincial Reconnaissance Unit. Only what you did wasn't so pretty, was it? You became what they trained you to be, didn't you? And you were the best there was at it. The government used you to get intel from senior members of the Viet Cong."

For the first time since he sat down, a flicker of doubt went through Mick Harter's eyes.

"If Rachel knew you've been lying about your disabilities, what else does she know? See ... there's one thing ... one piece of this I don't have."

Jake picked up the bag of Mick's personal effects again. He isolated the set of keys. There was one that stuck out from the rest. A small gold one with a round head.

"I know what a safe deposit box key looks like, Mick. It's not going to take me too long to figure out what it goes to. See, we never could figure out what was stored in that hole in the wall busted out of the barn. But you did, didn't you? Your safety net. Or Rachel's. Only ... if she knew ... even after the fact ... it'll all be for nothing, Mick. You can't protect her. Rachel's gonna go down for obstruction of justice, aiding and abetting ..."

"She's got *nothing* to do with this!" Mick shouted. "You leave that girl alone!"

"I don't want to do anything to Rachel. But you're leaving me with very few options. Your ring. This key. You didn't clean up your mess as well as you thought you did. Did you, Mick?"

Mick's eyes searched Jake's face. Jake felt the man was looking to see if he was bluffing. He wasn't.

"Tell me the truth," Jake said. "If you did all this to protect Rachel, those are extenuating circumstances. I can help you."

"Help me? Help *me*? Detective, just a block from here, a grand jury is set to indict one of the worst monsters you or I have ever seen. Do you know what happens if Matteo Torres ever sees the light of day again? He's gonna vanish. Vaporize. But he won't be gone. You're not naïve. That man? He's a serial killer who's found a way to get paid. You already know his killings have gotten worse. More grisly. He refines his technique. Comes up with new, more painful methods of torture. I think even the cartel is afraid of him now. They want him to fry because it takes care of their problem. And it takes care of yours."

Mick leaned far forward, close enough Jake could feel his breath on his face.

"Let it go," Harter whispered. "Do you really trust the feds or someone else to neutralize El Carnicero? It's you. This case. Your career. You can have it all. I gave him to you."

Mick sat back down. A thousand doubts flooded through Jake. Matteo Torres. Everything Mick said about him was true. He would kill again if he ever got out. It would be worse. It would be horrific. It would be bold.

"You, Jake," Mick said. "You. The power is in your hands to keep the devil locked away until they finally stick a needle in his arm. Do you really want to piss that away? Because it'll be on your conscience, the next victim that turns up along the border. You'll always know you could have prevented it. Me? I'm almost eighty years old. As long as my daughter, granddaughter, and yes ... even my idiot son is safe, no one has anything to fear from me. Because you're right. That's all this has ever been about. You said the Bardos take care of their own. *I* take care of my own."

"I believe that," Jake said. "I truly do."

The two men locked eyes.

"Here's your shot. We're not so different, you and me," Mick said. "We have to do the hard things other people don't want to face. Sometimes, you have to be dark to keep the darkness away from the people you love."

The people you love.

"She'll lose it all," Jake said. "If the feds come after Rachel. The house in Destin. Whatever you put in that safe deposit box. They'll seize it. She'll have nothing. And she won't have you."

Mick dropped his head. He looked a little like the frail man he'd been portraying. Only this time, Jake sensed it was real. He was also right.

Matteo Torres. Gable West's warning replayed in his head. The U.S. Attorney might not go forward with the drug charges. This case? The murder of Craig Albright? It might be the best chance of making sure Torres never walked the streets to kill again.

It was his choice. His power.

Right ... and wrong.

"You haven't booked me," Mick said. "That key? You can have it. Think about what you can do for the people *you* live to protect?"

Jake looked at the key. The light caught it, making it glint.

Light. Dark. Jake met Harter's eyes.

"It's over, Mick. I'm going to tell Corey Ansel he'll need to drop the charges against Torres. Because he's innocent of this. And it's the right thing to do. But I can do my best to make sure Rachel gets to keep her house. Whatever money she's got in the bank. If you cooperate. You did all this to protect her, didn't you? So finish what you started. Tell me the truth."

Mick Harter closed his eyes. When he opened them, Jake saw the change go through him. The man had played his last card and came up empty.

"He was never going to get out. I told him that from the beginning. Warned him. Begged him. But by the time I knew the full extent of it, it was already too late. I know these people. They would have used my daughter to send Craig a message. Then when he put my son in the middle of this ... I knew it was only a matter of time. The cartel would have ended up killing them both."

"Yes," Jake said. "They would."

"So Craig had to be sacrificed instead."

"And you did it in such a way you knew it would draw heat. A giant, blazing spotlight to Worthington County and the cartel's operation here. Because you knew me or someone like me would figure it out eventually."

"No. I hoped you wouldn't."

Jake paused. "Drew. You couldn't control him. Did he know? Does he know now it was you?"

Mick could have lied to him, but somehow, Jake knew he was telling the truth. "No," he said. "Drew doesn't know. He thinks Craig was killed by the cartel. Just like everyone else."

"He wasn't supposed to tell me about his involvement with Floyd Bardo. He wasn't supposed to flip so easily about Craig and his deal as middle man for the cartel and the Hilltop Boys, was he?"

"No. All he had to do was keep his mouth shut."

"I never would have put it together," Jake said. "I never would have started looking harder at you if Drew hadn't folded. I would have just chased cartel ghosts forever."

"My son is weak," Mick said. "You have nothing to fear from him."

"He has an immunity deal," Jake said. "It'll hold."

"I have your word?"

"You have the state of Ohio's word," Jake said. "Drew won't face prosecution if he truly didn't know you were involved."

"He didn't. You know a little bit about my son now, Detective. You've seen what I already knew. Look at how fast he flipped for you. You think I would have been dumb enough to trust my secret with him?"

"All right."

Mick sat back. "No matter what else happens, the cartel won't be doing business in this town anytime soon. Craig trusted the Bardos. Floyd promised him he'd get him out. But he's got protection. He's got his family. Rachel and Drew only have me. Floyd would have sold Craig out to save his own skin. He was a marked man anyway. But this way? Rachel has a chance to make it to the other side. You promise me. She gets to make it to the other side."

Mick hung his head. He buried his face in his hands. Was it an act? Jake would never be sure. But he reached for Mick, putting a hand on the man's arm.

"You have my word," he said. "I'll do everything I can. And I'll do what I can to make them understand why you did what you did."

Mick nodded, grateful. Jake wanted him to believe he had truly done all he could. For his daughter. His son. And for Blackhand Hills.

Jake hoped it would be enough.

THIRTY-FIVE

"On behalf of the citizens of Worthington County and the state of Ohio, we'd like to thank you for your service."

County Commissioner Rob Arden held the giant plaque with the replica of a detective's badge on the front of it. There had been other plaques and awards as well. A meritorious service certificate from the governor's office, though he hadn't appeared in person. Arden smiled for the cameras, shaking hands. Then it was Landry's turn. She turned toward the camera with the biggest smile Jake had ever seen, and extended her hand to Ed Zender.

His smile came in the form of a fake laugh as he shook the sheriff's hand and got his plaque.

Jake stood toward the door, ready to make a quick exit when the time was right. But they'd want his picture too, flanking Ed around Sheriff Landry's desk along with the day shift command and whatever other uniformed deputies Landry could scare up.

"Congratulations, Detective," she said. "Enjoy your retirement."

Zender beamed. When he tried to let go of Landry's hand, she pulled him closer and whispered something in his ear. His smile faltered but he recovered quickly. He moved out of the camera shot, making way for the next ceremony of the day. For this one, Jake moved closer to Landry's side.

"I'm pleased to announce the latest promotion. Deputy Rathburn, congratulations. This is well deserved."

Mary Rathburn's mother stood in the back of the room holding Mary's four-year-old son, Kevin. She'd plied the boy with candy while Ed took his time accepting his accolades. Now, he was relegated to the back of the room.

"Thank you," Mary said, her face flushed. Tears filled her eyes as Landry handed her her detective's badge.

"I know you'll make us proud," Landry said. Then she posed for pictures. A round of applause went up. Jake couldn't help but suppress a chuckle. Nobody had clapped for Ed.

Mary's mother and son moved in and got their pictures taken as well.

"You too, Jake," Mary said, motioning him over. Jake hated this, but appreciated the respect.

Finally, he posed with Landry and Mary. Afterward, Niel, Landry's press liaison, lowered his camera and the group in her office dispersed. Zender himself grabbed his plaques and certificates, gave Meg Landry a vile look, then brushed past Jake on the way out the door.

Jake held back, waiting for the room to clear. Mary said her goodbyes to her mother and son. She'd meet them for a celebratory lunch in a couple of hours at Papa's Diner.

"Will you join us, Jake?" Mary's mother, Connie, asked. She had a warm smile. "I'd love to catch up. You know, I was good friends with your mother once upon a time."

Jake stopped, caught off guard. "No," he said. "I guess I didn't know that."

Connie Rathburn touched Jake's face. He went rigid, unused to affection from strangers.

"She'd be so proud of you. So come to lunch. My treat."

"I'll try," Jake said. Mary moved in, kissed her mother and son, then bid them a temporary goodbye. Jake waited until they'd left and Mary closed the door before turning to Landry.

"What'd you say to Ed?"

Landry laughed. "Oh, I just wished him well in his retirement. And ... uh ... threatened to wipe the floor with him if he was serious about coming after my job. Told him to be ready because I've just about finished sharpening the knife he stuck in my back."

"Ah. Well. That'll do it. Good for you."

"Have a seat, you two," Landry said. "Give me the good news."

"I don't know how good it is," Jake said. "But I got off the phone with Corey Ansel about an hour ago. He just inked Mick Harter's plea deal. First-degree murder. He'll do life, but Ansel's taking the death penalty off the table."

"It's good work, Jake," Landry said. "It's justice."

Jake felt pensive. The other administrative task had fallen to Corey Ansel as well.

"All state charges against Matteo Torres have been dropped. He's off our books," Jake said. "But the U.S. Attorney's office just came through with an indictment against him on federal drug charges.

They're gonna hold him without bond pending the outcome of that case. So at least for the time being, that monster's not going anywhere."

"I hope they stick," Mary said. "Do you think they will?"

"It's out of my hands. I just hope the U.S. Attorney's office does their job. I'll be keeping a close eye on it. I can promise you that."

"It's a good outcome, Jake," Landry said. "Sure, I would have loved to be able to be the ones who put a needle in that butcher's arm. But Craig Albright, for all his faults, is getting justice. I just feel terrible for his family. Any word about how they're doing?"

"Drew Harter's like a cockroach. He'll survive. Though the word I'm hearing, nobody wants to do business with him. He may end up broke and homeless, but that won't be my problem. Doesn't mean I won't keep watching him. That slime has gotten a taste of dirty money. He's gonna be looking for an angle. With any luck, he'll just wither away or maybe slink off to Florida to sponge off his sister."

"Is she gonna be all right, do you think? Craig's wife?" Landry asked.

"I spoke to Alexis Albright, the daughter, just yesterday. She's moving to Destin to be with her mother."

"There's no danger the feds will seize any of her property?" Mary asked.

"I think she's safe. On the Florida house anyway. Not sure if she's gonna be able to keep it with no new money coming in. As part of Mick's plea deal, he told us where to find the bag he took from inside the barn wall. It was in a safe deposit box. We found a million bucks in cash. It's been turned over to the feds. You know, Meg, the sheriff's office is going to get a good chunk of that cash once it's forfeited. And that happened under your watch. Let's see if the *Daily Beacon* writes about *that*. But as for Rachel Albright, she's gonna get to keep whatever she can get for the house at Red Sky Hill, plus the one in Florida. She'll be just fine."

"Good luck getting anybody to buy that place now," Mary said. "Nobody in town will go near it."

"Trust me, I've heard. My poor sister's name and face are still on the sign on the front lawn."

"Poor Gemma," Landry said. "I hate that this whole thing touched her, too. Please let me know if there's anything I can do."

Jake smiled. "Well, short of coming up with a million bucks to buy Craig Albright's house, I'm not sure what there is."

"Still. Tell her just the same." She turned to Mary. "Your new badge looks good on you, Rathburn. I'm glad to have you on board. Now the hard part starts. You'll have to keep this jackass in line."

"I'll do my best," Mary said, rising. "If you don't mind, I'm gonna head over to Papa's Diner before my mother talks Tessa and Spiros's ears off."

"Tell them I said hello," Landry said.

"Sheriff, you're also welcome to join us. I know my mom would love that."

"I'll try," Landry said. Mary excused herself and left Landry and Jake alone. Her expression turned grim as soon as the door shut.

"Is it over?" she asked. "Let me know what you really think. Is the cartel going to be a continuing problem?"

Jake knew this had been Landry's central worry through all of this. It's what Tim Brouchard would try to convince the people of Worthington County was coming. That Landry had been too soft.

That she'd let the cartel move in under her nose. It wasn't fair. Floyd Bardo had started this mess long before Meg Landry ever moved to the county. But nobody would remember that if things got bad again.

"I think Mick Harter did us a favor."

"What?"

"He was smart. He knew the only way to get his daughter out from under anything her husband started was to shine a big fat spotlight right on our little town and Craig's business dealings. There's way too much heat now for the cartel to want to bother with us."

"Floyd Bardo is a problem," Landry said.

"He's neutralized for now. Just because the cartel doesn't want to do business here doesn't mean they won't be looking to make an example out of Floyd. I think he's going to stay out of sight in the hills for the foreseeable future. He'll leave it to his kids to oversee operations. He doesn't want to risk pissing off his brother too much, either. Make no mistake. Rex Bardo is still firmly in charge."

"Well," Landry said. "Then I guess this whole thing worked out pretty well for Rex, didn't it? He gets his idiot rogue brother out of the way. The cartel's been run off. And King Rex gets to establish that he's still in power. He couldn't have orchestrated this whole thing better himself."

There was sarcasm in her voice. Jake didn't respond at first.

"Jake," she said. "Has it occurred to you that Mick Harter might have gone to Rex in the first place when he found out what his son-in-law was doing? Is it possible that Mick and Rex were working together this whole time?"

"It's possible," Jake said. "And yes. I've thought of it. Only, that would presume that Drew Harter played a role. I'm telling you, that kid wasn't supposed to finger Floyd. He broke. It was real fear. I know the difference. I think Rex Bardo is just very good at finding the angle that'll serve him best. He's always two moves ahead of everyone else."

"So we're stuck with the devil we know," she said. "King Rex."

"Yeah."

"And Ed Zender."

"Ed's a puppet," Jake said. "Alone, he's no threat. It's Tim Brouchard who's the real enemy, Meg. He's coming after me. And he's using Ed to come after you."

Meg reached into her desk drawer. She pulled out two rocks glasses and a bottle of Johnny Walker Red.

Jake smiled. "You've been holding out on me."

"Shh," she said. She poured herself a shot and one for Jake, then slid a glass to him.

"They're coming for us, Jake," she said. She leaned forward and clinked her glass with his.

"Let them," he said. Then he and Landry sipped their drinks.

THIRTY-SIX

Red Sky Hill
One month later ...

"I don't know why you insisted on coming out here," Jake said. "It just makes you angry."

"I had to see for myself," she said. Jake parked near the big red barn, away from the main crowd assembling on the front lawn. A light drizzle fell. The weather lady said it would turn to snow by midnight. They could expect three inches on the ground by morning. An early snow. Six weeks ago it was eighty degrees. They were in for a long winter ahead.

"Do you get any piece of it? Anything at all?" Jake asked. "It was your listing. Don't you still have a contract with Rachel Albright?"

"No," Gemma said. "I don't even get what I spent on marketing back. A million bucks, Jake. Poof. Gone. I thought finally, you know? I'd get ahead a little. I'd be able to put something aside for Ryan's college fund. For Aiden's. It's coming fast, Jake. Ryan graduates in six months."

"Don't remind me. That kid was in diapers last week."

She smiled and leaned her head on her brother's shoulder in the front seat of the car.

"Ted Janowicz is good," she said. "I mean, this auction is really a fire sale. Rachel wants to be done with it. All the showings dried up. She lost confidence in me. I mean … how was I supposed to predict Craig would get murdered in the middle of the barn? How is that my fault?"

"I'm sorry," he said. He'd already said it a hundred times. And he was. In addition to Gemma losing her biggest listing to date, she'd gotten a reputation in town as a jinx. There'd been too many pictures online of this house with Gemma's sign front and center during the murder investigation. It was a tough optic to overcome. Though she hadn't said it, Jake knew Gemma had lost more clients than just Rachel Albright. It wasn't fair.

He thought of Mick Harter today. Something he'd said. "When it comes down to it. You'll do whatever you have to to protect the women you love."

Though Mick had taken that to a horrific extreme, Jake couldn't help but respect the man. Or at least, understand him.

What would he do if Gemma were in trouble like Rachel had been? Would he steal for her? Lie? Cheat? Could he kill?

"Do you want to get closer? Actually, listen to the dang thing once he gets going?"

"No," Gemma said. "I just want to wallow in my misery from a distance like a normal person."

"Gotcha. I can do that."

There was a commotion in the small crowd. Ted Janowicz, the auctioneer, walked up the porch steps and turned to face them. It was twelve o'clock on the dot. Time for the auction to start. From this distance, Jake couldn't hear the calls. He saw yellow tags go up as the bids were made.

"I can't watch," Gemma said. "She's gonna get screwed. It'll go for pennies on the dollar."

"She'll be fine. Rachel Albright's got a healthy bank account, thanks to her father and husband."

"She's no good with money. She'll blow it all unless by some miracle her daughter's got a brain in her head."

The frequency of the yellow cards raising began to dwindle. From Jake's vantage point, he could only see two cards now. He couldn't make out who they belonged to.

"It'll be over soon," she said. "Tell me when it's over."

"It's going to be okay, Gemma," Jake said. "You know I can help. I mean, with Ryan. And Aiden when the time comes. If you'll let me."

"What are you saying?"

"I'm saying let me help you send them to college."

"Jake ..."

"It's just me, Gemma. It's always gonna be just me. Gramps doesn't exactly charge me rent. I have some money saved."

"That money's for you, Jake. For your future family."

He laughed. "For the love of God, please don't tell me you've got matchmaking ideas again. Dominique Gill was your last chance."

"Oh no. I'm not letting you give up that easily."

"I mean it," he said. "Let me help you. I want to."

Gemma blinked wildly. She was holding back rare tears. He knew she wouldn't let him help her without a fight. For now, he knew to let it be.

A while later, the crowd up at the porch disbanded. Ted Janowicz had a huge smile on his face. He spotted Jake's car and walked right up to it.

"Crap," Gemma said. "I didn't think he knew I was here."

Jake rolled down the window. "Everything turn out all right?"

"She's sold," Ted said. "Gemma, I appreciate the referral. I'll have your fee deposited Monday morning."

Jake turned to her. "I thought you said ..."

"One percent," she said. "Of ..."

"Three hundred grand was the winning bid," Ted said. Gemma winced as if the number caused her physical pain.

"Who's the buyer?" Jake asked.

"She's local, I guess," Ted said. "She's paying with cash. It was a proxy bid. She sent a representative."

"You mind telling me who it is?" Jake asked.

"Who cares at this point," Gemma said.

"Just curious," Jake answered.

"Hang on," Ted said. He looked through the paperwork he held. "I know I've got it somewhere. I told you. They said she's local but I've never heard of her."

Jake had a sneaky suspicion he would recognize the name.

"Here it is. Buyer's name is Knox. Melva Knox. It's a local address. You know her?"

Jake smirked. "Checkmate," he whispered.

"What?" Gemma and Ted said it in unison.

"Nothing," Jake said. "Yeah. I know her."

"Anyway, I need to finish up some paperwork at the office. I'll wire your three grand to you tomorrow morning, Gemma."

"Thanks, Ted," she said. As soon as he walked off, she turned to Jake. "So, who is she?"

"Melva Knox. No one you'd know. She's just ... local."

Jake started his truck and turned the wheel. Gemma leaned against the back seat, staring wistfully at the red barn and the old farmhouse beside it. Empty now. The fields were overgrown and brown. As they drove away, a blazing sun peeked over the horizon, making Red Sky Hill look like it was on fire.

Don't miss Her Last Moment, Book 5 in the Jake Cashen Crime Thriller Series. A horrifying discovery on a quiet, winter morning will rock the very foundation of the Worthington County Sheriff's Department.

One-Click So You Don't Miss Out!

Turn the page and keep reading for a special preview...

Interested in getting a free exclusive extended prologue to the Jake Cashen Series?

Join Declan James's Roll Call Newsletter for a free download.

Sneak Preview of Her Last Moment

Her Last Moment
by Declan James

Two months later ...

"I just don't see why it has to be your responsibility." Sarah Hammer stood at the back door with a Yeti coffee mug in her hand, holding it hostage. Three times, her husband, Sergeant Jeff Hammer, tried to take it from her. Three times, she pulled it back, like Lucy and Charlie Brown with the football.

"It's not my responsibility," Jeff said. "It's just a nice thing to do."

Sarah wore a pink robe with a yellow duck embroidered on the lapel. She had a thing about ducks. Jeff bought that particular robe for her the Christmas before last.

"Nobody's coming to take me to work," Sarah said, pulling the coffee mug away from him for the fourth time.

"Sarah," he said. "Detective Rathburn's house is on my way. I've got a four-wheel drive. She doesn't. She asked. They're calling for another six inches of snow by noon. It's Jake's day off and I've got three other people out sick with the flu. I need Rathburn at work today. And you're not going into work anyway today. Schools are closed."

He moved to her, sliding his arms around her waist. She smelled good. Like roses and honeysuckle. She'd just gotten out of the shower and her hair was still wet. He kissed her on the neck, just below her left ear in the spot that always gave her goosebumps. She giggled and pressed her body against him.

"I love you," he said.

"Will you be home on time, or do you have to work over?" she said. "I'm not trying to nag. I'm just trying to figure out when to have dinner ready. I'll make meatloaf. It seems like a meatloaf kind of a day."

Jeff plastered a smile on his face. Sarah's meatloaf usually had the same flavor and consistency of a football. But like always, he would dutifully eat it and ask for seconds.

"I'm sure I'll have to work over. With everyone out sick and this storm not letting up. I'll text you when I have a better idea of how my day is going to go," he said.

Sarah pouted. "Jeff, it's not fair that they put all of this on you. Sheriff Landry needs to hire more deputies."

"The county can't afford them," he said. This was an old argument. One he didn't feel like having as he was walking out the door. He kissed his wife again. This time, she let him have his coffee mug.

"I meant what I said," Jeff cautioned her. "I don't want you driving anywhere today. Stay off the roads. We're gonna have our hands full with people not paying attention to the county snow emergency levels. The more accidents we have out there, the longer I'm gonna end up having to stay at work."

"So I'm supposed to stay cooped up here all day? I wanted to go grocery shopping."

Jeff had his hand on the back door. Every muscle in his body tensed. "Sarah, for God's sake. Please stay away from the stores. Every idiot in town is going to be in there stocking up on milk and toilet paper. We have plenty of both. Honestly. Just stay home."

He knew he was likely wasting his breath. Sarah would do whatever she pleased.

"I told you we should rent a condo in Fort Myers near my sister," she said. "Next year, we're doing it. You have six weeks' vacation. You're going to take all of them at once and we'll leave on February first. That way, we'll be down there until spring."

Jeff felt his shoulders tense. This was an argument they'd had a hundred times. "I can't take six weeks all at once."

"I don't see why not. Ed Zender did."

"I don't want to," he said. "Then I get no time off over the holidays or the summer when I like to go fishing."

"You, you, you. What about what I want?"

"We'll talk about it later," Jeff said.

"I still don't like it, Jeff. Here you are, leaving for work a full half hour before you're supposed to so you can go pick up that woman. What are people going to think when they see you driving in with her?"

"What people? And I don't know, maybe they'll think I'm being a nice guy."

"I know how the tongues wag in that department, Jeff. People are going to think you're sleeping with her."

"Sarah, please."

"I told you she was trouble."

"Who? Mary?"

"Yes. Mary. She's a single woman with a kid. Women like that are always on the prowl, Jeff. Today it's you picking her up and driving her into work. Next, she's gonna start asking you to do her yard work or whatever. You watch."

"I promise you," he said. "Mary Rathburn's not my type." He meant it as a light joke. He saw fire coming out of his wife's eyes. She jabbed a finger in his chest.

"Oh, so you have a type?"

Jeff could have kicked himself for walking right into that one. He tried to lean in and give his wife another kiss. She twisted away from him, eyes still blazing.

"I don't like it, Jeff. Not one bit. After this, you tell that woman to find somebody else to pick her up. Or better yet. Tell her to get a better car. I don't care."

Sarah was still yelling at him when he closed the back door and hit the remote for the garage door. A cyclone of white powder hit him in the face and it was still a more welcome storm than the one he'd left in the kitchen. He could barely see to the end of the driveway. The mailboxes were already buried. He felt bad for not being able to stick around and shovel after the snow stopped falling. Sarah would end up plowed in by noon. He just prayed she'd actually listen to him this time and stay off the roads.

Jeff climbed into his brand-new Toyota Tundra and engaged the four-wheel drive. The engine revved as he headed down the hill and out into the storm.

The plows hadn't yet made their way down Marigold Drive where he lived. They likely wouldn't until this evening. It meant that Sarah wouldn't be able to get out in her little Prius even if she wanted to. A small blessing. Only he wouldn't put it past her to try to then get stuck. Which meant he'd get a frantic phone call in the middle of his work day and he'd have to send a crew to dig her out. He should have thought to remove her distributor cap before he left. It wouldn't have been the first time.

County Road Ten was much better as soon as Jeff made the turn. Though it was near whiteout conditions, the salt trucks had done their thing. He didn't envy them their job and knew they felt the same about his.

It was normally just a short, ten-minute drive to Mary Rathburn's house at the end of Lassiter Road. There were only four other houses on this street though developers had just bought up the acreage on the north side. Rumor was, they were trying to get approval for a mobile home park.

The plows had been through. Jeff grumbled. The sister of one of the Road Commission board members lived here, two houses down from Mary.

Jeff hit a patch of ice as he rounded the curve to Mary's house. He swore as he gripped the wheel and struggled to keep the truck from careening into the drainage ditch on the right-hand side. That would be just his luck.

Up ahead, he saw lights on at Mary's two-story home. As Jeff approached, he realized he wouldn't be able to make it up the drive as a giant mound of plowed snow was piled in front.

"Great," he mumbled. He hit the horn in two quick bursts and waited. A minute passed and Mary didn't come out.

He picked up his phone and dialed her number. It went straight to voicemail.

"You gotta be kidding me," Jeff said. With a good four inches of new snow on her walkway and driveway, he knew she hadn't left the house yet. Unless she hadn't come home last night. Anger warmed him.

Jeff got out of his truck but left it running. He pulled his coat tighter around him and trudged up the sidewalk to the covered front porch.

"Mary?" he called out. He pounded on the door and waited. Nothing. No answer. Had she overslept?

His patience gone, Jeff pounded on the door harder, then tried the knob. The door was unlocked. He shook off his boots and went inside.

"Mary?" he called out. He could hear a television set tuned to a morning show in Mary's den at the back of the house. He didn't want to track snow through the house so he waited on the mat by the door.

"Come on, Mary. We're gonna be late!"

No answer.

Frustrated, Jeff walked through the living room and toward the kitchen. The hallway to the bedrooms branched off to the right.

Jeff froze.

The smell hit him first. He looked down. He was standing in a pool of blood. The hallway walls were painted red with it. The kitchen floor too. Red. Everywhere.

Jeff took a staggering step backward. His stomach roiled. He lurched toward the front door and barely made it outside before doubling over and puking in the snow drift off Mary Rathburn's front porch.

Click Here or scan the code below to get your copy!

ABOUT THE AUTHOR

Before putting pen to paper, Declan James's career in law enforcement spanned twenty-six years. Declan's work as a digital forensics detective has earned him the highest honors from the U.S. Secret Service and F.B.I. For the last sixteen years of his career, Declan served on a nationally recognized task force aimed at protecting children from online predators. Prior to that, Declan spent six years undercover working Vice-Narcotics.

An avid outdoorsman and conservationist, Declan enjoys hunting, fishing, grilling, smoking meats, and his quest for the perfect bottle of bourbon. He lives on a lake in Southern Michigan along with his wife and kids. Declan James is a pseudonym.

For more information follow Declan at one of the links below. If you'd like to receive new release alerts, author news, and a FREE digital bonus prologue to Murder in the Hollows, sign up for Declan's Roll Call Newsletter here: https://declanjamesbooks.com/rollcall/

ALSO BY DECLAN JAMES

Murder in the Hollows

Kill Season

Bones of Echo Lake

Red Sky Hill

Her Last Moment

With more to come...

Stay in Touch with Declan James

For more information, visit

https://declanjamesbooks.com

If you'd like to receive a free digital copy of the extended prologue to the Jake Cashen series, sign up for Declan James's Roll Call Newsletter here: https://declanjamesbooks.com/rollcall/

Made in United States
Orlando, FL
27 February 2024

44165336R00200